THE CURSE OF SELTEMVER

A Collection of Short Stories

Tales from Lythinall: Book 2

By Michael D. Nadeau

The Curse of Seltemver

First paperback edition March 2024 Michael D. Nadeau

Cover design by (shutter stock) Denis---S
Editing review by Curtis Alan Provance
Typography and Interior Design by Michael D. Nadeau

ISBN (paperback) 978-1-960654-02-1

ISBN (eBook) 978-1-960654-03-8

Also from Michael D. Nadeau

<u>The Land of Lythinall Series</u>

The Darkness Returns
The Darkness Within
Tales From Lythinall
The Darkness Falls

<u>Rise of the Archmage Series</u>

Dragon Caller
Dragon Master

<u>Angels Among Us</u>

Acknowledgments

This is dedicated to my wonderful wife, Sheila, for putting up with me and my imagination. Without her support and love, these stories would never be possible. Shout out to my friends for always having faith in me and supporting my many stories I wrote them as gifts. Our many adventures play out in my head as I write these exciting stories. Special shout out to my fellow author B.K Bass for the accidental inspiration for this character.

Index

Prologue: To Tell the Story — 6

Across the Wide Seas — 11

Any Orc in a Storm — 35

Journey to the Isle of Ximn — 75

The Witch's Isle — 118

Jail Break — 157

Interlude: The Story Teller Falters — 202

The Shattered Sea — 205

The Wizard's Tower — 245

As the Gears Turn — 260

City of Mystery — 303

The Last Storm — 339

Epilogue: End of the Story — 364

Prologue: To Tell the Story

His slender hands held the ancient book with the utmost care, its fading pages held together by old magic. Calling this a book was a bit of a stretch, as the bindings had rotted away a very long time ago, and all that was left was a collection of parchment. The pages of the once infamous book were ripped and torn in various places with no discernible way to tell where they had been originally. Still, this was a treasured find; the original stories of the cursed elf Seltemver.

Karsis the bard, legendary rogue, warrior, and general hero of the downtrodden pulled out a chair and sat down, carefully laying out the pages on the wooden table. He couldn't believe that he was still alive, never mind the new Incarnation of Magic. His name had already spanned centuries, his deeds the stuff of legend. His auburn curls were as recognizable as his, exquisite burgundy longcoat. He had played for kings, slain tyrants, and even won the heart of an ancient dragon. That's what all the songs had said; he should know, he wrote most of them.

He stood a hair above five feet with long auburn curls draped over his slender shoulders. His stylish clothes were finely made, especially the burgundy longcoat that he was quite fond of. He had a ruffled shirt with tiny pockets, and his black pants fell to his black polished high boots, decorated with tiny charms. He focused his wandering thoughts and went back to work, knowing that he wouldn't have long to sift through them in peace; the twins would be on him the minute they came back from their evening walk with Tierra.

Karsis took a minute to look around the room and had to chuckle. It was Rhoe's old room and it had been converted into a guest room specifically for when Karsis visited. This was where it had all started almost a decade ago; a young Rhoe finding out that he was also a wizard and leaving to cross the land. The bard brushed his auburn curls from his face and started assembling the pages in some semblance of order. This would take him a while, but he was confident that he could put this back to its original form and restore the tale for all to read once more; just like he had when he was young.

Padding footfalls alerted him to the oncoming storm before they hit the door, his smile somehow widening despite the oncoming lack of peace and quiet. The twins were exactly like their parents in almost every way. The door burst open and the young boy and girl came spilling into the room, their eager eyes wide with expectation.

"Uncle Karsis!" they both shouted at once. Brinn and Braelyn Whitehair were almost eight years old and had the temperament of their mother as well as the curiosity of their father.

"I've said before, dear children, that I am not to be called 'Uncle'," Karsis admonished rather forcefully. "You may simply call me Karsis." In truth, he was their grandfather, but they were too young to understand that right now.

"Father says..."

"I know, but I would rather he didn't sometimes," Karsis interrupted, leaning back in his chair as the twins came around to see what he had brought them this time.

"What did you bring to read to us this time Unc...Karsis?" Braelyn corrected herself as she leaned over the scattered pages. She had Liss's eyes and her impatience.

"Is it an ancient spellbook from an evil sorcerer?" Brinn asked coming around the other side clearly annoyed that his sister got to the table first.

"It is ancient, yes, but it is certainly not a book of spells," Karsis said with a frown. "I've told you before, those books are only in stories. Real magic is asked for, not memorized as spells."

"So what is it?" they both asked in concert.

"It is a story about a cursed elf and a cursed ship," Karsis told them. "It was a favorite story of all the children when I was your age. We loved it so much that we would act out the parts of the characters in the streets."

Sadly, the only copy of the book was spirited away with Ill'lyth G'harr when she was banished and the stories were lost to the ages. Karsis thought as he was spinning the tale now, keeping them focused on his words rather than the book in front of them; It was the power of bards to be able to weave a tale so powerful that the listener could actually feel themselves in the story. "Imagine my surprise when I stumbled across this hidden in a secret room in G'harr while visiting the Sorcerer King."

"Why is it all in pieces?" Brinn asked as the twins jumped up on the bed in the room. They both got comfy and awaited the story that they always got when Karsis visited the northern village of Daelyn.

"It is in pieces because it has started to fall apart. I will have to assemble it as I tell you the tale, but the parts may be out of order," Karsis told them as he turned his chair around to face the bed. He may be the Incarnation of Magic and a powerful wizard, but these two kids had become his world of late. Ten more years and he would have to train them like he did their father. *And may the gods above help me when that time comes.*

"Why don't you put it together first then?" Braelyn asked as she kicked Brinn to get him to give up some blankets.

"Because it would take me *days* to do that," Karsis admitted. "And I know you are impatient to hear it correct?" The twins nodded and he put his feet up on the bed as he selected the first page.

"Is this a real tale?" Brinn asked kicking his feet with excitement.

"Some say that Seltemver did indeed exist, but as always, some truths are embellished. You will have to listen and form your own opinions on that matter,"

Karsis said with a flourish. "The beginning of each tale has a description of the story and notes from one of the characters—Amonar, the imp—that supposedly wrote the tales."

"So we can try and guess where they all fit as we hear them?" Braelyn asked excitedly.

"Yes, dear one," Karsis said as he flipped the first page over and found the scribbling in the hand of the imp. "Now, where were we? Oh yes. Once upon a time..."

Across the Wide Seas

This story is fun. Seltemver and I have been together for a little while at this point, but the ship and crew are relatively new to us. He decided to leave the crew on board when we found this port city so he could negotiate repairs with the local lord or whoever was in charge; the crew isn't exactly good around people. It was the second place we had been to and we weren't altogether convinced that we were being transported to different worlds yet. I went with him because he's bonded to me, but also because I find him fascinating, despite the violence he always gets himself into.

Repairs you ask? Well, let's just say that the time before this we came out of the storm in the middle of a heated exchange between two other ships and both of them thought we were the enemy. There was some yelling, some cannon fire, and then I had to work my magic, scaring most of our crew in the process. It was the first time I had used my infernal magic around them and it sure shocked Seltemver as well; thank the gods above that he was elven and was used to magic. Anyway, yeah...so we needed some repairs to the ship and of course, nothing went as planned...

—Amonar

Arrival in a Strange Land

He shook his head as he walked into the tavern, his short white hair spraying seawater over the patrons nearest him. He whipped off his worn brown longcoat and spun a chair around to sit, slinging his longbow on his back. His old friend, Amonar, fluttered up as he took off his coat, then settled back down on his shoulder with a huff that was ignored with practiced ease.

That was the worst sailing he had been through in a while, and they were lucky to be alive, though where in the heavens he was *this* time was anyone's guess. The elf laid his sheathed sword in his lap because the patrons were looking a little gruff about him being here. He would hate to kill someone his first day in this town. As if that was some sort of cue to the gods above, a rather large man came striding over.

"Hey, elf. Where'd you come from anyway? Ain't never seen anything like *that* thing there." The big man pointed to the creature on the elf's shoulder.

"You've never seen a longbow?" The elf asked sarcastically, knowing full well that the man was talking about Amonar, the tiny winged imp on his shoulder.

"Seltemver, he thinks I'm a thing," Amonar said, looking around the place for another exit just in case it came to blows. The poor thing hated violence.

"To him, you *are* a thing."

"Hey!" Amonar said with mock indignation.

"I'm just saying." Seltemver looked at the man and smiled, which never helped—or so he was told. "My friend here is harmless; and no, I'm not from around here." The elf kicked out the chair opposite him and gestured for the man to sit.

"Humph," the big man grunted. The rest of the patrons waited silently as the man sat hesitantly...the mumblings going back to normal once he had.

"My name is Seltemver Ashblade and this is my friend, Amonar. Amonar, say hello."

"Hello," Amonar said, imitating a parrot.

"Anyway," Seltemver said, smacking his friend lightly to make him behave, "would you tell us where we are, good sir?"

The man scratched his head and looked at the ceiling for a minute. "What did I do to deserve this?" he asked under his breath, then fixed his gaze on Seltemver once more. "You don't know where you are? How did you get here if you didn't know where you were going?"

"You always find the smart ones, don't you?" Amonar asked as the imp stared at a passing serving girl with his tiny black eyes.

"Hush Amonar." Seltemver sighed and waved his hand for the girl to come over as she walked by. "You see, good man, we were on my ship, the *Seahaven*, sailing for Larishan Cove when we hit a terrible storm. We fought our way through it with some casualties and limped into port here...wherever here happens to be." It helped that most of that was the truth. All right, sixty percent truth at least.

"Oh. Well, in that case, you happen to be at the port town of Gnashar." The man said with a lopsided grin; a grin that never touched his narrowed eyes. The man leaned back as the serving girl came over and he put down four copper pieces. "Ale, Filden."

"Yes, sir. And you, good sir?" Filden asked, averting her eyes from the table.

"I'll have whatever is standard. House ale or mead," Seltemver said, eyeing the rest of the bar with suspicion. It had gone quiet once more and he didn't know why. What was he missing?

Strange Place Indeed

"Mead?" the serving girl asked with a confused tone.

"Where have you brought me?" Amonar asked, feigning a grievous wound and teetering on the elf's shoulder as if he was about to plummet to his death. "She's not heard of Mead!?"

"All right, that's enough," Seltemver growled, as he felt the imp stiffen on his shoulder. Seltemver looked at the big man across from him with more attention this time, knowing he must've missed something. The man had plain breeches and a tunic, nothing special there. His hair was short and well-kept, his muscles honed from regular use, and his skin bore a dark tan. *Probably a farmer or some such,* the elf thought. The big man's eyes didn't show any spark of great intellect, but Seltemver had gathered that from the conversation already. In fact, the man was the perfect example of normal. *Too normal.* It had to be an act. "I never got your name, sir," Seltemver asked nonchalantly.

"That you didn't, stranger." The man pushed his chair back and stood slowly, flexing his arms and cracking his back and neck. He held out his hand towards the serving girl. "Filden. Ale. Now." The girl grabbed an ale from the table next to them without asking and handed it to the man and he drained it in one shot.

Seltemver hooked his foot around the bottom of his chair as he sat back, ready for trouble but trying to look comfortable. More patrons got up, but this time came over to the big man's side. *Well, there goes the 'no killing on the first day' thing*, he thought sardonically. Then it clicked. "Gnashar, I presume?"

The man called Gnashar smiled and took a large club from one of the men nearest him, testing it for balance and weight. "You see, stranger, this is my town and newcomers with strange pets spell trouble; especially *your* kind."

"Seltemver, he called me a pet," Amonar said looking to the rafters—probably for a safe place to fly to. Not only did the imp abhor violence, blood made him squeamish. If it came to blows—and honestly, when did it not lately—the imp would bolt for the highest beam and wait it out like he always did.

"Not *now*, Amonar.," Seltemver said, sizing up the other men that had joined Gnashar's side. They didn't seem overly competent, mainly the type that used overwhelming numbers and intimidation to cower their opponents; they would die quickly.

"So, you want me to leave? Fine, I'll be going," Seltemver said, knowing they wouldn't let him leave. He could see that they already had weapons drawn and fire in their veins, but it did give them pause. *They are so used to immediate violence that I confused them,* he thought as the men started to look at each other. *Where in the deep hells did I end up?*

"Too late for that, elf. Your kind always spells trouble," Gnashar said as he advanced upon Seltemver. "I just wanted to see if you were here for Lord Masonel or not. Since you're not here for him, I can just kill you and be done with it." He raised his club and started to bring it down, but Seltemver burst into action.

Seltemver stood, flexed his leg, and sent his chair flying into the man to his right. He drew his blade and slashed at Gnashar in one fluid movement, the magically sharp blade opening the man's belly, as he grabbed another chair and threw it at a third man. The elven warrior backed up, avoiding the splash of blood and entrails as Gnashar dropped his club and grasped at his innards spilling from the wound.

"Wha...," Gnashar started to say as his guts slipped through his fingers and splashed to the ground around his blood-soaked boots. The man dropped to his knees, swayed for a moment as his eyes glossed over, then fell to the ground dead.

Seltemver spun and danced with his sharp, thin blade, parrying blows with ease. No words were spoken as they danced around the table. Fear slowly crept into the faces of his opponents as one after another fell to his overwhelming skill.

Amonar had flown straight up, probably hiding until it was over. Seltemver would never get used to an imp that hated violence. Imps, by their very nature, were violent and malicious, yet this one had always been a bit of a coward. A club struck the elf's shoulder, snapping him out of his thoughts. He spun with the impact and came around with his sword to take the man in the leg. He finished the man quickly and a second man after that; the whole fight lasted less than a minute. The attackers were all down and the rest of the patrons had fled out the back door. All but the serving girl.

Filden, I think her name was, Seltemver thought as he wiped his blade on one of the dead men and smiled.

Tough Choices

Filden stood right where she was, daring not to move lest the elf see that as a sign of aggression. The elf had been talking so nicely and then suddenly he had turned into this...killer. Worse, he was good at it. *Very* good. Lord Masonel would come down on the town with a vengeance now; Gnashar was his pet enforcer. Filden saw the elf looking at her and swallowed hard. "You're not going to kill me too, are you?"

"Why would I kill you?" Seltemver met her eyes as he sheathed his sword.

Filden leaned back against the bar. "I don't know, just... you killed all of them and so quickly." She had to sit down, the scene getting to her finally. Yet she was awkwardly happy. Gnashar was an absolute brute, and she would never have to suffer his meaty touch again. Now they just had to survive the lord's wrath.

"Well, I have this thing about people attacking me," Seltemver said as he spied his friend in the rafters and signaled for him to come down. "I tend to retaliate with extreme force. It works very well, as no one that attacks me ever does it a second time." He moved to her side with caution and laid a tentative hand on her shoulder. "You, my dear, have nothing to worry about."

She smiled up at him as he comforted her. It was odd being cared for by a complete stranger. "Well, then we have to get out of here," Filden said as she sat there trying to process all that she had seen. It's not like she had never seen a dead body or anything, yet this was somehow different. "Lord Masonel will know about this soon and probably send down a force to deal with you."

"I thought this was Gnashar's town?" Seltemver asked slowly.

"That oaf liked to think it was his, but he served Lord Masonel."

"Great, more violence. Why do I stay with you Seltemver?" Amonar asked as he alighted upon his friends shoulder once more.

"You stay because you are bound to my soul."

"Ah yeah, there *is* that."

Filden shook her head and got up to get her meager belongings. She didn't have a room, per se, as she slept on the floor in the back room, but she kept a bag behind the bar with what she held most dear. She knew that if she could get away from this damned town she could truly start a life and be free of slavery once and for all. She had heard of other places from travelers and dared to hope for a life free of groping hands. Now it seemed that day had come; now she just had to survive. *Let's just hope that this elf is as good as he seems...*

Fight or Flight

Seltemver waited as Filden stood and walked to the bar to grab her bag. The girl had said that the lord would send a force and that meant he wasn't done yet. *Maybe I should've taken some of the crew with me*, Seltemver thought as Filden retrieved a pack from behind the bar.

"Does he protect you?" she asked taking off her apron and letting down her hair. Her demeanor had changed, and Seltemver thought she seemed relieved to be free of this place.

"Amonar is supposed to, but he doesn't like violence," Seltemver said, looking at his friend and smiling despite the remark. He grabbed his coat and shook it out, spun it around his shoulder, and settled it over his bow once more.

Amonar leapt up and came back down as the coat came on, clearing his throat loudly and puffing out his little chest, trying to look dignified. "I am bound to keep him alive at all costs. If he dies, I would be thrust down into the pits of the Hells forever; burning endlessly in torment until time ends."

"Drama hound."

"Psychopath."

"So," Filden interjected before they got into it, "do you have a ship we could take before the lord comes?"

Seltemver smiled. She didn't say 'take me home', or 'let me leave before you', she had asked to go with him. He looked at her and noticed for the first time how stunning she was. She had long blond hair and a slim build with piercing green eyes. Pity that he wasn't thinking of leaving just yet.

"No, the ship was heavily damaged and needs time to make repairs." Seltemver noticed her frown and couldn't help but laugh. "Don't worry I know how to handle a *lord*."

"This one is not a noble by any means; he is a warlord." Filden sighed and hefted her bag over her shoulder. "Well, I'm going with you no matter where it is. My life here is done after all this." She gestured to the carnage.

"You can't just work for the bar still?" Amonar asked, seeming interested in her dilemma. "It doesn't seem to be that big a deal."

Filden chuckled and patted Amonar on the head. "You don't understand. Gnashar was my owner, and a slave can't live when her owner has died and there was no transaction. I'm free property, and free property is always cashed out."

"Slavery," Seltemver swore with disgust. He hated that trade and it was the one thing he would never stoop to. "Well, warlord or not, I'm still not worried about this Masonel." He walked to the door and opened it, stepping out into the overcast morning.

The little town of Gnashar—if that was what it was actually called—seemed nice at first glance. A wide, packed earthen road ran from the docks up through the center of town sporting what businesses there were. Off of this were side roads that presumably led to houses with women hanging clothes and doing other such chores as the distant ring of the blacksmith busy at work echoed in the evening air. Ahead, in what could only be a merchant's area, boys cried out deals for their prospective masters as dusk approached and vendors started closing up their carts.

Seltemver smiled. It looked quaint actually, until he saw the row of horses with armed men riding towards them with a heavily armored man in their midst. They moved with purpose and were bearing down on the trio, staring with smiles that had no mirth in them. Lord Masonel and his men, no doubt.

"Speak of the Demon," Amonar said, looking around for another place to hide.

"Seltemver are you sure we can't run for the ship anyway?" Filden asked nervously.

"It's fine, I'll take care of this; just stay behind me." He had faced odds like this before, but admittedly not while protecting someone as well. Seltemver drew his enchanted slim blade slowly, to add effect for the men watching. Seltemver's blade never needed to be sharpened, always having a wicked edge that would slice through most things with ease. The blade had even cut through things that most swords never could, severing metal if swung with purpose. As the approaching men slowed down, Seltemver spread his feet apart and made notes on which ones looked brave, and which ones seemed unsure. This was when reading people came in handy.

Heavy Heart

Jacen Drake rode point with his lord behind him. This stranger had reportedly killed Gnashar—Gods above take that man's soul anyway—and the lord meant to deal swift and harsh justice; at least what Lord Masonel considered justice that is. Jacen shifted in his scale armor and fingered his short sword in its worn leather sheath. Jacen had been leading the men under Gnashar—that enormous pile of filth of a man—for over four years now as Captain of the Watch, and he despised Lord Masonel just as much as his dead superior. His family, however, depended on his income. So here he was, killing another person for no good reason other than probably defending himself.

"Eyes front, Captain Drake. This man is dangerous and must be taken seriously."

The tone of his lord told Jacen that the pompous bastard wasn't taking any chances. Admittedly, When he had heard it was an elf, he had worried as well. Lord Masonel summoned all his guard under the Captain of the Watch and rode out immediately. Twenty trained cavalry would have no trouble against a lone swordsman, even if it was an elf.

Jacen kicked his horse in front of the other men signaling for them to slow. He proceeded carefully, keeping an eye on the elf as he neared. The stranger had already shifted his feet, a sign that he was skilled. Assuming a stance to sidestep any charge that the horse would make, and opposite his shield arm at that, showed Jacen that his foe was well-trained, and then some.

"Hail, elf. I, Jacen Drake, Captain of the Watch, hereby place you under arrest for murder." He had barely finished the sentence when the elf ran toward him at full speed. He had missed the movement until the stranger was halfway to him, that slim blade gleaming despite the overcast weather. Jacen whistled and pulled the reins of the horse, spinning the beast around in a blink to get his shield to bear and block any incoming blow. When the elf ducked under the shield and slashed low, Jacen knew he was doomed; the elf was going for the saddle straps!

"Kill him and the woman!" Lord Masonel yelled from behind him, inciting half of the men to charge while keeping some around him as a shield.

Jacen thrust his short sword to parry the slim blade as the elf slashed and their weapons rang out across the earthen road. To his shock, when he pulled his blade back once more, he saw that it had been cut in half! The horse reared as Jacen pulled the reins again, spinning the horse away from that deceptively sharp blade, yet the elf had rolled under the deadly hooves and slashed once more at the straps holding the saddle in place. Jacen tried to leap clear, but his heavy armor prevented such agile movements. As the saddle came free, he tumbled from the beast and hit the packed road hard, his breath leaving him in a rush. Before he could roll away, the horse came down on his right leg with its front hooves and crushed it. Jacen cried out in shock and pain as the elf leapt upon the beast and took off towards the men charging at them.

Among the Enemy

Seltemver slashed carefully, severing the strap to the saddle without hitting the animal, and watched the captain fall to the dirt. He could tell the young man had no heart in this fight and he wanted to spare as many that didn't rush to their deaths as he could. Sometimes, however, it couldn't be helped. He saw the horse crush the man's leg and winced, knowing that he was done in this fight. Seltemver leapt onto the horse bareback and kicked it around to meet the charging cavalry, guiding the animal with his knees. Seltemver had been riding horses for over a hundred years and felt right at home despite being on a ship for most of his life.

The move surprised the men, as usually a lone rider tried to flee. Seltemver was among them then, taking three of them down right away in the confusion, his sword slicing through their leather effortlessly and sending them to the dirt. Seltemver felt blades bite into his arm and back as he spun this way and that, slashing with methodical savagery. The wounds he took were minor, so he grimaced through the pain and killed two more that came at him. He spared a glance back at Filden and Amonar, seeing the imp behind the girl and holding onto her leg. "Don't worry he does this all the time," the imp said loudly.

Seltemver could tell whose heart was in this fight and who's wasn't, so he turned the horse towards the main host surrounding the lord still and kicked forward in another rush, He slashed left, taking another man out but not before a man with a spear stabbed him squarely in the shoulder; the blow almost taking him right off the horse.

Missed that guy, I must be getting old, Seltemver joked to himself. *And I won't be getting any older if I miss spear guy again.* Seltemver swung his horse around and slashed the spearman across the back, cutting clean through the leather armor and into his spine. He spun the horse and kicked it towards the lord, parrying blows from the remaining three soldiers as he charged.

"Fight me so that these men will live, coward!"

Lord Masonel laughed as he shouted back, "You surprise me, elf. I had expected a summary execution, but instead, you treated us to a display of expert swordsmanship. Challenging me might be the only mistake you made today." The Lord guided his horse out from behind the ten men around him, waving them back. "I would've let you off with a quick death, but now? Now you will learn what pain is." The Lord charged then, the two warriors meeting as the overcast sky opened up and poured rain down on the town.

Seltemver swung his sword and caught the lord in the chest as he passed, his sword ringing off the ornate armor like it was a mountain. The sword sounded almost like it was crying, denied the blood that it yearned for. The elven warrior came around and found that the lord was ready for him, slashing at the elf's horse. Seltemver knew the animal was doomed, so he pulled his feet up and pushed off, leaping for the side to get clear of the falling beast, lest he get caught under the animal as the Captain did.

Seltemver landed in a roll, his sword flying away to his right, and came up covered in dirt and blood; he knew he was in trouble. Seltemver saw Lord Masonel dismount slowly; giving him time to gain his feet. A sense of dread crawled down the elf's back. The man had the advantage of being mounted and gave that up...this man wasn't even worried.

Seltemver lunged for his sword, rolling again and coming up as the big man charged him, his own sword whistling through the air in a deadly arc. Seltemver parried the sword, notching it badly, and riposted, his blade bouncing off of the man's armor once more. *Not good,* Seltemver thought backing up slowly. *That never happens.*

"Give up, elf, no weapon may pierce this enchanted armor, and many have tried. Even the joints are impervious to penetration; you have no chance." Masonel laughed as he advanced once more, his notched sword swinging for Seltemver's head. It was a feint though—and one he missed, sadly—for as soon as Seltemver ducked, Masonel's other hand punched low, catching him hard in the sternum. The air rushed out of his lungs as he was hefted up with that same hand, easily held aloft in the grip of the armored lord.

"Little... help...Amonar?"

To the Rescue

Amonar was horrified. Never had he seen his friend and master thrown around like this. Then he heard the lord say that the armor was enchanted and he knew Seltemver was in trouble. He saw the big man heft his master up in the air like a child's doll and tried to stop his wings from shaking. The remaining guards had all stopped and were watching the exchange with eager eyes; at least some of them were. Some were looking at the ground; unwilling to witness what they knew would come next.

Amonar didn't want to even guess what that was. If it could turn hardened warriors to look away, then it was bad. The imp was still trying to figure out if he needed to intervene when Seltemver called for help and Amonar sighed; the choice had been taken from him. It helped to know that he had to act, or his friend would perish. He closed his eyes and concentrated, pulling his power up from deep within. He hated this part the most. When the power rose to the surface, he opened his eyes; eyes that now had a deep red glow to them.

Amonar looked out from behind Filden and pointed straight at Lord Masonel. "Ackresh firan sistern dwon ta hellin!" he said, his voice resounding across the open road for all to hear with a deep resonating echo. The sound of the hellish power cowed man and beast alike, the remaining guards fleeing rather than face whatever could've uttered those words. When Amonar felt the power take hold of Masonel, he looked away.

"I'm sorry," Amonar whispered to himself more than anyone still nearby. He held onto the girl with preternatural strength, lest she flee as well. Filden resisted only slightly, then relaxed and crumpled down in the dirt sobbing in the rain.

Seltemver smiled at the sound of Amonar's voice. He alone, out of anyone here, knew what was coming. "Swords...can't get to you...Masonel," the elf said with gasping breath. "But how...do you feel about fire?"

Amonar watched as the lord's eyes widened in horror dropping Seltemver and backing away. Masonel spun in circles, calling out for mercy as flames began to consume him from within.

Fire gushed out of the gaps of the enchanted armor, even coming out of the neck, licking his flesh like a hungry lover. Lord Masonel screamed, thrashing on the ground now as he tried desperately to remove the armor that had only moments before protected him, but now entrapped him with the burning wrath of the deep hells. Masonel's screams echoed across the entire town as the flames took his flesh first, then worked down to the bone, burning him to a cinder; the infernal magic kept him conscious past the point where he should have blacked out from the pain; such was the hellish power.

Around the thrashing lord, flames sprouted from the ground, forming hands that curled around the agonizing lord and pulled the burning body into the earth itself, the dirt closing in after, sealing him away. It was over in moments, yet Masonel's screams continued to echo as if from very far away, adding to the horror.

Decisions

As the rain poured down, finally quenching the remaining flames now that the infernal magic had dissipated, Seltemver looked at the only people left near them: Filden, who couldn't run because Amonar held her. Amonar, who was looking at the ground with tears in his tiny black eyes. And finally, the captain, who couldn't run because of a shattered leg.

"What have you done!?" Jacen asked in a hysterical tone.

"I've... *we've* stopped a tyrant that was holding your town in an iron grip of fear and slavery," Seltemver said as he walked over and helped the man up, wincing at the sound of grating bone and the man's whimpers of pain.

"But..." The captain was at a loss for words.

"Belt up, Captain; or should I say, Lord?" Seltemver smiled despite his injuries. "Let's go to my ship, I have a healer there that can help you." Seltemver turned to Amonar and Filden. "Come on, you two; we can rest on the *Seahaven.*" He saw the reluctant, fear-filled, eyes of Filden and knew that she had changed her mind about going with him.

"Seltemver I..." Filden began, then stopped as Amonar fluttered off and landed upon the elf's shoulder once more.

Seltemver raised his hand to stall her. "Filden, I'm sure that as the new Lord of..." He shook his head and laughed, looking askance at the new lord. "You need a new name for this town, by the way."

"Freeport," Jacen said through the pain of his crushed leg. "That was what it was called before Masonel came here with his warriors years ago."

"Good. So, Filden, I'm sure the Lord of Freeport will let you live now that slavery is going to be abolished. Right, Lord?" Seltemver asked with an edge to his voice, implying that if it wasn't, there could be more trouble.

"Of course." Jacen turned to Filden, who took his arm from Seltemver. Jacen smiled as best he could as they hobbled to the docks.

"I'm fine. No one bother to comfort me or anything," Amonar said sullenly as he sat on Seltemver's shoulder, sulking.

As the group made their way to the docks, Filden and Jacen could not contain their shock and surprise at the sight of Seltemver's crew as they looked upon the *Seahaven* docked below; Seltemver seemed to be the only elf. Orcs worked busily at rigging, supplies, and other tasks as one larger orc stood near the wheel shouting orders in a gruff manner.

"Don't be alarmed, The orcs of the *Seahaven* have no problems with humans, but I knew how they would have been greeted, so they stayed on the ship when it docked," Seltemver said laughing at their faces. Amonar went flying ahead, waving at the orcs, but seemed to be invisible to them as they ignored the imp and his gestures.

One orc, a grey-skinned female with braids, came down the plank as they neared, shaking her head. "We heard Amonar's voice...just couldn't resist causing trouble could you Seltemver?"

"Shut it, Grunhilde," Seltemver said laughing. He turned to Jacen and Filden as the orc approached. "Lord, Lady, this is Grunhilde, the *Seahaven's* healer.

"Is that an amulet of Dava?" Jacen asked incredulously.

"Yes. Do you have a problem with the God of Protection and Life?" Grunhilde asked, her tusks showing through her wide smile.

"No...just,"

Seltemver patted Jacen on the shoulder lightly. "I know. You didn't think Dava would have an orc for a follower. Well, He does and she channels his power with skilled hands and a full heart." Seltemver caught Filden staring at the orc healer's figure and laughed again. Grunhilde may be an orc, but she was in fine shape for a female of her kind and he had often wondered why no one else on the ship had hooked up with her—aside from the bruises they would get trying that is. "Let's get aboard and tend to your wounds, we have some things we want to ask the new Lord of Freeport and some wine that is itching to be had.

Setting Sail

Grunhilde had the new lord's leg splinted in record time, her healing hands working miracles on the wounded lord and making it easier for the breaks to heal. Bones would take a while to fully seal, but her power made it easier for the body to do that. The cuts and bruises were gone in minutes though, much to the lord's shock.

Filden helped Jacen with his recovery as the orcs repaired the ship, but Seltemver knew that it would turn into something a lot more than that. He was good at reading people, after all. The new lord had some questions about the damage done to the ship, as most of it did not look to be storm-related. Cannon fire had wrecked most of it and the mast was charred from fire. Seltemver explained it away as an attack before the storm; again, at least half of it was true.

Ten days later the *Seahaven* eased out of Freeport, its damage repaired and the crew in good spirits. Filden stayed behind in Freeport as expected, holding onto the lord's arm as they waved goodbye. Now the *Seahaven* was sailing on foreign seas and with the charts that Lord Jacen had provided, they would try for the shore of someplace to the west called Handonin.

"Captain! Storm on the horizon!" The lookout, a smaller orc named Crak called out.

Seltemver frowned as the sea breeze blew his short white hair. He was afraid of this. He knew they were cursed, always getting caught in this strange storm and being sent someplace *else*, just the time it took to show up was different. "Well Amonar, where do you think we'll end up next?" Amonar never answered the rhetorical question. No one could know.

"Great, here we go again," was the only thing the imp ever said.

Any Orc in a Storm

This time we came out of the storm near a northern chain of scattered islands, with snow and everything. Most of the crew had never seen snow, and it was a rare thing for me as well, though I'd seen it once or twice with my old master. This last time through the storm was the worst...we were in a world with land but absolutely no people. It was unsettling that we sailed around all these towns but no one at all. There were shops with supplies in them and even fresh food...yet the people were just gone. They had some cool items we had never seen, but all in all, it was creepy.

So here we were, a new land and that was exciting after all that boredom, mainly because we could see people and other boats. This time we took Grunhilde with us when we went ashore. She is the healer aboard the Seahaven and the toughest orc I've ever met, besides Toth that is. By now we've realized that we are being transported to different worlds through that storm and most of us try not to think about the implications of that.

I was sure that we couldn't get into that much trouble in this world...boy was I wrong. So get ready for some good old-fashioned sarcasm and of course, trouble, Seltemver style.

—Amonar

Coming Out of the Storm

The ship rocked on the massive waves and righted as the spray hit his slender elven face. He could see sunlight ahead; the sign that they were coming out of this supernatural storm once more. This was always the part that he dreaded, the 'where are we now' dilemma. He shouted orders to his crew, a finer bunch of orcs you couldn't find. "Tighten that line, Toth!" he called over the crashing seas around them, the wind whipping his short white hair about like a rowboat in a whirlpool; his brown longcoat wasn't doing much better in this storm.

"Aye Capt'n. I never thought of that," the burly orc replied, more venom than usual in his deep voice.

Seltemver Ashblade, elven pirate and Captain of the *Seahaven* smiled at the snarky tone of his first mate. This trip had been a rough one, better than usual, but rough all the same. Their eighth since being cursed, his crew was getting downright depressed about ever finding a way out of the strange predicament they were all in. *At least this time we won't have massive repairs to worry about,* he thought. *Let them get snarky for once, they deserved it.*

The *Seahaven's* crew was made up of orcs that knew their way around a ship like some know how to breathe. They had been with Seltemver on this cursed journey for gods above knew how long now. Time seemed to be different every time they came out of the storm, and with strange worlds, it wasn't always tracked the same.

"Seltemver, are you going to take that from him?" a voice on his shoulder asked, clawed hands digging into the captain's coat as the ship rocked back and forth.

"Amonar, they are just vexed, let them blow off some steam," Seltemver told the imp on his shoulder. He knew that his friend was just as wound up as the crew, hating sailing as much as he hated violence. The imp wanted this curse to end as much as the orcs did, so they could all get back home. Not that Amonar wanted to get back to *his* home; he was just as cursed as the ship was.

"You know, for an elf, you're a lot more forgiving than most." The imp said, closing his eyes as the sunlight washed over the deck of the *Seahaven* as the storm shut off like blowing out a candle. Then the cold air hit and they all knew they were somewhere else again.

"Yeah well, my upbringing was a bit skewed." Seltemver shook the sea spray out of his hair and straightened his longcoat. He spun the wheel and brought them around, watching the seas change before his eyes. A 'huzzah' went up from the crew as they stopped rocking and settled into a more steady rhythm. "Amonar, fly up and see what you can see with those eyes of yours," Seltemver told his friend as he looked at his compass with skepticism. They were headed north when they left the last port town, now it seemed that they were headed due south, and they were obviously in the far north, as large ice flows could be seen to either side in the distance.

Amonar flew up to the crow's nest—renamed Crak's nest for the small orc that usually took post up here—without arguing, which was astounding to any that would've witnessed it. *Not that they would pay attention to me,* the imp thought sadly. *Most of the crew hates me, and the ones that don't, are afraid of me.* His thoughts drifted to poor Crak, who still wasn't completely healed from the broken leg he got in the everlasting storm world they had been to. Just thinking of how much their ship had been tossed around in that place made Amonar's stomach turn.

The red-skinned imp settled down far above the deck of the ship and folded his wings, peering into the distance and focusing his eyes to see what lay ahead of them. He could see impossibly far when he wanted to, a gift of his infernal legacy, and it was one of his powers that he didn't mind using; the others made him sick to even think about. Amonar could make out a large mass in his vision, maybe a couple of hours due south.

"Land!" Amonar called down to Toth, the burly orc that was Seltemver's first mate. Toth was the only orc on board the *Seahaven* that talked to him without disdain in his voice. Toth had umber-colored skin, as most orcs did, and curved tusks protruding from his mouth. His long hair fell across broad shoulders and his heavily muscled arms bore tattoos of various weapons.

"How far, Am?" the orc asked, using the nickname he had come up with for the imp, his booming voice carrying across the deck.

How can they talk so good with those tusks in their mouth? Amonar thought before he answered. Some things just mystified him in this world. "Maybe a couple of hours? Is that how you guys say it?" Amonar never got the seafaring lingo they used, it just baffled him. He guessed it was fine because Toth just laughed and shook his head. The imp settled in and kept a lookout, just in case there were any ships that might see them.

Seltemver heard the call of land and let loose a genuine smile. They came out of the storm that time without too much damage, everyone in one piece, and land ahead. "Maybe my luck is starting to turn?" he asked the gods above as he looked up to the clouds.

"Wouldn't that be a nice change," Toth said, coming up to the helm.

"Yeah, well, I'm not putting any gold on it."

"Seriously though, Capt'n, how many times do you think we have to do this?" The worry in Toth's voice was plain to anyone with ears, never mind the ears of an elf.

"I honestly don't know, Toth. You were there when that sea witch cursed me. She said I was doomed to sail distant waters until we found a home." Seltemver looked right into the grey eyes of his first mate, wishing that he could tell him something different; he just couldn't.

"I do remember, and we all thought it was weird that she said you, then followed with 'you all'." The orc stood by the wheel and laid a hand on Seltemver's shoulder. "Yet, we said it then and it still stands. You saved us all from that bitch, so we are *all* with you until death...and beyond." The last part was said as Toth looked up at Crak's nest, apprehension furrowing his sloping brow.

"Listen, I know most of you don't trust Amonar. Just know that the ship isn't my only curse, and he means no harm to anyone who doesn't try and harm me." Seltemver knew that his crew was a superstitious lot, and having a tiny demon-like creature on board was difficult. Some of the crew had warmed to the imp, though Amonar didn't see it; yet there were still some that gave the sign of Dava when he flew by.

"No, it's all right. That little guy has saved us time and time again, it's just *how* he did it that doesn't sit well with some of the crew." Toth nodded and walked back down to the deck, calling orders to the rest of the crew in preparation for land.

Seltemver watched him go with an odd sense of pride. They were a good bunch of orcs but if you had ever told him before all of this that he would be sailing with an orc crew, he would've laughed himself to death.

"Stop feeling sorry for yourself and get it together." A stern feminine voice said from behind him.

Seltemver jumped then laughed as a female orc slapped him on the shoulder. "Hey, I'm allowed once in a while you know," he said to the orc healer. Grunhilde was a huge grey-skinned orc with long braids and a fierce smile. The best healer he had ever seen, she had a good eye and a bedside manner that could level a mountain. She got the job done though, and it still amazed him that she could channel the healing power of the gods, even a little; his upbringing had always said that it was impossible. Of course, it also said that all elves could cast magic when clearly he couldn't. "I'll feel better once we get into town and find out where we are this time."

"You always say that then you end up in trouble and we all have to save you," Grunhilde said, her tusky grin unnerving.

"That was one time...and she was a shapeshifter. How was I supposed to know?" They both laughed as the ship sailed on towards a fate that neither of them saw coming. What else was new?

All Ashore that's Going Ashore

Within a couple of hours, just as Amonar had guessed, they came within view of the island; or more importantly, islands. There were two of them, separated by a two-mile channel. He thought about heading through there, but he could see the waves crashing upon the rocks on either side. Anyone worth their salt would know the currents slamming together at the mouth of this little channel, as well as the rocks littered among the edges, meant certain doom for a large ship. It would be pure folly to try and sail through it without scouting it out first. The *Seahaven* could probably do it, but it would take all the training of his expert crew to make it in one piece.

Seltemver spun the ship to starboard and aimed for the snowy shore near the mountains. They stood out like a triple monolith in the white expanse that stretched out before him and he wondered if he even *had* any fur cloaks on board. *No matter, I'll just pick one up in port*, he thought, as he angled the ship in quickly.

Seltemver ordered the anchor dropped about two miles out, just to be sure the strange tides didn't pull the ship in too close, and saw the small port near the town up on the hill. Smaller ships were docked and loading something, while a huge ship stood even further out towards the channel like some sort of sentinel. The ships were unlike anything he had ever seen.

"Orcish, if I'm not mistaken," Toth said, coming up to the helm once more. "Though that type of ship is like nothing I've ever encountered."

"Good, It's not just me," Seltemver said, bowing to the first mate and indicating the wheel. "You're in charge until we come back and I let you all know that it's safe."

"It's never safe."

"Hey, our luck has to turn at some point Toth, have faith."

"Luck has nothing to do with it, you always kill people."

"He's not wrong," Amonar chimed in, grinning from long-pointed ear to long-pointed ear, as he flew down from the Crak's nest and alighted on the elf's shoulder.

"You want to stay here with them?"

"Here's me shutting up." Amonar pouted and folded his little arms.

Toth smiled wickedly. "At least take Grunhilde with you this time, those orc ships might mean that she could help talk us into some good trade, and when something happens, she can patch you up." Toth was trying not to laugh and failing miserably.

"Actually that sounds like a good plan, and this time I'll cover up in case this place hates white hair like that gear world did." Seltemver clasped the arm of his first mate and walked off to get ready, silently praying that they could have a peaceful time in a new world for once. *Not that the last place wasn't peaceful, but it was so empty that it was unnerving,* he thought.

Hours later, as the sun was going down, Seltemver pulled the small boat up to the docks at the bottom of a high cliff. He made sure he kept his hood pulled over his short hair and his hands inside of his cloak just in case. The cold didn't affect elves that much, yet even so he was feeling himself start to shiver. Amonar, of course, was perfectly fine as always. Grunhilde argued, but grudgingly came, if only to keep them out of trouble. That remark had the imp laughing for an hour.

"I'll go on ahead and see what there is for shops," the orc healer said, her braids click-clacking as she bounded out of the boat. Her huge battle axe hanging at her side looked almost as menacing as her tusky smile.

Seltemver nodded and continued to tie up the small boat, making sure the knot would hold before setting out. If he lost another boat he wouldn't hear the end of it.

"It's real quiet around here, huh?" Amonar asked, looking around suspiciously.

"Yeah, maybe we came at some festival or something? I don't know. Let's catch up with Grunhilde and find out." Seltemver walked on, up the path, Amonar on his shoulder and his hand on his slim blade. He had left his longbow back on the ship, mainly because he couldn't hide it under his cloak. So if he needed range he was out of luck.

From the docks, it was a hike up a long set of stone steps that wound back and forth up the high, stone cliff. The snow on either side of the steps was fairly deep and the ice on the stone made his progress slow going. About halfway up he could hear the distant cheering of a large crowd and smiled despite the unknown. It was good to hear people cheering, that meant they were enjoying themselves. *Maybe this land won't be so bad*, he dared to think.

At the top of the stair, it opened up into a wide walkway, with huge tusk-like bones, covered in snow, serving as an entry arch. The houses were mostly stone and wood, decorated with tusks and other animal bones and hides. He was no expert, but it all looked orcish, much like the ships. There was no sign of anyone else in the street. Despite the ominous feel of the area, the wonder of the snowy landscape put him a little at ease. He hadn't seen snow like this since he was young.

The drifts were massive near some of the houses, the wind whipping it around this high up on the mountain, and he could see some of the figures made out of the snow decorating the fronts of the houses; children having fun always meant a relaxed environment.

"I don't like this..."Amonar squirmed on his shoulder.

"You never like anything."

"True, true."

"You there!" A gruff voice called out from the far left. "Why aren't you at the auction?"

Seltemver glanced that way, still keeping his visage hidden under his cloak, and saw a huge green-skinned orc dressed as some sort of guard hailing them. *Green skin, now that's different,* Seltemver thought as he turned and walked on, ignoring the guard and heading for the cheering crowd. "Headed that way now," he called back in an unassuming voice, trying not to say too much in this unknown land. Hells, in one land Amonar had said the word mead and it put them under suspicion.

"Hey what is that thing on your shoulder?" the guard asked, closing the distance quickly.

"Why does everyone call me a thing!?" Amonar shispered—a word that Seltemver came up with for the way the imp could whisper and still seem to shout at the same time—

"Just my new pet," Seltemver called back, grabbing Amonar's mouth as he said it, knowing that the imp was going to protest quite loudly over that one. He looked and saw Grunhilde up ahead and whistled a two-note shrill that would tell her he needed help.

"Ah there you are," Grunhilde said as he neared, "and who is that handsome thing you brought with you?" The healer's voice, normally gruff, had toned down to a husky pant at the sight of the burly guard. She walked right past Seltemver and Amonar and laid her hand on the guard's chest, letting her tusky smile touch her deep grey eyes.

Seltemver walked on towards the crowd, looking back to see the guard obviously smitten with the orc healer and knowing that he would owe her big time for that save. He never noticed the crowd makeup until he was amongst them, then froze. They were *all* orcs. Every last one of them.

"Mm mm," Amonar said under the hand that was still clamped down over his mouth.

Seltemver didn't say a word, he just backed up the way he came and went off behind one of the dwellings, plowing through the knee-deep snow; he never even bothered to look up on the stage of the auction. As he came around the stone house and into what could only be called a garden, he saw a female elf tending the frozen soil. The snow back here had been cleared for some sort of planting; what they could grow in the frozen ground was beyond him, though. Seltemver was relieved that he had found someone that wasn't an orc, yet his elation lasted exactly three seconds.

As the female elf turned at his approach, Seltemver could see the chains that bound her to an iron post not ten feet away. "Damn them to the deep hells. It just *had* to be slavers again didn't it?" he asked with a hint of sadness in his voice. "Are you all right?" Stepping closer, he lowered his hood so that she could see his face.

The elf made some sign with her hands and shook her head as if in panic. She was dressed sparsely, wearing only a thin overcoat that seemed torn and shredded.

"She can't speak, you should know that," another voice said coming around the other side of the house where a path had been cleared through the snow. This voice belonged to a human man, roughly average height with short black hair. He too had chains on his hands but wasn't tied to a post thank the gods. He was dressed a little warmer than the elven female, but still, the clothes didn't seem to afford much warmth in this climate. He had a thick cloak that was filled with holes and gloves that seemed ripped in three places.

"I have no idea what you're talking about," Seltemver confessed, "we have just arrived on my ship and have no clue as to where we are."

"This is Duoskar, in the nation of Harn." The human said, clearly expecting Seltemver to know what that would mean.

"Well, I don't know what that means but I *do* know that I hate slavery." Seltemver walked over and pulled on the iron post with everything he had, straining his toned muscles but finally uprooting it from the ground. The elven pirate tossed it to the side and turned to look at the man. "How many of you are enslaved here?" the elven pirate asked as he pulled his thin blade and slashed the elf's chains, his enchanted blade severing the metal links neatly.

"You jest! There are over thirty thousand slaves on Duoskar alone!" The man laughed hysterically.

"Seltemver...we have to go," Amonar said weakly, fear creeping into his normally sarcastic voice.

Seltemver nodded in agreement, knowing that they were in over their head. He turned to the female elf and flashed his best smile despite the grim circumstances. "Well, you are free to come with me and...what do I call you?" he asked her as she rubbed her wrists. She moved her fingers again and he shook his head. "Silence. I'll call you Silence." He saw her nod and stretch her legs, possibly trying to warm them up. How they could work in the snow with barely anything on was beyond him.

"Now, let's see if we can get to our ship." Seltemver turned to go when two orcs came around the corner, trudging through the snow behind them, weapons clearing their sheaths.

"What is this? An elf?!" The guard charged as he said this like it was the worst thing they could've seen.

New Friends, Old Enemies

Amonar flew up off Seltemver's shoulder, knowing confrontation was imminent once more. "Why is it, everywhere we go, people want to kill you?" the imp asked, his voice rising with every note; he hated violence.

"My winning personality?" Seltemver answered without skipping a beat. He slashed an orc with his blade and spun around another as they came at the pair, dodging through the drifts of white powder.

"Yeah, that has to be why," the imp finished dryly; flapping his wings over to the elf girl they were calling Silence. He watched his master finish off both orcs and knew that they were in some very serious trouble this time. Thirty thousand slaves with orc masters didn't exactly spell 'Pleasure Island.' Amonar heard a deep horn blare, then an answering call from the sea as the huge ship started towards the

Seahaven. Both he and Silence exchanged grim looks. "I think they know which boat is yours Seltemver."

"It's a *ship*, not a boat."

"Semantics."

"Look Amonar, a boat is..."

"You two are insane," the man said interrupting them both with a raised brow. "You know that right?"

Seltemver laughed but ultimately ignored the human. "Amonar, Toth knows how to lose a bigger ship, he'll head for that channel we saw and lose them in the currents, even though he knows I wouldn't want him to. Let's make for the coast and free as many slaves as we can along the way, then steal a boat and meet up with him there."

"Did you say Toth?" the man stopped dead, turning towards them with an ashen look on his already pale skin.

Amonar had that bad feeling again, the one when everything goes to the deep hells— metaphorically, thank the gods above— "Do I want to know why he is looking at us like that?" the imp asked.

Seltemver ignored him with practiced ease, instead focusing on the human. "Yes, I did. He is my First Mate...why?" Seltemver led them to the eastern side of the house and down a back alley as he talked in hushed tones. The snow had been cleared on this side and they passed a few sculptures made of snow resembling orc warriors.

"The Nation of Toth lies to the west; they would surely help you if you know one of the great line." The man turned and hung his head. "Free them if you must but leave me. This life is all I know and I'm content here."

Amonar flew over and hovered in front of the man. "What's your name?" Amonar asked, worried that the man was indeed content with slavery. *I should've stayed on the ship...*

The man looked down at the ships with a mix of wonder and trepidation and turned to towards Amonar. "My name is Karel."

"Well, Karel, you may only know this life, but trust me. Someday you will want freedom," Amonar said with his voice tinged with sorrow. He knew how it felt to feel this way. He had been a slave to an elven archmage before Seltemver saved him. *Well, saved is a stretch but...* With that, they turned and headed out with their new group. Before they got too far they ran into more slaves.

Seltemver saw the slaves, one elf and two humans, chained up to a similar iron post as they worked the frozen ground. They were dropping tiny purple seeds the size of a coin into the dirt and covering them back up as best they could. He was about to just yank the post out like the other one when two orcs came out of the back door. He pushed Silence behind him protectively as he approached the orcs with his slim sword out, ready for anything; he wasn't ready for their response though.

"Oh! An elf. Mercy me. Hammon, would you look at him!" the female said, clearly not dressed as a guard, nor angry with him. If anything, she seemed interested...like he was a toy.

"Never mind him, Bernice, would you take a look at *her*!" The orc male said pointing behind Seltemver. He wasn't dressed as a guard either, in fact, they looked just like farmers, both bundled up in thick coats and gloves.

Seltemver heard heavy footsteps behind him and turned to see Grunhilde catching up with them.

"About time I found you. Did you see the ship leave?" Grunhilde asked as she came running up. She had acquired a heavy fur cloak, lined with red fur. There was blood on her hands and her weapon, a huge axe, was steady in her grip. She had clearly seen some sort of battle, yet there were still no general alarms sounding in the town other than that initial horn blaring out over the cliffs. Odd.

"Yes, I did, we're going to try and get out of town and head to the coast near that channel," Seltemver said as he looked ahead to see if anyone else was coming.

"I see we've found slaves again. Can't help yourself can you?" Grunhilde slapped him on the back then saw the green-skinned orc staring at her and smiled at him.

"No, I can't. I will let a lot of things slide, gods above know I'm not a good person, yet slavery is not one of those things." Seltemver sheathed his sword and gestured for Grunhilde to pull the iron post out of the ground, then he turned to the orcs. "I'm freeing these slaves, I don't want to hurt you, but I will if it comes to that."

"Slavery is embedded into the very society we live in, where could you take them so they could be safe?" The orc named Hammon asked.

Seltemver noticed that the orc's tone sounded like he was simply curious; puzzling, to say the least. "I'm grabbing as many as I can and getting to my ship. Once we set sail, well, let's just say we kind of have this curse and won't be around here much longer after that."

"That's a unique way of putting it," Grunhilde said, taking the post and pulling it up in one heave of her muscled shoulders without straining at all.

"Do you think we could come with you?" Bernice asked, looking back at the door of the house like they were being watched.

Seltemver stared for a couple of seconds before answering. This place was just plain weird. "If you want freedom from this slave society and don't have qualms about working for it, then yes."

"Bernice..."

"Hammon, you know we hate this, we just don't have the stomach for it," Bernice said, almost pleading with what had to be her husband. "And there are more of us," she said, turning to Seltemver and smiling. "I know some of them that would join us."

"Well let's get moving, they haven't sounded an alarm yet, but they should any moment."

"They don't sound alarms."

"What now?"

"They just send runners ahead and let all the guards know that they want the gates locked down. They do have a sea horn though; when that is blown the entire region knows there's a slave revolt."

"We're doomed," Amonar said, fluttering back onto Seltemver's shoulder.

"Well, there's nothing to do about it now. It's going to be a hard run to the coast," Seltemver said, feeling that knot in his stomach when he started to worry, which wasn't often.

Captain Ulargth shouted at his men again, mainly because he wanted to shout at someone. He had known that sleek ship was trouble, but his commander had said to let it pass. Once the riot horn sounded he knew that the strange ship had caused the trouble. Rogue orcs from another nation had probably snuck in and disturbed the slave auction, but they would not get away that easily.

"Get those slaves rowing, Hargen!" Ulargth bellowed at his first mate. Over forty orcs manned the sails and the many slaves down below deck worked their backs rowing as they turned towards the smaller ship. It was probably faster, but once the rowers got their rhythm, they would catch them.

"Sir they are turning towards the channel with full sails," Hargen said, amazement in his voice. "And if I'm not mistaken, I do believe they are preparing to fire upon us."

Ulargth was shocked as well. A smaller ship would usually race for distance, rather than engage a larger ship... *What was that captain thinking?* "Well, prep the cannons and prepare to return fire when they close the distance."

He peered at the ship in the distance as they were turning towards the channel, a foolhardy move to say the least; they would never make it past his ship in one piece. He felt the ship lurch faster as the sails were filled with the wind coming out of the west. He turned his own ship to match the smaller one, then he heard the cannon fire. "Incoming!" he yelled, watching for the cannon shot that was coming. It would not breach the hull, but if they targeted the deck he could lose men. He worried for nothing as the shots fell short, splashing into the icy water on the port side.

"Horrible shot that captain is. Right, sir?" Hargen asked. Then he lost his balance and grabbed the rail as the ship turned violently to port, heading away from the channel.

"Swing the sail!" Ulargth yelled, trying to figure out what happened as more cannon shots fell short on the port side as they turned. He watched the orcs swing the sails and try to right themselves to no avail. Then the smaller ship sailed by and ran for the channel, the ship passing out of range of the larger ship's cannons. Captain Ulargth ran and looked over the rail at the port side and saw the handiwork of this rogue captain. They had shot at the oars of the slaves! Until they stopped the starboard side from rowing, they would just list to port.

"Stop the rowers!" Ulargth commanded, but it was useless. That ship would head into the channel unopposed; they would probably ground on the reefs to one side or another, though. Maneuvering those currents in deep winter was difficult at best. He would catch them when they did and then he would string them up for all to see. The large orc captain stomped off to see about replacing those oars and knew that he was going to be yelling a lot more now.

Almost Made It

Seltemver crept along the side of the snowy road, staying behind the snow-covered bushes as much as possible as he tried to keep his little group of freed slaves and odd companions quiet. Only the elven female they called Silence was doing what he asked, and technically she was cheating. They had found a slave transport heading towards the village of Largeth that Bernice had told them about. If they could catch the guards by surprise and take the transport, then they would have a better way into the village and a chance to grab a boat unnoticed; a small chance, but anything was better than nothing.

The transport was a large wagon, enclosed in the back with iron bars for a door. It was pulled by six huge horses and the six orc guards all walked as one hooded orc drove the wagon from a seat in the front. Snow covered most of the wagon and icicles dripped down the sides like teeth.

"Your hand..." Grunhilde said ominously to Hammon. The orc farmer had laid his hand on her muscled shoulder again and by the look on her face, she was ready to hit him. He had kept doing that ever since they had met up and Bernice was getting irritated as well.

"You are aware that she can probably pick you up and throw you right?" Amonar asked the hapless orc male.

"Sssshhhh!" Seltemver moved his hand across his throat signaling them to kill the talk. Too late. Three of the orc guards were walking quickly to them and pulling their weapons. "Well, when the dark one rides..." Seltemver started, pulling his slim sword and stepping out of the bushes. So much for stealth, now they had to do this the hard way.

"...The only thing you can do is hold on and pray." Grunhilde finished as she pulled her axe as well.

"I'll just stay here and guard the slaves, guys," Amonar said, hiding behind Silence.

Seltemver had no time for the imp as the three orcs broke into a run, their long pike-like weapons already swinging as they spread out to flank him. The other three came a bit more slowly, waiting to see if they were needed.

This might   hurt, Seltemver thought, still running right up the middle of the group. These orcs seemed to have good training and looked competent, and with reach weapons, his normal prowess was cut down a bit. He slid to his knees as one weapon came whooshing overhead and sliced with his sword, cutting the haft in twain, then spun around to block another weapon. He took a cut on his side from the third, but thankfully their long weapons got in the way of each other in these close quarters. "I heard you chaps go to brutality school. They don't teach you how to actually kill or what?" he taunted, trying to get them angry enough to lose their focus. It worked.

One brute grabbed him in a meaty fist as another kicked at his side. He slashed the incoming foot, but the hand picked him right up off the ground with ease. An orc's head came in like a flash, head butting him and sending his eyesight into a dazzling spin. "Well then..." Seltemver said, trying to get his vision to clear. He saw Grunhilde with the other three orcs, doing a slight bit better than he was at the moment, yet even she had taken a fair amount of cuts due to the reach of those weapons.

Seltemver brought his sword up and tried to cut the arm of the orc holding him, but didn't have the angle. He did cut the brute, but that only annoyed the big orc. *Okay, so this isn't my day,* he thought as the orc slammed him down on the frozen ground, kicking the slim sword away from his loosened grip. These orcs were very well-trained and he had never seen a group work better together. He had underestimated his opponent, and it may well cost them.

"Hey, I think it's that elf from the slave auction!" the orc said to his buddies, stepping on Seltemver's back to hold him down.

"Definitely not dressed as a slave that's for sure," another replied.

Seltemver looked up as Grunhilde swore, the orc healer down and weaponless as well. Two of her opponents were on the ground, but the third had her on her knees with his weapon at her throat.

"Amonar, little help here," Seltemver whispered, knowing that the imp would hear him regardless of the distance. Their bond came in handy from time to time.

Amonar winced as he saw the beating his friends were taking. Seltemver was one of the best swordsmen he had ever seen, and after one thousand years, he had seen a lot of warriors. These brutes however were coordinated and well-trained, despite his master's bravado. Amonar was trying to keep the others hidden behind the snow-covered bushes, but they kept peeking up to see the action. Then the battle turned ugly.

Both Seltemver and Grunhilde were down, and solidly from the looks of it. The big brute with the black hood was getting off of the wagon and pulling a huge curved blade, obviously moving in to finish the fight.

"Amonar, little help here."

The imp flinched at the sound of his master's voice and wrung his hands together. He was hoping he wouldn't have to do anything this time. It always made him feel...dirty somehow. In the end, Amonar saw that he had no choice or his bond would shatter. Amonar was bound to keep Seltemver alive at all costs. If his master died, the imp would be thrust down into the pits of the Hells forever; burning endlessly in torment until time ended. Not high on his 'Things to do' list.

Amonar hung his head and flew out of the bushes, snow falling over his red wings. He closed his eyes and concentrated. He pulled his power up from deep within, knowing what he must do; he hated this part the most. When the power rose to the surface, he opened his eyes; eyes that now had a deep red glow to them.

"Ackresh firan risal en shiran ea orkan!" Amonar said, his voice resounding across the open road for all to hear. The sound of it cowed orc and beast alike, the slaves backing up behind him and the orc in the hood dropping to a knee and bracing his hands on the icy ground for balance. Two of the orcs on Seltemver fled rather than face a beast that uttered those words, while the others just whimpered.

The orc in the hood stood after a moment, looking at his hands; hands that were just on the frozen ground; they were burnt and smoking. The next instant, flames roared to life under each orc; a pillar of flame that spread to nothing else and refused to be extinguished, despite the cold or the snow around them. Some of the orcs rolled on the ground while the others ran for their water skins, screaming for help and dying hideously in front of the group no matter what they tried. Even the ones that had fled, burned, the flaming bodies lying among the deep snow where they had fallen as the fire slowly went back from where it came.

Amonar heard Hammon throw up behind him and Bernice swore softly while Silence clapped. The imp flew back, head hung down once more and feeling sick to his tiny stomach.

"What did you do to them?" Bernice asked in a horrified whisper, holding her husband's hair out of his face as he retched again.

"I'm sorry, I had to save him or else," Amonar said, averting his eyes from all of them. "He was cursed years ago for saving my life. The wizard that kept me transferred the curse as he died, binding us together until one of us dies...funny story, I'm immortal."

"So what does that mean?" Bernice asked quietly

"It means that he has to protect me until I die or he gets dragged back down to hell, roasting in the pits assigned to oath breakers and slavers. I hear it's not a fun place," Seltemver said, walking over with Grunhilde, rubbing his neck.

"But what happens when you eventually die? Like of old age or disease?" The female orc was trying to get a handle on what had happened, but they weren't helping at all.

"If he dies naturally, then I just go back to my normal life in hell, sans the torture and eternal damnation; so to speak," Amonar said, sniffing loudly to let everyone know he was upset; no one was noticing however. He flew up and landed on Seltemver's shoulder once more, his small tail wrapping around the elf's arm.

Grunhilde walked over and looked Amonar straight in the face with a stern expression. "Well I, for one, have something to say about this," she started, her voice hard and uncompromising.

Amonar knew this was coming. Stirrings around the ship were already bad enough. This would make it unbearable for them to be around him. They had seen him use his power before, but not to kill their own kind before. "I'm sor..."

Grunhilde kept talking, cutting him off. "I think this little imp...should have my eternal gratitude." She patted him on the head and broke into a tusky grin.

Amonar physically relaxed and let out a tiny breath. *Okay, that one got me,* he thought as loud banging came from the wagon. Silence was pointing to the slaves in the back and motioning for the group to get over there.

"Hey, it looks like we have some more recruits for the boat Seltemver," Amonar said playfully, his mood brightening quickly with Grunhilde's acceptance.

"It's a *ship!*"

"Potatoes, or whatever."

"You guys *do* need help you know that right?" Bernice told them walking towards the wagon with Hammon in tow.

"Yeah, we hear that a lot," Amonar said. He saw the road winding down to the coast and couldn't wait to be miserable on that boat, instead of being miserable around these orc slavers.

Channel Running

Seltemver sat in the back of the wagon and felt every damned bump. Bernice and Harmon were driving while everyone else pretended to be 'slaves' in the enclosure. The door was latched but unlocked so they could exit quickly if need be. This way, upon minor inspections, they would be unmolested by the guards. Seltemver was covered in a heavy cloak—a *mostly* unburned one, taken from a fallen guard—and Amonar was curled up on his shoulder. The other slaves stared in open horror at the little imp until Grunhilde snarled at them; then they took turns filling Seltemver in on how slavery started in what they called The Shards.

The gist was that many of the stars had fallen from the deep sky centuries ago and devastated the main land masses, fragmenting them into dozens of smaller islands. The orcs took the initiative to rebuild and enslave the other races who had been relying on their societies and advancements instead of brute strength and endurance like the orcs; dwarves, humans, and elves. The dwarves were controlled by torturing their families—using their strong ties to the family bond to break them—but Seltemver was more curious about the elves. He knew that most elves had magic, so it confused him how they were enslaved so easily. That's when they talked about the horrible way that the orcs used to keep the elves in line; they cut out their tongues. Worse was what they did to the young infants when they were born.

A stout dwarf, named Morn, talked as Silence hung her head, his long red beard stained by years of blood and dust. "You see, when they is born, the orcs wait fer about two tendays, then cut out the baby's tongue, burning the tip to stop tha bleeds," he said in a slight accent.

"Cauterizing it," Seltemver said quietly, that feeling in his stomach boiling its way up to his throat. How could they? *No wonder Silence doesn't talk,* he thought as he looked upon the ragged elven woman hanging her head.

"Don't be knowin that wurd, but mebbe."

Seltemver couldn't wait to be gone from this horrendous world. What started out a perspective happy place with cheering had turned into a nightmare beyond anything he had ever encountered. *And yet another world with dwarves,* he thought. *That's the second time we've seen them.*

In his world, they had vanished centuries ago, but not so in other worlds it seemed.

Seltemver tapped Silence's leg and got the attention of the other elves he had with him in the enclosure and held their steady gaze. "We will get you out of this nightmare, I promise you." Seltemver hated making promises—he was no hero—but he couldn't abide this. *A real hero would stay and fight them all. Probably die doing it too,* he thought to himself.

As the wagon started to slow, no doubt finally pulling into Largeth, Seltemver stood and pulled off the cloak, determined to make the orcs pay all the way to the docks. He had originally thought to sneak in, but who was he kidding; his plans never went that well anyway. Now that he knew how well-trained they were, and how good they were at fighting together, he had a better idea of how to fight them. He wouldn't underestimate these slavers again. "Does anyone want to back out? Now would be the time," he asked, looking from free man to free elf, "It will get pretty dangerous from here until we sail out of the channel." He looked at the ragged faces, amazed at what his fellow elves had to endure here in this world.

Silence stood and placed her fist inside of her other hand, then bowed. A sign of some sort, maybe fealty...or service. Then two others stood and repeated it. Soon they were all standing, all except the dwarf. That's when Seltemver remembered the dwarven control method.

"What about you Morn, will they kill your family?

"Heh, they all reda have, I was going to Largeth to be hung, so this is freedom fer me."

Grunhilde slapped the dwarf on the shoulder a little too hard and laughed. "Well, I will gladly swing my axe in your cause dwarf. I have never seen your kind in battle, but I've read about the grit and honor of your race."

Seltemver felt good about the imminent battle and looked around the group of warriors he had assembled. "It's settled then. We will grab Bernice's friends that want to come with us, and then fight our way to the docks. Grunhilde and I will take point, then toss you back weapons as we find them," Seltemver looked to Amonar on his shoulder, "Just stay with me and you'll be fine. If you go off, I may lose you in the chaos."

"Oh great, me, right in the thick of it...I'll get maimed I just know it," Amonar said rolling his little eyes. That made some of the freed slaves laugh and break what tension was left. They all went out quickly once past the gates and headed to the docks, not even bothering to be quiet anymore.

Bransh heard the clang of weapons and slapped his companion awake. "Hey, Margth, something's coming."

"What'd you wake me for?"

"It sounds like fighting," Bransh said, pulling his halberd and stepping away from the gate. Guard duty here was just a formality, as no orc in his left mind would try and steal another orc's Slave Runner. The penalty for that was the loss of slaves and a public flogging...if you were lucky.

Bransh hadn't gone more than ten feet before an elf came around the corner, fighting another guard and cutting the orc's head clean off! "Margth, to arms!" Bransh called to his companion as he rushed forward. This elf was different, dressed in a longcoat and good clothes with a gleaming sword as thin as an icicle.

"What the hell is on his shoulder?" Margth called, pulling his halberd and moving up shoulder to shoulder with his fellow guard, "Is it a rat?"

"Seltemver, that orc called me a rat?!" the thing said in a high-pitched voice, screaming in fury.

Bransh faced a gorgeous orc woman with an axe and cute braids, her chest cut in various places with her armor half falling off. Her breast and entire right side lay exposed pulling his gaze to the sweet flesh. Too late he realized his error as she laughed and swung her axe Bransh tried to parry and took a cut across his right arm. His numb hand dropped his halberd and he fell back as Margth faced the elf with the strange pet. Without two hands Bransh was forced to draw his side blade, which meant his advantage of reach was lost.

Margth swung for his opponent with a slow arc, bringing the weapon around quickly for a trip, but the elf hopped over it and slashed out with a slim sword. The blade took Margth's arm clean off as the elf spun, running the orc through. The elf kicked the body off his sword and smiled in Bransh's direction.

Seltemver walked towards the wounded orc and pointed his blade at his throat. They had done well, getting Bernice's friends and gathering up more slaves to take with them. The main gates were where most of the guards were because of the lockdown, and the wagon got them past that. Those guards were undoubtedly on their way down here now with the sounds of battle, but they had a good head start. "So, you get to be the lucky winner today, friend orc," Seltemver said calmly, "You get to tell us which ship we can take that will make it out into that channel the fastest."

"That one. The *Cutter*."

"Well, he folded quickly," Amonar said, a mix of sarcasm and fear pervading his voice.

Seltemver laughed and ran the orc through the heart, pushing him aside and limping through the gate. They had fought another ten or so orcs to get here after getting the other slaves and had almost twenty with them now. "Good, that saved us some valuable time, let's get the ship ready and start looking for the *Seahaven*."

Between the orcs they had with them, and the slaves willing to help, they sailed out of Largeth just as orc guards stampeded the docks in force, throwing spears and firing crossbows; yet the *Cutter* was well out of range by then.

"They'll be followin ya with those other ships ya know," Morn said, blood still dripping from his wounds. He was still holding a small spear they had given him and refused to let his guard down until they were far gone.

Seltemver grabbed the wheel and spun the ship towards the north, laughing into the spray from the canal. "Just look for another ship, then we can board and get out of this hellish place." The view from the channel was even more stunning than from the sea. Here the snows cascaded down the mountainsides and into ice flows that sparkled and gleamed in the sunlight. The white caps of the majestic mountains to either side just seemed to look down on the tiny ship as he held his course.

Amonar flew up to the mast and perched on the cross beams, kicking ice off the wood. "There, Seltemver, hard to starboard!"

"You don't even know what that means," Grunhilde called up, making sure the other orcs were tying off the right ropes and sails. "Just point."

"That way," the imp said, pointing to the northeast.

"Huh, it *was* starboard. Lucky guess." Seltemver said, wondering if the little imp was finally learning. Then he saw his ship, running strong down the side of the channel, fighting the current and trying to lose the big ship behind it without running into those ice flows. He could see now that the orc ship was made of stone, not wood, and his brows furrowed. "Amonar, I may need a favor."

"Oh, this can't be good. You've never asked me that before." The imp flew down and landed upon the wheel as he corrected his course. "How bad is it?"

"We won't be able to dock with the *Seahaven* running like that..." Seltemver left the sentence open, knowing his friend would get it without him having to say it. He hated asking, but none of them would make it unless he did.

"Oh gods below, you want me to wreck that big ship don't you?" Amonar shrunk down, shaking and trembling.

"Please, Amonar, it's the only way."

"Fine, but not for you," the imp said slowly, avoiding the elf's pleading gaze. "I'll do it for them." Amonar pointed at the slaves who staring at the oncoming ships with a mixture of awe and dread.

"I'll still owe you..."

"No, that's not how this curse works. Just never ask this of me again." The imp flew off towards the bow of the small ship and closed his eyes, spreading his arms out wide. He opened his eyes a minute later; that deep red glow staring at the ship behind the *Seahaven*.

"Ackresh wanar krakon, fris en vessah tal!" Amonar said, his voice resounding across the open water for everyone to hear. There was a dreadful quiet, almost like nature was holding its breath, then, within a three count, there was a hollow boom under the water and thunder without sound. The big ship fractured, leaning slightly as its stone frame split asunder; a large spear of ice spouting up, ringed with tiny flames, high into the sky. Orcs leaped from its sides as it floundered and sank quickly, almost like it was being dragged down. The huge ice spear retracted slowly, back under the waves and down to the hells from whence it came without a sound.

"Gods above, I've never seen a thin like tha before," Morn said, finally resting his spear aside and falling to his knees.

The people gathered on the *Cutter* felt the same way. More than one slave, and a few orcs, leapt into the icy waters rather than be on board with the tiny demon after seeing the infernal power wielded against the massive ship. Seltemver let them go without a second thought; right now he needed to get to his ship.

They sailed towards the *Seahaven* and within the hour they were aboard, the *Cutter* left drifting. They sailed out of the channel, pursuit holding back at the horror of the demonic power that echoed throughout the channel, and the crew was never gladder to have their cautious captain back.

"I knew you'd take the channel," Seltemver said to Toth as they cleared the islands and headed back north to their waiting fate.

"Oh, you did? Why is that?" Toth asked, amused at the guess.

"Because I never would have, and you knew that when we saw it."

Toth laughed out loud, his booming voice startling the newcomers. "You got me on that one. So where do you think we'll end up next?" the first mate asked, staring at the growing storm coming right at them. It never failed, once they sailed into an open sea, that storm came for them, sending them somewhere else.

"Honestly? I don't care as long as it doesn't have slavers," Seltemver said, looking out at his newly enlarged crew. He threw back his head and laughed at the dark clouds coming for them. *One more time into the dark,* he thought, quoting his favorite book. Then they were in it and the ship was gone.

Be Good or Else

Orath walked down the hallway to her daughter's room, her heavy steps reflecting her anger at the child. She banged the door open and stepped inside, making her child dive under the covers. "I told you to go to bed!"

"I tried, but I can't fall asleep, mommy."

"Granta, you don't want Seltemver the Wicked to come and take you away...do you?" Orath said to the eight-year-old orc. She hated to use this on her, but it worked for the boys when they disobeyed. Sadly her daughter was a bit smarter.

"Mommy, he didn't actually exist, that was centuries ago." The child said, peeking out from her blankets.

Orath sighed. Her daughter had grown more defiant as the years rolled on. *This one is going to be trouble in her teens,* she thought, feeling her tusks as she stared sternly at the young orc. "It was over seven centuries ago to be exact, and it still frightens *me*," she admitted to the young one.

"It does? Why?"

Sitting down on the bed she patted her daughter's knee under the blanket and had her sit up to listen. "Because Granta, no one knows where he came from, or where he disappeared to."

"But isn't that good? That he's gone?" The child struggled to find a solid footing for her argument, but at eight it wasn't going well. Then a spark showed in her eye. "Wouldn't he be dead by now?"

Orath smiled, anticipating this; after all, she had used this same argument when she was a child. "Well dear after all he was an elf, and they can live for a very long time." She saw the horror set in finally, realizing that she had seen elves that were said to be almost five hundred years old as personal slaves of their rich friends.

"But...but he wouldn't come back. He wouldn't. Would he Mommy?"

"Well, legend says, that on nights like this, when the snows are deep in the mountains, his ship comes in from a storm looking for young orc slaves to sail his ship." Orath got up and tucked her daughter in tight, walking over and locking the window out of habit. "After all, he may live forever but his orc slaves surely die. Every so often he has to replenish them wouldn't you think?"

"I'll sleep mommy, I'm sorry!" Granta rolled over, fake snoring and shaking a little.

Orath closed the door after blowing out the lamp and left her daughter to think on that. That would keep her from sneaking out of bed to play in the toy room for a couple of months at least. The orc mother shivered herself as she walked down to the kitchen. That story always got to her, *especially* as an adult. When she grew up she learned that it *was* a true story and not made up just to scare children into listening. Somehow that was even worse.

"Everything all right dear?" her husband asked as she passed the living room. He was staring out at the falling snow and sipping his ale.

"Yes dear, just a naughty child and a scary story," Orath said, smiling to herself. *I wonder what ever happened to that elf,* she thought, as she made sure the back door was locked as well.

Journey to the Isle of Ximn

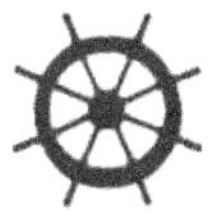

This is one of the weirdest places I've seen yet, and that is saying a lot for an imp from the deep hells. I've seen some bizarre things in my immortal life but this island was the strangest! We had just spent three days inside the storm that usually transports us to another world—a record so far—and I was looking forward to a quiet place, especially after that fiasco with everyone being arrested! I should never get my hopes up like that. It was a nice tropical island but boy was it hot! This world had not one sun, but two, and the island had to be at the world's equator; thank the deep hells I can stand the heat well.

So, here we were, paradise. We took Silence with us this time so the rest of the crew stayed on board and watched us through the fancy spyglasses we picked up in that empty world a ways back—they had the coolest things there. Of course, paradise is never what you think it is...So get ready for weird, and that's an understatement.

—Amonar

Surviving the Storm

The ship heaved back and forth as the sprays of the ocean soaked the orcs battling the forces raised against them. Every time they passed through the veil between worlds, another storm battered them senseless. The rain pelted the elf behind the wheel ceaselessly as the ship rocked back and forth. He flipped his white hair out of his eyes and saw bright skies off the starboard side. "Hold on, I see the end!" he called out to his loyal crew as he spun the wheel and aimed for the sunlight. The deck tilted and the orcs grabbed what they could as the ship turned sharply, the elf's long coat flapping in the storm.

"I *am* holding on," a tiny voice on his shoulder called out over the storm. "What else can I do with the way you steer this ship?"

Seltemver grinned at his companion despite the danger. Leave it to the imp to make him smile even in the middle of a crisis. "At least you called her a ship this time, Amonar," he yelled over the noise of the storm.

"I'm too scared to be snarky!" the imp countered.

"That's a first." Seltemver looked out over his ship and saw the winds and rain subsiding as they neared the rift. *Where are we going to end up this time?* he pondered as the crew went about securing loose ropes and checking on the damage to the *Seahaven.* They had been battling this storm for almost three days, a record in their travels to say the least. and the last world they were in was an endless fog for over two months. As the ship came fully out of the storm and set sail on this foreign sea, the change in the air was shocking. The sheer humidity, even on the ocean, was palpable.

"We must be near this world's equator or something," Amonar said, fluttering down from his shoulder and landing upon the wheel now that it was steady. His red skin and long tail were dripping water like the rest of them, yet he seemed acclimated to the humidity already. "I haven't been this hot since I left the Deep Hells."

"I'm surprised the water doesn't just steam right off of you." A voice said as someone came up the stairs to the deck. Grunhilde was a well-muscled orc, who happened to be the healer on the ship. She had grown fond of the imp, even though some of the crew still made the sign of Dava when he passed them.

Seltemver laughed as Amonar stuck his long tongue out at Grunhilde in jest, just as she called to the small orc lookout climbing up the main mast.

"Careful, Crak; you don't want to break that leg again!"

"That's it, distract him as he climbs..." Amonar ducked the orc's hand as it came lazily by his head.

"All right you two. Grunhilde, go see what Toth says about the damage."

"Aye, cap't."

Seltemver watched her walk back down and turned his attention to the sky. It was hot, yet the sun wasn't even directly overhead. Not a good sign. That's when he heard the sound he always dreaded when they came out of the storm.

"Land ho!" Crak yelled from the Crak's Nest—named after him since he was the only one besides Amonar who fit up there. Crak was a smaller orc and was always chided for it by the rest of the crew, but only in jest; too bad the young one took it to heart all the time. He worked twice as hard though, to make up for his inexperience and youth, and back when they were all imprisoned, he pulled through for them. *Who would've thought Amonar and Crak could've staged a jailbreak,* Seltemver thought as he spun the wheel once more.

Seltemver turned to see the dark shadow in the distance and was baffled when he saw that there was another sun coming over the horizon that way as well. "Well dye my hair and call me human. That could be why it is so damned hot here."

"Hey, this is the first world we've been to with more than one sun. Cool!" Amonar was excited for once, mainly because there hadn't been any fighting yet.

Seltemver took off his longcoat and saw others similarly undressing because of the heat. Normally on the open ocean the air was cooler, and he frowned thinking how warm it must be on land; he hated being hot. "Well? Can she make it there?" he called down to Grunhilde and Toth, his first mate. He figured the ship was good, especially after the extensive repairs on that gear world, but one never knew after a lengthy storm like that.

Toth looked up, his tusks sticking out to show he was smiling, and gave the thumbs up. He was a burly orc and had been with Seltemver since the beginning of this crazy, cursed, journey; most of them had. Of course, they had taken on some others here and there, as they visited other worlds and lands. They had even freed a dwarf and some elves a while ago from a world where orcs had enslaved everyone. Because of that, most of the elves were having trouble dealing with the orcs on the ship. It was against their nature to like any orc at this point, yet they were trying.

"Why do we always find islands?" Amonar asked, flying back to Seltemver's shoulder once more. "I mean it's always an island or something like that."

"Not true, that town with the lord in enchanted armor wasn't an island."

"All right, so it's most of the time…"

"To answer your question though, little friend: I have no idea. The witch's curse didn't seem to come with a handbook; and if it did, she never gave it to me." Seltemver remembered that fateful day when he had forced the witch to free the orcs she had enslaved. Of course, one *more* curse couldn't hurt, he had thought…gods above was he wrong.

"She couldn't have. You cut off her arm and she was too busy screaming curses at you to offer you the book," Amonar said, patting him on the head.

"Yes, well, we all know how much I hate slavery."

"And that's another thing...why is it always slaves? So far, every place that had people, except for when you all were imprisoned and that one world with that lady that waylaid you..."

"She was a shapeshifter!" Seltemver said loudly. "And it's not like we had a choice when we were taken into custody." He took a calming breath and spun the wheel towards the island. "Let's just get closer and see what is in store for us this time. We're low on stores and could use some fresh water." Seltemver waved to Toth to come take over and when the big orc had the wheel, Seltemver went to go find the elf they called Silence.

Amonar waved at Toth as Seltemver walked away and looked out over the ocean towards the land mass. For once he didn't have a bad feeling, and somehow that was even more troubling than when he did. He just couldn't win sometimes. *Just once,* he thought, *can it just be a happy place with parties and mead?* The gods denied him an answer, as was common.

THE ISLE OF XIMN

Seltemver pulled the small boat onto the sandy beach with water sloshing in his high leather boots. It was the only such boat left as he had lost the other two in past excursions. Besides Amonar, he had brought Silence with him to check out the island. She was a female elf that couldn't speak, who they had rescued from orc slavers in another world. She was teaching Seltemver her strange sign language while learning to fight with a spear. He smiled when he thought of how well the orcs had taken to her and turned his attention to the beach. He secretly prayed there weren't any slaves for once. *I'm tired of playing the hero when I'm not anywhere close to that*, he thought as he surveyed the tree line. The foliage was tropical, able to withstand the hot temperatures and humidity. What drew his eye, however, was the flora that grew all around the edges of the trees. They were unlike any type of bush he had ever seen, and he had been around.

The short bushes only came up to his knees and were obviously in bloom. The pretty blue flowers were open wide and staring at the twin suns as they rose into the sky. The blue coloring was made all the stranger by the light pink of the leaves. In fact, the only green thing on the entire bush had to be the very center of the flower. Strange pink vines curled around the ground near these and seemed to number in the hundreds.

"It's like the gods just had some drinks and decided to create things half-blind," Amonar said, flying around the bushes and sniffing them.

"Amonar, we *are* in a different world. Mayhap the gods here always do things like this?" Seltemver laughed when the imp's face came up with a serious look on it, like he was suddenly worried about the gods. "Don't worry friend I'm sure they will leave us alone."

Silence made some gestures and passed her hand in a circle. *We're too exposed here in the wide open.*

Seltemver gestured, pointed to the trees, then his eyes. *We'll go check out the woods now.* He had learned some of the silent language that she spoke with her hands on their trip and was getting better as the days went on. Others had picked it up as well, even the stubborn Toth had learned to say 'thank you' with his hands.

"There you go fidgeting with your fingers again," Amonar said as he flew back to Seltemver's shoulder, sneezing from the pollen he had sniffed.

"It's a silent language."

"It's made up and she's messing with you." Amonar stuck his tongue out at Silence, and she grinned back.

Seltemver ignored them both, as he heard movement in the brush. He drew his slim sword and crouched down as the other two argued. He saw Silence hush the imp, and Amonar flew behind her as the sound grew louder. This was not a rodent trudging through the trees, but something larger. Then he heard the voices and relaxed a little.

"Akoo mira?"

"Akan san ri."

Great, they're speaking a form of Ling, he thought as the pair came into his view. They were about the height of a ling, only three feet or so, but the facial hair was all wrong.

The ling were a diminutive race of people that resembled human children but with much more facial hair. Most of them favored long mustaches and sideburns, as well as a few beards—much to the chagrin of the dwarves who knew how to grow a good beard. These two were clean-shaven and had long black hair twisted into braids. *No weapons that I can see, that's good at least. Well, here goes nothing,* Seltemver thought as he stood up and sheathed his sword. He put his arms out wide but kept his footing squared and balanced in case he had to dodge. "Hira akoo akan si, peka wi coma."

"Rana!" the smaller one said, bolting for the deeper trees as Seltemver stood out in the open.

"You come...just three?" the other one asked in broken common. His eyes were gleaming in concert with his broad smile as he looked them over.

"Yes, three. You speak my language?" Seltemver was impressed. The level of advancement didn't appear to be that great, especially since they wore woven vine clothes, yet this one had learned common from somewhere.

"Ya, the Xa show us. Teach us of Ximn to talk funny." He scratched his head as he stepped forward, and cocked his head to the side as he pointed at Amonar. "He funny. What it?"

"Why does everyone call me an it, or a thing?" Amonar huffed.

"Amonar, shush." Seltemver lowered himself down to the ling's height, still wary of what it may do, yet trying to seem non-threatening; something he wasn't very good at. "Is your name Ximn?"

"No, elf. The island is called Ximn. This one's name is Ral," A deep voice said from far behind the ling.

Seltemver rolled backward, coming to his feet quickly and hearing Amonar squeal in fear as he took flight at the unexpected movement. The man that walked towards them was tall, broad-shouldered, and hooded. "You must be the Xa," Seltemver deduced as he shifted his balance, just in case.

"Well, you got one right," the Xa said, his voice calm and controlled. He looked down upon the ling and patted him on the head. "Go, Ral. Tell Ven it's all right." The man waited until the ling was out of sight, then continued. "You are from the ship that came out of the rift storm?"

Seltemver sheathed his sword, still keeping his feet balanced. "Yes. We were coming to see if there was a town or village on the island." He looked back at Silence and moved two fingers, curling them and straightening another one. *Stay ready, and alert.*

Silence shook her fist and opened it quickly. *No shit.*

"At least you were walking in the right direction. The town of Galsin is just over that high ridge. Come, we can eat and talk. I'm sure we both have many questions."

Silence trudged along behind them and scowled to herself. She could almost smell the magic coming off the man called the Xa, and she didn't like it one bit. She might not be able to cast anymore—she would need to talk to be able to do that—but she sure as the deep hells could spot someone well-versed in it. Seltemver had given her freedom she hadn't known in centuries, and she would die to protect him. For now, she walked behind and kept her eyes and ears sharp. No one would take them by surprise as long as she was there.

The Hospitality of the Xa

Seltemver and his companions followed their enigmatic host through trees that were thinning out dramatically the farther from the coast they went. The heat was oppressive, yet the canopy kept most of the direct sunlight from them at least. After an hour of walking, they came to a small village bustling with the little people; running to and fro with buckets of water, fish, and other things. They seemed happy and at peace, something none of the three visitors had known for many decades.

"Hi, eh, do yous want drink?" a small female ling came up to them and asked. She held out a bucket made of tightly woven reeds lined with what seemed like baked clay.

"No, thank you," Seltemver said, smiling down at her. "My name is Seltemver, what's yours?"

"Me is Syn, I call you Selt." Syn smiled and ran off, giggling to herself.

"It's like they're all twelve," Amonar said, a tone of disgust in his voice. He flew down and landed on a bench, folding his wings with a humph.

"Hey, no one is trying to kill me, so you should be happy." Seltemver heard Silence chortle and started laughing himself. *This place is infectious*, he thought, *The lighthearted feel of the village making me relax for the first time in a long while.*

"Give it time," Amonar quipped.

The Xa cleared his throat to get their attention, and Seltemver noticed that the man seemed impatient. "What kind of stores did you have in mind for your ship?" he asked, leading them on through the village to the larger structure on the western edge of the village.

"Mostly fresh water and dried meats; any food. My crew isn't picky, except for Amonar here." Seltemver patted the imp on the head as he landed on his shoulder once more.

"Aaa, Picky!" Amonar repeated like some sort of parrot, just to be smug.

The Xa ignored the scene and carried on. "Well, I would assume he would be, being an imp and all. They only like the hearts of animals; and raw at that."

"Hey, he knows about me." Amonar perked up at that and flew over to hover next to the mysterious figure. "Have you met an imp before?"

"No, I haven't, but I was quite the scholar before I came here." He stopped at the door to the structure, opened it, and waved them all in; holding the door for them like a gentleman. "I will let the ling know what you need, and have them start gathering things together for you. It should all be ready by tomorrow evening. Is that all right?"

"Thank you, that would be wonderful. I can send Amonar back to the ship and let them know to expect us late." Seltemver was shocked at how easy all of this had been. It had been so many trips through those cursed storms since they had a smooth trip, that he felt like this was a dream.

"No need. I can send Ral in his coracle—his boat—and let them know. He is going fishing tonight once the first sunsets." The Xa whistled, and Ral came bouncing up to them. "Ral, tell the people on the boat that our visitors are sleeping here tonight."

"Tell boat that Selt is staying here for sleeps," Ral repeated, getting the message in the barest of terms.

"Yes, Ral, thank you." The Xa turned to them as Ral ran off, and ushered them the rest of the way into the building, closing the door behind him.

Seltemver shook his head. Why had he let this man tell him what to do? That wasn't like him at all, yet he couldn't argue with the logic of it all. "Thank you, Xa, we are in your debt," he said, silently signing to Silence behind his back as he did. *Something's wrong, not sure what.*

"No trouble. Now, let us sit and talk. I'm sure you have questions, as do I." He pulled up a chair made from woven reads. It looked like a hollowed-out turtle shell sitting on an angled stump. He gestured towards more chairs like his and crossed his legs.

Seltemver took one and crossed his legs. "I must say, I was surprised to see ling here of all places. I always thought they hated the humidity." Seltemver said, going over in his head what he wanted to ask and how to ask it without seeming offensive.

"Ling?"

"The small people of the village. Where we come from, they were called ling," Seltemver said. "But they all disappeared with the faeries shortly after I was born."

"Ah, I see. They call themselves the Kana, though I like ling better. It seems to fit them somehow." The Xa gestured towards the fire pit and flames came to life as though by magic, though he spoke no words."

"How did you do that without asking the elements to help you?" Amonar asked, sitting up at the display. The imp looked intrigued and frightened at the same time. Magic was cast by asking the elements to do certain things, and only those with elven blood could even attempt it.

"Ah, you know about magic, I see." The Xa chuckled, "I have mastered the smaller art to the extent that they know what I want without asking."

Silence held her hands up and made quick intricate gestures. *Impossible, magic doesn't do that.*

Seltemver concurred, but kept it to himself. "And you called me elf; have you met other elves before?" Seltemver knew how magic worked as well, but didn't want to give that away yet. After all, they may be in a completely new world, and the rules of magic might be different here.

"He's half-elven. Now that I'm looking for it, I can smell it from here," Amonar said. It was a gift of his infernal legacy; one that he always said he didn't mind using. The other ones made him sick to even think about sometimes. "By the way, what does *the Xa* mean anyway? Is it a title?"

"A title of sorts; the kana called me that when I arrived here. It's their word for 'savior.'" He sat forward and removed his hood, letting his long, white hair spill down. His blue eyes seemed so bright with his trimmed white beard. "And yes, I am half-elven, though I never knew imps had such amazing senses." He cleared his throat and looked at Silence. "My turn. How is it that you are mute? I have never seen an elf that couldn't talk, let alone cast magic."

Seltemver looked to his companion and waited for her to nod her consent. He was used to being her translator, though he knew this story from heart by now. "She was disfigured at birth by her captives so that she couldn't cast magic. We rescued her from an entire civilization of orc slavers." He shivered as he remembered that place; the prevalence of slavery there was like a horrid dream.

"And it has never returned? That is indeed a shame." He sat back and let out a long breath like he truly was saddened by her circumstance. "And you can't cast magic?" he asked Seltemver.

"No, and I've never known why. The elements simply refuse to listen to me," Seltemver said, biting back an angry retort. It was a sore spot with him. *Why am I telling this man my secrets?* Seltemver wondered. It was something he had never talked about, not even with Toth and the others.

"Intriguing, but enough for now. It's getting late, and I'm sure you would like to discuss what you have learned." The Xa winked and took his leave. "I will see to the water before I retire, that way you have the house to yourselves to talk freely." The Xa closed the door behind him softly, leaving them alone for the first time since discovering the ling.

Strange Occurrences

Amonar flitted over to the chair that the strange man had been sitting in and sniffed carefully. *Strange that I can't smell much of anything except the odd tinge of elven blood*, he thought to himself. He had an exceptional sense of smell, when he focused it. Here though, it was almost like his senses were muted. "I don't like this, Seltemver. Something is wrong, and I can't put my wing on it."

"You always worry when there is someone out to get us. Now, the first time it's peaceful, you worry too?" Seltemver laughed and put his feet up on the table between the chairs.

Amonar huffed and flew over to the braided rug near the fire. Seltemver seemed way too relaxed here like he was under some spell. Amonar knew that was impossible because he'd know. The imp stood there and brushed his red skin with his hands, trying to get sand out of places he wouldn't have invited it into. It was like he was covered in the scratchy stuff, even though he couldn't see it. "Is anyone else regretting that beach landing?" he asked, shaking himself like a wet dog.

Seltemver ignored his friend and tried to piece the meeting together in his mind. *What am I missing?* he asked himself, finally noticing that Silence was trying to get his attention.

She made some gestures, once he was looking at her. *He is right though, something is off.*

I know I'm just teasing him. I'm trying to figure it out, Seltemver signed back. He knew that his friend was the worrier of the group, but truth be told: the imp had a sixth sense about danger that he envied greatly. "All right, so what do we know by watching our new benefactor?"

He is intent on pleasing us at any cost. He never even asked us how many crewmen we had to feed, or how much water to prepare, Silence signed, sitting back and crossing her legs underneath her. Her short white hair was getting longer now that she wasn't forced to chop it off every month.

"And that trick with the fire was worrying," Seltemver said aloud to keep Amonar in the loop.

"Yeah, I've seen some things in my time, but that one was the weirdest," Amonar said, finally sitting down after dancing around to get the sand out of his wings.

"Okay, so he's placating us. What else?" Seltemver squirmed in his seat, his wet pants making him uncomfortable. *They'll dry soon enough,* he thought.

"For starters, all the ling—or kana as he calls them—are related. That's just plain weird." The imp settled down and sighed. "And I wish I had a fresh heart now that the Xa brought that up and made me all hungry."

"What do you mean?"

"Well, I haven't had a good heart in decades, and now..."

"No about the ling."

"Oh. Well, that one that we met, what was his name? Ral? There were six others we went by that looked *exactly* like him, down to the crooked smile," Amonar said proudly.

Are you' sure? Silence asked, waiting for Seltemver to translate.

"Yeah, and I saw at least four others that looked like each other. Creepy, if you ask me."

Amonar curled his tail around him and settled in basking in the fire's warmth.

"All right, that is something I missed; and that's *my* major problem. I usually don't miss this much." Seltemver admitted.

"Um, there was that one time with that girl..."

"Amonar, don't bring her up. I hear enough about her from Toth," Seltemver said, shrugging to Silence when her questioning eyes met his. "Anyway, it's like my focus is being purposely diverted or misled." Seltemver wished Amonar had taken Silence up on her offer to teach him her sign language. The little imp could be stubborn sometimes.

So, what do we do? Silence signed.

"For now, we stay alert and try to keep each other focused. If we can get the water and stores, we can just leave and never look back." Seltemver knew it probably wouldn't be that easy, but he could hope. *And, why do I still feel soaking wet?* he asked himself, taking his shirt off and wringing it out by the window. His bare chest was covered in sweat. *Is it that humid?* He turned to look at Silence and saw that her shirt was also soaked to the point of dripping on the floor under her chair.

Before he could bring it up, the door banged open and Syn came rushing in, all smiles and dancing eyes. "Oh Selt, you bare for all to look?" She covered her eyes, yet he could see her peaking through her fingers.

Seltemver laughed as Silence rolled her eyes, then shook out his shirt and put it on slowly. He could see Syn's eyes following his movements through her fingers and thought it was cute. "Just getting dressed, little one. What can we do for you?"

"Maybe our water is ready?" Amonar asked, flying up and spinning around. "Then we can leave this weird island."

Syn looked askance at the imp and frowned. "Nah, me just want to see if you need eat." She pulled out a half loaf of black bread from her shoulder bag and placed it on the small table.

"What kind of bread is that?" Seltemver asked, intrigued at the dark color. He had never seen any type of grain that would be almost black.

Silence held up her fist, *Stop!* She slapped his hand away from the bread and eyed the Ling carefully.

"What is it?" Seltemver had never seen her so perturbed over anything.

This is from my world. The orcs grew it to feed us in the slave towers. Her eyes looked from the bread to him with concern. *It can't be here.* Her hands made the gestures with urgency.

Amonar flew over and sniffed the bread, wrinkling his nose at the smell. "Weird, no smell whatsoever."

Seltemver drew his sword slowly, looking around for anything out of the ordinary. "That's it, I knew it was too good to be true." He saw it then; the problem with the house and why he felt so very comfortable here. Those paintings were from his own house where he grew up, and that shelf of books was something he had in his cabin aboard the *Seahaven*! "They're taking things from our mind and showing us what we want to see..."

"...and telling us what we want to hear." Amonar finished for him. He lunged for Syn, but she was already running for the door with tears running down her face.

"Hemma! Hemma akan!" she yelled in her own tongue, sprinting for the group of ling in the center of the village.

"Hells, there goes the element of surprise," Amonar said, shrugging and flying over to Seltemver's shoulder. "I suppose someone will want to kill you now."

"Wouldn't be an adventure if they didn't," Seltemver said, walking calmly towards the open door.

"He 's always like this," Amonar said turning to Silence as the elven woman shook her head and followed.

Worse than they Thought

Silence walked out the open door behind Seltemver, her eyes sweeping this way and that. She was looking for the rush of small bodies, possibly with spears or something similar. Seltemver was striding towards the center of the village like nothing could touch him, and that damned imp sitting on his shoulder was babbling away as usual. *I swear that thing talks more than his master,* she thought to herself as the crowd of ling gathered around them warily.

Ral stepped forward, his legs shaking as he hefted a small sword. "What you do to us now?" he asked Seltemver.

Silence looked at the crowd. Now that Amonar had said it, she could see the resemblance in all of the ling. It was like they were copies of only three or four individuals. She moved her hands pointing at her companions, then sideways and in an endless loop. *Your friend is right, the ling are like copies.*

"We're not going to hurt any of you unless you force us to," Seltemver said while moving back towards Silence and gesturing, *I see it too, what could it mean?*

The female elf shrugged and pulled her weapon, a short spear with white leather wrapped around the handle. She set her feet and stared death at the little folk, trying to scare them.

"We just want to get some supplies and go home," Seltemver told the gathering crowd. The surprising look they gave him showed that most of them had no idea what he was talking about. *The Xa probably never even asked them, just promised and drugged us*, he thought as he scanned the buildings for the enigmatic ruler.

"You have nothing to worry about," the Xa said from behind them. He was coming out of the house they had been in like he was there the whole time. "It isn't what you think."

"So, tell us what it is then. Why have you have misled us so?" Seltemver turned and spun his sword through a quick warm-up as he stepped towards the man. He heard the ling gasp at his display, and he couldn't help but smile.

"I have merely brought you here to keep myself and my friends company."

Seltemver looked around at the faces of the ling and couldn't believe that they were friends. They looked horrified at the man now, almost like they had seen him for the first time. "They don't look like they're your friends anymore, Xa," Seltemver said as he took three more steps towards the robed figure. The man's hood was up again, but he could see his smile. *He isn't worried in the slightest...this is going to hurt,* he thought as his eyes swept the area.

"The ling?" the Xa laughed, a deep throaty laugh that made some of the diminutive creatures back up a step. "They were merely a tool used to get you here." He waved his hand, and all but four of the creatures disappeared. "No, you haven't been formally introduced to my friends yet, Seltemver."

"How *are* you doing that?" Amonar asked, his voice ringing out in the stunned silence of the remaining ling. "Magic doesn't work like that."

Seltemver had run out of patience. He lunged forward the rest of the distance to the Xa and slashed across, taking the man clean in the stomach. The robe exploded and dozens of vines came streaming out of the wound to entwine both his sword arm and his legs. Seltemver struggled and twisted, but they held fast.

Silence's spear came down, slashing some of the vines, yet the Xa gestured and more of them sprung from the ground and entangled her legs. She tried to roll and slash with her spear, yet more vines crawled up her legs, and wrapped her arms up tight before she could free herself.

"Damn, I so wanted to avoid this," Amonar said in a sad voice as he drew on the power from deep within himself; he hated this part the most. When the power rose to the surface, he opened his eyes; eyes that now had a deep red glow to them. "Ackresh firan risal en shiran eo huma!" he said. His voice resounded through the village and reverberated into the dense forest. The sound of it cowed the ling that were left, two of them weeping openly on the ground. The very earth shook and rumbled...then nothing. The light faded from Amonar's eyes and he was left dumbfounded. *That can't happen, I have a pact...* he thought before everything went to the deep hells.

The Xa lashed out, sending a thick mass of vines hurtling towards Amonar, slamming into the imp and sending him sprawling across the sandy ground. He felt like he had been hit with a mountain, point first, and his whole body was cold and sandy. *Sandy?*

"Amonar!"

The imp looked up, hearing Toth's voice. It sounded distant, but Amonar could hear him plainly with his demon ears. The imp saw Seltemver slice the vines with a hidden dagger and roll away, also cutting with his sword as he did. "Seltemver...I hear Toth!" But it was fruitless. More vines engulfed the elf, even muffling his words by covering his mouth.

Silence turned towards Amonar and cocked her head, then nodded vigorously.

"I'm going to guess you hear him too," Amonar said, leaping up and hiding behind a prone ling. The unknown ling took one look at him and feinted dead away. "Great, there goes my cover."

"Meet my real friends. The very forest around you all!" the Xa said, his voice even louder than before; like it was coming from all around them at once. "They obey my every thought and command, so there is no way you can triumph here." He fired vines at them again and again, raising roots and trying to snag Amonar.

"Wait...thoughts and commands?" Amonar asked, more to himself than to anyone else. He was pretty damned smart when he needed to be, and when it came to the mystical and arcane things in the known world, he had seen more than any five elves. *He knows our thoughts, our dreams, even things we've never shared with anyone.* Amonar's thoughts were firing fast now as he flew from barrel to rock, avoiding shooting vines and grasping roots. A lifetime of cowardice was finally paying off; no one could dodge like Amonar.

"That's it!" he flew high over a mass of twisted roots and came crashing down on Seltemver, knocking some of the vines from his mouth. "We're dreaming!" he yelled, then took the sharp point of his tail and rammed it into his master's eye.

Seltemver screamed and disappeared in a flash, dropping Amonar onto the ground with a thump. He rolled as more vines came at him, then scrambled towards Silence, beating his weary wings. "Don't worry, I'm *almost* sure this won't hurt," Amonar said, as he flew up and rammed his fingers into both of her eyes, his claws driving deep. Her mouth stretched open wide in a horrifying, silent scream; then she flashed away as well.

"You think you have won, little fiend, but this is only the beginning. *You* are still mine." The Xa stalked towards the tiring imp but stopped suddenly.

"You no hurt us. No more." Ral said.

Amonar looked up and saw two of the ling behind him, tears drying on hardened faces. "It seems like you're losing your following there, Xa. What are you, anyway? You're not a demon, so..."

"Demon? No. Those beings are formless wastes of power, always fighting for souls and entrance into your world. I am far older than that." He opened his robes all the way, shedding them like some sort of second skin, and revealing himself fully to the remaining audience. His form was all vines and roots, like some massive plant brain pulsing with energy and purpose. It looked humanoid, but without the robe to keep that form, it melted into a writhing mass. "I was the one that gave plants their life, their purpose. I have seeded entire worlds, grown planets, and now I have come here to take it back from humanity." The Xa stepped closer, his vines forming crude arms to grasp at them all. The pulsing mass was speaking through the very air around them.

"And you've made this island your home. Got it, thanks!" He grabbed the two ling, stabbing one with his claws and ramming the other one with its own spear, then flew for the forest as fast as he could. "Toth! Wake me up!" he screamed, focusing on the burly warrior's voice; praying the big orc could hear him.

Back in the World

Toth swung his axe with a fervor born of desperation. The sharpened blade bit through the pink vines and spewed ichor all over the sand. He stood over the limp form of Amonar, newly freed from the mass of vines that had entwined the imp and slowly dragged him across the sand; he still had not woken up.

"I've got him!" Grunhilde called out, dragging the body of their captain past Toth and into the saltwater of the ocean washing up on the beach. Vines were still wrapped around Seltemver's legs where Grunhilde had severed them, and he was covered in the strange ichor.

"Little help here," Crak said, coming right behind the healer. The smaller orc was cradling Silence as he fought the vines that were now wrapping around him with his free hand.

"Morn! Help Crak with the elf!" Toth yelled to the stout dwarf.

"Aye lad, I'm on it." Morn ducked under the reaching vines and sprinted towards the smaller orc, whose hands were too busy holding Silence to use his weapon effectively.

"I'm not your lad," Toth retorted, swinging again to keep the vines from grabbing the imp again. They seemed more interested in Amonar than the others, and Toth was near the limits of his skill keeping them at bay. Once he saw that both the captain and Silence were in the water, Toth breathed a little easier. For whatever reason, the vines hated the water. He was ready to call a formal retreat when he heard Amonar speak.

"Ackresh firan risal en shiran eo huma!" the prone body of Amonar spoke in a harsh whisper, but power was behind the infernal voice nonetheless.

"Amonar!" Toth yelled as flames shot up his right side, igniting his tunic and breeches. He dove to the left, rolling on the sand and ripping off the burning clothes. When he looked up he saw that the vines were retreating into the woods, drawing back unexpectedly.

Grunhilde was there, extending her hand to help him to his feet. She was breathing heavily, but smiling. "Damn, that was fun," she said.

Toth ignored her and stood slowly on his wounded leg. "All right, let's get them into the boat and back to the ship before those damn things come at us again." He was about to say more when Seltemver sat up screaming, thrashing in the water and holding his eye.

Seltemver screamed, then realized the pain was gone. He opened his eyes. They burned like he had saltwater in them, but were otherwise intact. He blinked a few times and looked around to figure out what the deep hells was going on. He was sitting in the shallow surf, the waves lapping at his back, surrounded by some of his crew from the *Seahaven*. "What in the briny hell is going on?" Seltemver asked as he tried to stand.

"Toth was watching through the spyglass and saw you all fall. He dove into the water, making for the beach while I gathered some volunteers to follow suit." Grunhilde said as she walked over to him. "Those vines had completely entombed you and were dragging you all off into the woods. When we got here, Toth had pulled Amonar out and was going back in for you."

"You saved *Amonar* first?" Seltemver asked incredulously, turning towards his first mate.

"He's my little buddy," Toth said, not even looking sorry. "Besides, he's the one with the power. If we needed it, I wanted him free first."

"All right, I can agree with that," Seltemver muttered.

"Anyway, we ran up to get you out, but then the vines exploded in fury trying to get Amonar again. Thankfully he did his fire from hell trick and almost killed Toth," Grunhilde said, winking at the burly orc.

"Why am I in the water?" Seltemver asked. *Though now I think I understand why I felt wet in....wherever we were,* he thought. "And why are you naked?"

Toth laughed as he stood there with only his short clothes on. "Amonar's fire burned most of my clothes off, and as for the water. The vines didn't seem to like that we were soaked so I figured they didn't like the salt."

"She's up!" Crak called out.

Seltemver looked over and saw Silence sit up and promptly get sick on the beach as she crawled out of the water.

"It's the smell," Morn said, coming over with a blue-stained axe. The blade was dripping ichor and matched Seltemver's clothes. "Almost upchucked meself."

"That's wonderful," Seltemver said, looking around for Amonar. Seltemver could see his old friend lying on the sand still and felt a pang of concern. He had rarely seen the imp down for any reason. That was when Toth tilted his head and rushed for the imp once more. "Toth?"

"I hear him," Toth said, falling to his knees in the sand despite his burns and shaking the small red body gently. When that didn't work, Toth slapped the imp.

Amonar sat up, back on the beach, and drew a deep breath of air into his lungs. He rolled frantically to his little feet, looked around, and oriented on Toth. "You slapped me?" He didn't wait for an answer, just hugged the orc then looked around. Amonar spied Seltemver and half ran, half flew to his side, wrapping him in a tight embrace. "I'm sorry...I'm sorry..."

"It's fine Amonar, you saved us."

"Look, the vines are gone for now, but let's not get cocky. Can we get off this cursed beach now?" Toth asked, standing up and wincing in pain. He held his right arm close to his chest and shook his head slowly.

Amonar's eyes went wide, finally noticing the burns. "Oh, gods below! Toth, was that from me?"

"It's fine, Am," Toth said. "Your flames drove the vines back into the woods." He patted the imp on the head and motioned for Grunhilde to check on him as they dragged the boat over.

"If only we had more boats," Grunhilde said as she smirked at Seltemver.

"I didn't lose this one did I?" Seltemver quipped.

"Wait, we can't leave yet. They're still in there," Amonar said, staring off into the woods. He remembered now. It was the pollen from those bushes that knocked him out.

"Who is?" Seltemver asked, concern heavy in his voice.

"The Ling."

Silence moved her hands and pointed to her head, then at Seltemver's head.

"You're going to have to translate that for me, Seltemver," Amonar said. They were all looking at him now, and it made him worried; worried, and a bit afraid. He knew that some of the crew still made the sign of Dava around him, thinking he was wicked. All this might just prove them right.

"She thought they were just made from our minds," Seltemver said, shaking his head. "You should learn some of that."

"Yeah, yeah, I know. If we live through this, she can teach me." Amonar smiled at her, then looked at Seltemver. "Okay, the original four Ling were all that was left at the end, and I think they are still in there. Besides, I talked with the thing that did this...the Xa. It has to die." Amonar's voice grew somber and damn near violent towards the end. In fact, two of the orcs backed up when they heard him talk about what did this.

Toth shook his head when he realized no one was getting into the boat. "Fine, but we hit those vines with everything we had the first time and barely kept them at bay. Only your fire seemed to vex it enough to make it retreat, that and the water."

THE END OF THE XA

Amonar looked around at the still-smoldering remnants of the vines, then at the waves coming in. *It must be the salt water the vines don't like.* Now he had a plan. Amonar nodded to the burly, naked orc, an air of sadness to his voice when he spoke. "Then I have no choice."

"Won't your flames burn everything in the forest?" Seltemver asked as he stood on shaky legs. "The Ling would be just as vulnerable...if they are still alive.

"It comes!" Morn called out, brandishing his weapon and pointing to the tree line. Dozens of pink vines came rushing out, snaking their way across the sands as they avoided smoking piles of ash. Morn and Crak rushed to meet the oncoming vines with Silence taking a slender sword from another crewman and following.

"We would need a sizable fire to burn all of those," Grunhilde said as she finished her work on Toth's wounds. Her hands were still glowing with the healing prayers of Dava when she pulled out her axe.

"I don't need fire," Amonar said, backing away from the oncoming vines. He didn't want to fight, yet he couldn't leave those defenseless ling in there; he was torn. *Seltemver usually takes care of the plotting and killing, I just hang back and hide,* Amonar said to himself. "You just have to ask me," he finished, his eyes downcast at the prospect of handling that power again. "I can't use my power on my own like this."

One of the orcs that was afraid of him, Sombra, stepped up before anyone else could speak. He had his hair done in long braids entwined with black beads and a kind smile despite the tusks. Sombra laid his hand on Amonar's shoulder and knelt as the others started fighting the incoming vines. "We need your power, Amonar. Would you help us, and kill that thing?"

Amonar was shocked. "You're not afraid?" he asked. "You trust me?"

"With our lives. I'm sorry if we don't show it, or even fear you sometimes, but you're one of us and we trust you," Sombra said, his tusks sticking out even more as he smiled.

Amonar nodded, a tear sliding down his red-skinned cheek, and pulled the power up from deep inside. His eyes turned red and he turned towards the ocean as the cries of his crewmates echoed from the beach. "Ackresh wanar, risal en wes eo foren." Amonar felt the power shake down below him and backed away as the saltwater rose and formed into huge, tentacle-like appendages. They raced past the imp, dozens of them, and snaked their way into the forest. They soaked everything they touched, the saltwater reacting with the vines, and withering them on contact. On and on they drove, into the woods, searching for the heart of the Xa. Then came an awful, soul starling, scream.

✦

Seltemver kept his balance as the ground trembled. The forest seemed to shake in answer to the screaming, and the very trees were swaying as if a titanic battle was taking place within their canopy. The vines doubled in ferocity, even more coming out of the trees, as if trying to escape. Orcs were snagged and pulled, their weapons slashing about them to no avail. There were just too many.

Seltemver fought his way up the beach towards Grunhilde. She had been dragged off her feet and had lost her axe. Toth beat him to her, though. The recently healed orc grabbed her hand and pulled her straight up, almost ripping the vines from her legs by the sheer strength of his pull.

"Easy, big boy, I can't swing my axe with only one arm," Grunhilde said, gaining her balance and hacking through the taut vines.

Seltemver slashed more vines coming for the pair then pointed to the boat. "I'll get the others, get her into the boat," he said as he turned and ran to the orcs that were struggling. The ground started shaking even more now, and as he freed Sombra, he saw there was a growing ball of bluish-green in the woods coming towards them. "All right, that's it, time to go!" Seltemver called out, helping another orc and then grabbing the dwarf, Morn. He had a nasty gash on his leg and was having trouble walking. Seltemver kept him up, deflecting or slashing the vines that came at them as they went.

"What is that thing?" The dwarf asked, trying to catch his breath as they ran.

"I don't know, but it can't be a good thing; I know that much," Seltemver said as he slashed another vine. The constant spinning around as he ran was making him dizzy, but he didn't want to get snatched up again by the vines. He saw Toth still farther back, tangled in at least ten vines and struggling. "Damnit," Seltemver swore.

"I got him, Captain!" Crak said, sprinting pastthem.

Seltemver nodded to the brave orc and retreated to the boat with Morn. He threw the dwarf to the waiting orcs and turned, sprinting back to help Crak. Seltemver saw the young orc cut through the grasping vines and push Toth free, his face grinning with accomplishment. As Seltemver raced to join them, two heavy vines wrapped around Crak's neck and yanked him back violently. There was an audible snap, and the orc's body went limp and fell to the sand. Dead eyes stared back at Seltemver for a moment, then the vines dragged Crak's body into the forest.

"Crak!" Toth screamed, "No!" The orc rushed after the body of the small orc, heedless of the danger.

Seltemver cursed and ran faster, finally getting to Toth as the big orc tore his way into the woods. Toth already had at least twelve vines on him again, but he kept his footing and slashed wildly, refusing to give up. "Toth, we have to go!" Seltemver called out as the bluish sphere grew closer. He could see it was some kind of sac, or body that was expanding.

Toth turned to him, tears falling down his tusks, his eyes fierce and unyielding. "Captain..."

All the vines went stiff then, as a deep concussion pulsed through the ground. They looked deeper into the forest and saw the bluish sphere turn white, spreading out towards them even faster. "He's gone, Toth. We have to go, *now!*" Seltemver grabbed the orc, dragging him towards the beach. The others were already in the boat, and Amonar was waiting for them perched on the bow with his head down. Seltemver and Toth grabbed the boat and pushed it off the beach, sliding in over the sides once it drifted free. Once in, Sombra went at the oars with a ferocity born of desperation.

"He's screaming...I can hear him," Amonar said, "The Xa. He's dying, and he can't stop it."

"Well, we'll have to come back and see what's left, but for now that white sphere is still coming," Seltemver said.

Amonar flew up and onto his shoulder as he crawled into the boat. "That's the Xa's power. He's trying to banish the water I sent, and the two powers are escalating. He's old, like a demon, Seltemver, but that Infernal power is just as strong. It's going to be bad, but only on the edges...like where we are.

"Of course." Seltemver turned to watch as Toth took over for Sombra and rowed as hard as he could, trying to get far enough away from the beach just in case. Now that he could study the white sphere, he could see that it was more like a blob; moving around the trees like a liquid or an ooze. Once it hit the sand it detonated with an ear-splitting scream, blowing outward with such force that the boat was blasted with sand as well as ichor. The small boat capsized, throwing them all into the waves.

Then, quiet descended upon the isle of Ximn.

No Rush

A few hours later Seltemver, Amonar, Toth, and Sombra, sailed back to the isle of Ximn in the boat. They had gone back to the Seahaven to change and inform the rest of the crew what had happened, then returned to retrieve Crak's body and see what was left of the ling; no words were spoken on the trip back. They left the others to tend to any wounded, except Toth, who refused to be tended to until he brought back the fallen crewman.

Once they had beached, Seltemver looked at the group and sighed. "Alright, we're sticking together and keeping our weapons out," he said, looking at Toth mainly.

"Aye cap't' I know. I won't run off." Toth seemed somber, yet anyone who knew him could tell there was a fierce rage boiling inside.

Amonar flew over to Seltemver's shoulder as they walked up, cautious of anything that could come at them. It only took a few minutes to discern that the isle was devoid of anything that may want to attack them. The forest was littered with withered vines, and a clear path led towards the center of the woods.

A short time later they reached the heart, where a massive battle had taken place. Twisted, withered vines lay around the broken ground where a large crater now stood. It looked like a giant tree had been uprooted, with broken roots and shattered branches scattered around the edges of the still-damp hole. The entire place stunk of sea salt, and the ground was muddy, yet the mood was still and somber.

Toth found what he was searching for right away, pulling the body of the young orc out of the withered vines near the edge of the forest. His sobs echoed through the clearing as he wiped mud from the younger orc's face. Everyone let him grieve and walked around looking at the devastation. Specifically, Seltemver and Amonar were looking for the ling.

"Would they just be buried in the ground?" Seltemver asked. He wasn't sure that they even existed, but if there was a chance...

"I'm not sure. Maybe in a pod-like thing?" Amonar flew over to the other side of the clearing and poked a couple of the larger trees.

"Seeing if they're hollow?" Sombra asked as he came over to help.

"No, I figured I'd poke them in case they were sleeping."

"All right, I deserved that one," the orc laughed.

"If you two are done, I think I found something," Seltemver said, kneeling in the far eastern corner of the clearing. Here, he could see the remnants of a couple of buildings, even a ruined fire pit. He found a buried blue pod, its severed vine sticking out of the ground. As he dug it out, something within stirred.

"Seltemver, I think that's one of them," Amonar said, flying over and landing on the elf's shoulder while he dug at the edges of the pod.

"Wow Amonar, and here I thought I found a three-foot pea pod."

"Bully."

"Must you two *always* do that?" Toth asked as he walked over with Crak's body on his shoulder. The first mate's eyes were bloodshot, but no more tears fell from them.

"It's just what we do Toth," Amonar said. The imp stared at the ground, seemingly trying to avoid looking up at Crak's body or Toth.

Seltemver glanced up at the body cradled on the big orc's shoulder, and memories of Crak climbing the mast of the *Seahaven* flooded his mind. He remembered that little orc from when he first met them all on the isle of the sea witch, and the small lookout had earned his place among the crew easily, despite his misgivings; Seltemver admired him. He shook the thoughts away, then turned back to the pod. "Anyway. Help me with this, Sombra. I think I have it loosened up."

"Mmm mmmm mmm." A muffled voice called out from within the blue pod.

Seltemver pried the leafy mass open with his sword, and inside was the tiny form of Ral. "Take it easy, little one, you're alright."

"Lan akan owa!" Ral said, looking frantically around.

"I hear another one," Amonar said, flittering over to a broken beam sticking out of the ground. "The ground must've kept them safe from the shockwave."

Toth reverently set down the body of Crak and went to help. Within an hour they had freed all four of the Ling, who were all very alive, if not a little confused.

Seltemver had to talk with them, as they actually didn't know how to speak the common tongue; that was just another lie the Xa had perpetrated. They learned that the isle of Ximn was their home. A wandering mystic came some time ago, preaching of peace and oneness with nature. He corrupted the plants and bushes, and killed most of the Ling, keeping these four as mind puppets in case of visitors. The good news was that the island was rich in resources, so the *Seahaven* could resupply with water and stores; the orcs would just have to learn to like coconuts and blue banana-like fruit.

Seltemver offered to take the four ling with him, but they declined, wanting to rebuild their island home; he could respect their determination. It took three days to get the supplies and water aboard the ship, and in that time the crew also helped the ling start to rebuild. In fact, the elves that they had rescued back on the orc slaver island wanted to stay and help. The elves were all mute like Silence, but the ling showed great promise with learning their silent language.

Days later, they were sailing out into the sea once more. The ship was heavy with food and water, but missing a few passengers. It was the way of the *Seahaven*, always changing and growing in ways that they could never anticipate. The clouds came then, with the distant thunder heralding the fateful storm.

"So, what next, captain?" Toth asked, coming up to the wheelhouse as the orcs battened down the ship for the coming rains. He had started to regain his gruff outer shell, but everyone could tell he was profoundly changed by the loss of Crak.

"Oh, probably land somewhere with yellow dragons or such," Seltemver said, laughing at the darkening clouds as if challenging them.

"You joke, but we almost died from blue plants," Amonar said, flying over to Toth's shoulder. The burly orc looked over at Amonar, smiled his tusky smile, and patted the imp on the head.

"Come Am, let's get these orcs into shape," Toth said as he walked down to the main deck.

Seltemver's eyes lit up as the clouds swallowed the ship. *Into the dark one more time, and let's see where we end up,* he thought and laughed as the ship started rocking.

THE WITCH'S ISLE

Witness the beginning of the Seahaven and its odd crew. This is the tale that started the curse—on the ship at least; Seltemver's curse with me happened before that, but that's a different story. Now you get to see the story as it happened all that time ago and witness the beginnings of the lasting friendships that came of this adventure.

Shipwrecks, giant skeletons, dark caves, sea witches, enslaved orcs...you've heard how Seltemver and I met, but this one is something altogether wild. Get ready for a sarcastic jaunt across the island of the sea witch and the meeting of the elven captain and his orc crew. Buckle up and grab your mug of ale, this one will make you wonder how they ever survived as long as they have.

—Amonar

Sand in My Mouth

He awoke with a start, coughing salt water out of his abused lungs. The elf rolled over on his elbow to look around, immediately sinking into the soft sand as the waves came up and over him again. He sat up, flipping his short white hair out of his eyes and looking about in confusion. He was sitting in the surf of a black sand beach, all of his clothes soaking wet. His body felt like he had fallen overboard, hit with the bow of the ship, and been dragged through a sandbar...twice. Seltemver Ashblade coughed again, as he searched for any sign of why he was sitting here like this, as his memory had decided to take a vacation. He closed his eyes and strained his elven ears for any sound that might help, but he only heard the soothing sound of the waves around him.

Where the hells is everybody? he asked himself as he tried to stand, thought better of it, and sat back down with a splash. *And what hit me?* Seltemver looked out over the sea for any signs of a ship, but saw nothing there either, which was bad because he definitely came on a ship; he just couldn't remember getting off of it. He checked for his sword; still there, then realized why the quiet was so bothersome. He didn't hear Amonar complaining.

Amonar was an imp and was bonded to him in a curse that had been with him for the last year. The little demonic pest was his constant companion and the rest of his elven crew hated him on general principles for it. The little fellow was decent enough, but it was his disdain of violence that surprised Seltemver the most, as most things of demonic nature enjoyed the torture and pain of anything with a soul; not so with Amonar.

Seltemver finally got up on his feet, under extreme protest from his knees, and shook his worn longcoat free of sand; or at least tried to. He needed a fire and to get out of these wet clothes or he could very well be worse off. He took three steps towards the tree line and saw a dark red splotch in the sand not more than twenty feet from him. The splotch had a pair of bat-like wings and a tail that flicked with lazy precision as the flies landed around it. "Working on your tan Amonar?" Seltemver asked the imp as he got closer. He got no response to his sarcastic question. The elven pirate slowed his pace and pulled his sword free, the cold fingers of worry creeping up his spine. "Amonar, it's me Seltemver," he said as he got close enough to nudge him with his boot.

The imp burst out of the sand in a whirlwind of arms and wings, spinning around and falling back down. He got up again, looking at Seltemver and shaking his head. "Seltemver? Where are we? What happened?" The imp looked down at his chest and saw that he had a cut across his chest. Not deep, but enough that it stung. "Oh my gods I'm bleeding!"

"Calm down Amonar, it's all right." Seltemver wasn't worried about the imp being hurt. The two-foot-tall imp had been wounded before and had healed so quick as to not even notice. "Right now I need you to focus. Now, breathe, and try to remember what happened to the ship?"

"The ship is *missing*?"

"Well, I mean..."

"Oh gods above what have you done *this* time?"

"Me? Why do you always assume *I'm* responsible?"

"You have been so far."

"Anyway, as I was saying. I can't remember what happened to the ship, or why we're here alone."

Amonar rubbed the sand free of his red skin, then folded his tiny arms across his already healing chest. "You don't remember the song?" Amonar asked.

Seltemver sighed knowing that this was going to be a *very* long day. "What song?" he asked, yet the minute the words came out of his mouth he did indeed remember. It was a haunting tune, coming through a fog bank as the *Ravencrest* cut through the waters. He recalled it all now; the tune that drew his crew towards the railings, abandoning their posts to stare out at the mysterious fog and the eerie music. That's when he saw the reefs through the fog and spun the wheel, but they were running too fast.

"It's all coming back to you isn't it?" the imp asked, flying up and hovering in front of him.

"Yeah, I think we're the only ones that survived, though why is a mystery to me," the elf said, looking down each end of the black sand beach with interest. He needed to figure out shelter and fire very soon. He should never have come looking for this lost island, but the temptation of treasure was too great. The legend told of black sands and hidden gold, and with that, he could retire and look into this curse of his.

"Not a mystery," Amonar said, tapping Seltemver on the head. "It's the bond we share now."

"Curse."

"Semantics." The imp retorted, "Anyway, it protects you from some things, like being charmed for instance."

"Listen. It's been a year and you're fine and all but I'd rather get this curse dissolved or removed..."

"What am I a wart?" Amonar asked, flapping his wings and flying away to the east.

"No. Wait, you know what I mean." Seltemver hung his head as the imp flew off in a huff. He didn't care, but he needed the imp; at least for now. He trudged after the little guy, not bothering to call out. He knew he would be ignored with practiced ease anyway. It wasn't more than fifty feet when people broke the tree line heading for him.

Welcoming Committee

Seltemver stopped as three orcs came walking out, led by a massive specimen carrying an axe. They were umber-skinned, with tusks protruding from their mouths, and dressed in leathers and sashes. The orcs, who resembled pirates, angled right towards him with smiles that showed very little humor.

"What's this then?" one of the orcs asked, trying to step out in front. He was strong-armed back into place by the lead orc, The burly leader's massive arm sending the smaller orc stumbling back.

"Sombra, calm down," the big orc said, turning his attention back to Seltemver. "Who are you, stranger, and what are you doing on the witch's island?" he asked, leaning on his axe as he planted the head in the sand. He couldn't have looked more uncaring if he tried.

"My name is Seltemver Ashblade and my ship was led onto the reefs by some eerie song of doom. And you are?" Seltemver asked the last with a flourish and a bow, intended to draw his blade in a flash so that when he stood he was ready. Thank the gods above that he did because the orc wasn't being polite when he asked his questions. As Seltemver came up, sword in hand, the orc was charging silently across the sand, eyes full of malice. *I almost fell for his relaxed pose like a human*, Seltemver thought as he set his feet apart, ready for battle. Seltemver wasn't worried about the fight, but he also didn't want to get blood on his already wet longcoat. He waited until the axe came crashing down as part of the charge and dove past the orc, rolling to his feet behind his opponent.

"Oh, you're one of those flashy warriors are you?" the orc asked, turning slowly, shifting his axe from one grip to another. It was a common practice to keep others from guessing one's handedness, whether they were a righty or lefty, and thus gain the upper hand.

Seltemver didn't care. He waited until the orc was close enough then lunged, expecting a parry. When he got it, he spun under the haft of the axe and swung his elbow up into his opponent's jaw, mashing the tusks into his upper mouth. The elf danced out of reach, then slashed with his enchanted blade, catching the orc on the arm and cutting deep. "Easy now, big fella, I could take that arm clean off, but I still want answers. May I remind you though that orcs don't need two arms to talk, so I'm being generous."

"Get him, Toth!" a small orc called out as they all drew closer to the spectacle.

"Ah, then you must be Toth?" Seltemver asked, backing up and getting ready as he could see the orc wasn't giving up quite yet

"She doesn't let us answer questions fool. She just wants you brought to her, warm or cold; it makes no difference," Toth said advancing once more.

Seltemver could now see why the warrior, evidently skilled, was making so many mistakes; this wasn't what he wanted. They were being controlled somehow and he was fighting against it. *This could hurt, but I can still take him without killing him; maybe,* Seltemver thought as he sheathed his sword and raised his hands in mock surrender. "All right, you win. Take me to her." When Toth got close enough, the agile elf grabbed his big arm and swung down between his legs, swinging out the other side.

He gained his feet quickly and kicked out at the back of Toth's knee. The orc went down, and as he did, Seltemver rammed both fists into the big orc's head, sending him face-first into the black sand. When Toth tried to get up, Seltemver kicked him in the head…twice.

"Hey, you found orcs!" Amonar said as he flew over to the gathering.

The orcs cried out in horror, scattering as they did. "Demon!"

"Where?!" Amonar yelled, fleeing behind Seltemver and shaking with fear.

"They mean you…" Seltemver said, rolling his eyes. *What have I done to deserve this?* he asked the gods above; who, of course, deemed not to answer.

Amonar came around and landed on the prone orc's head, puffing out his chest with indignation. "I am *not* a demon," the imp said, stomping down with his little clawed foot into the back of Toth's head. "Those guys are evil and twisted."

"Mmm M mmm mm mmm," the orc mumbled into the sand.

Amonar jumped off onto the sand next to the orc's head and put his tiny hands on his hips. "We can't understand you with your face in the sand like that, orc."

Toth raised his head, spitting sand. "I said. Can I get up now?"

"If you can behave," Seltemver said, hand on the hilt of his sword. He wouldn't draw it unless he had to, he needed information on what was controlling these orcs and why it wanted him. *And if this is the same thing that sang that song*, he thought.

"Well I don't know what you did, but I can't feel her in my head anymore, so you have my thanks," Toth said getting to his feet. He looked down at Amonar and smiled, his tusks sticking out more than usual.

"Ah, the mystery woman was controlling you with magic? That makes sense." Seltemver looked around to see if the other orcs were coming back, but there was no sign of them.

"The sea witch," Toth said evenly.

"What now?"

The sea witch. She was controlling me; is controlling all of us." Toth turned to look up at a distant cliff, pointing with his axe.

"What's she look like? Is she a withered old hag?" Amonar asked, interest gleaming in his eyes.

"We've never seen her, only her mouthpiece, Helarna."

"Mouth piece?" Seltemver asked, curiosity tugging at his mind. This place was getting stranger by the second.

"Yes, she too is controlled and serves the witch directly. She comes down and gives us orders, telling us what to do. She hates it, but she has no choice," Toth said wringing his hands on the haft of his axe. "We've been working on fixing up a ship for the witch so she can finally escape this island."

Slaves. The one thing I can't abide, he thought as he looked at the cliffs. There seemed to be only one way up and of course, it was wide open. There would be no getting there without her knowing. "Well then, let's go meet this sea witch shall we?"

Walking into a Trap

"So let me get this straight," Amonar said as the three of them walked up the twisting path. "We're going to just walk up to this sea witch—whom these orcs have never seen—and say hello? That's your plan?"

"The imp has a valid point," Toth said

"Thank you."

"You stay out of this, Toth," Seltemver said to the burly orc. "Look, Amonar, there is no way to get up there without her knowing we're coming. She already sent these orcs to bring me, so I'm just doing what she wants."

"What if she won't meet us?" the imp asked, clearly starting to worry.

Seltemver sighed inwardly, forgetting that Amonar hated violence. "Don't worry Amonar, I just want to talk to this sea witch and find out what she wants with me. She could've just killed us if she was powerful enough to enslave a whole tribe of orcs."

"We're not a tribe."

Seltemver stopped dead and turned to look at Toth. "What do you mean?" he asked, cold fingers tapping on his spine.

"We were the same as you. Pirates," Toth said looking out over the sea as he did. "We ran into the reefs after hearing her song, our ship breaking apart on the jagged rocks just like yours. Twenty-three of us survived and made it to shore, only to be captured by her magic and enslaved."

"So there was no life here but her?" Amonar asked

"No. Only the bones of those that had been slaves before us."

"Great, more questions. This day just keeps getting better and better," Seltemver said, continuing his walk toward the unknown. "Come on then, let's get this confrontation over with."

"He's a cheery one isn't he?" Toth asked the imp as they followed behind.

"Oh yeah, a real ray of sunshine that one."

"I can hear you both."

"I wasn't whispering," Amonar quipped.

An hour later the three of them crested the top of the cliff path and crossed the threshold into the witch's land. It was small, only holding a single house and some trees, yet the feel of it was palpable. It was like they walked into a place that despised life, the feel that everything here just...*hated* anything that drew breath. The trees, the grass, the small flowers, all of it seemed to radiate a loathing stench that they could feel on their skin. Small cages hung from the trees, bones piled at the bottoms of them from long-dead captives, and blood stained the dirt path leading to the steps of the house.

Amonar shivered while looking around. "It's like I'm home," he said as he flew up to Seltemver's shoulder. "Sans the flames."

"You're not a parrot Amonar. You can't sit on my shoulder," Seltemver said, drawing his blade slowly in anticipation.

"Last time I swear," the imp promised.

"How can you two function?" Toth asked, clearly irritated by their lack of care.

"It's a gift," Seltemver said with a weak smile.

"Welcome, elf, to the sea witch's home," a beautiful woman said as she walked around the far corner. She was dressed in a long flowing black gown with bare feet. Her raven black hair fell loose as it cascaded down past her shoulders and onto voluptuous breasts. Deep blue eyes bore into them as she sized them up, her smile holding no mirth whatsoever.

Seltemver saw Toth bow and step back, obviously knowing who she was. "The witch's mouthpiece I presume?" Seltemver asked with a casual tone in his voice.

"Helarna, if you please..." she said, letting the unasked question of who he was hang in the air.

"Seltemver," he said answering her as he pointed his bare blade at the imp. "And this little fellow is Amonar."

Amonar waved and winked at her like he was flirting. "Hi there wicked, live around here often?"

"Gods above do you two take *anything* seriously?" Toth asked from his position behind them all.

"Not particularly, no," Seltemver said looking over his shoulder at the burly orc. When he turned back to Helarna he flipped his hair and smiled. "Now what can we do for you?" he asked, "Since your boss was *so* enthusiastic about meeting me."

The woman came to a stop in front of them, just out of sword reach, and spread her arms wide open. "I assure you, she just wanted to meet one such as yourself and see what your business was on this island," Helarna said, eyeing the naked steel in his hand. "You see, she is in a particular quandary and an elf would be just the solution to her problems."

Seltemver laughed and turned towards Toth. "I thought you said you have never seen this sea witch?" When the orc shrugged his shoulders the elf turned back and raised his eyebrow at the human addressing them.

Helarna bowed her head reverently. "What I see, she sees. What I hear, she hears."

Amonar flew forward without pretense and flicked the woman in the arm with his tiny clawed finger, "What you feel, she feels?" the imp asked, then held his other hand up to his pointed ears. "Nope, no distant scream."

"Enough!" Helarna's voice rose, then her eyes turned pure white and her voice dropped in pitch. "*I have need of you and your magic, elf. There is a seal in the Caves of Despair that holds me to this place.*

Break that and you may leave the island with your life. Refuse and I will unleash the might of the Gramarye upon you and your familiar." The voice came out of Helarna's mouth, yet it clearly wasn't her.

He was about to respond when her eyes turned back and she inhaled like she had been underwater, gasping for that breath of life. Seltemver fought the fury building inside of him, knowing that if he lashed out now, he would doom this human and the orcs. Besides he wasn't about to tell her that he couldn't cast magic, that would be a surprise.

It was common knowledge, for anyone that knew of elves, that they could cast magic. As a race, they were inherently attuned to the elements, thanks to an ancient pact, and all they had to do was ask a certain element for something and it would obey. Unfortunately, Seltemver was born with a rare defect. The elements couldn't, or wouldn't, hear him at all. There were even rumors of some very rare elves that were immune to magic this way, but he was not one of them. It was why he took to life at sea very young. Anything to escape the disappointment on his family's faces and a society that called him an abomination.

"Fine. Tell your *witch* that I will do this, but there is one condition. I want the orcs to go with me," he said, hearing Toth gasp from behind.

Helarna closed her eyes, then opened them, smiling once more. "It is agreed. Break the seal and the orcs will be given to you as payment."

Seltemver sighed, knowing that he would have to play along for now, but he had no compunction about keeping these orcs as *his.* "Tell Amonar where these caves are and we will get going tomorrow morning," he said turning away from the woman and walking close to Toth. "Listen, I'm going to get you guys out of here but don't worry, I don't do slaves."

Toth nodded and clasped arms with the elf, smiling. "I will tell the others the plan. Are you sure that you can break this seal? We have never heard of it."

"Nope, but I'm not used to losing a bet so just get ready. Is that ship you've all been working on seaworthy?" Seltemver asked as they walked towards the path down the cliffs.

"No, but we will make sure that the hull is at least sealed for when you're done. If it can float, we can figure the rest out later." Toth laughed then and shook his head in disbelief. "I've always dreamed of coming up with a way out for my people and now that it's finally upon me, it sounds crazy."

"Stick around, Toth, crazy is normal around us," Seltemver said as Amonar came flying over. "Lead the way to your camp. We'll sleep the night there and Amonar and I will set out at first light."

The Orc Camp

As they walked to the camp, Toth explained about the charm that the witch put on the orcs. It seemed that they could normally do what they wanted; farming, fishing, and working, but anytime she needed them to do something for her, they had no choice but to obey. Convenient to say the least and something that didn't surprise him now that she had used the word Gramayre. The Gramayre were an ancient sect of blood mages that made pacts with dark forces to use magic. So long as they had blood, they didn't need to be elven to cast, which led to some pretty nasty practices.

An hour later they walked into the orc camp and even Seltemver was stunned. They had made huts and even tables out of the trees and lashed them with vines. He had heard orcs, or oran as they were called in the northern continents, were intelligent, despite what he was taught growing up about their savagery, but this level of ingenuity surprised him. There was a clean water source coming from a spring in the back, and even a small farm in the dirt under the trees. Nothing extravagant, but enough to survive. "So with no other life on the island, I bet you're all sick of fish right?"

"Wow, Toth you found a regular genius didn't you?" a tall orc female asked, coming over to greet them as they walked into the encampment. She had grey skin as opposed to the umber color of the other orcs and she seemed ready for battle by the look of her.

"Grunhilde, this is Seltemver. Seltemver, this is our healer, Grunhilde Strongheart," Toth said as he stepped back from them as if he was expecting violence.

"Healer? Odd, you didn't say, Shaman," Seltemver said, walking around her like he was admiring a fine sculpture. He knew it would irritate her, but he needed to keep these orcs off balance until he could come up with a plan. Too many questions and the witch might start to expect that he was bluffing.

"Toth, tell me you brought him here so I can hit him?" Grunhilde asked, clearly bothered by Seltemver's staring. When Toth shrugged she growled and spun around, facing the elf. "He said healer because that is what I am. I have heard the voice of Dava and he has touched me."

"In the no-no place?" Amonar asked, clearly poking the preverbal bear with a stick.

Seltemver watched the large orc woman close her eyes and take a deep breath, then turn towards Amonar; he couldn't help but smile. *Thank god that little guy is immortal,* he thought

"You're a little small for a demon," Grunhilde said, looking down at Amonar with a grin that had no mirth in it.

"I'm not a demon, I'm an imp. You're a little big for a boar aren't you?" Amonar asked, immediately regretting it as she advanced upon him with murder in her eyes. He shrieked and flew behind Seltemver.

"All right, that's enough, children," Seltemver said holding up his hands like a mother breaking up siblings. "Listen, we're just here to get some rest before we go and try and set you all free if that isn't too much of a problem." Seltemver saw the assembled orcs perk up at that and start to whisper. Most of them, no doubt, cursing him.

"It's true," Toth agreed, turning towards the gathering crowd. They all came out to see what the commotion was and now looked upon Toth with something akin to hope. "This elf is going to do a favor for the sea witch and in exchange we can go with him when he leaves."

"Oh, so we exchange one master for another?" a small orc in the back asked. He was only about five feet tall and skinny compared to the rest of the orcs here.

"No." Seltemver stepped up next to Toth and looked them over slowly. They looked tired and worn, but not broken. They were proud, even in the grip of the witch's charms. "I am no slave master; first things first though. Let's see if I can pull this off before you start packing," he said, looking at Toth with a wink. "In the meantime, I need you to finish as much of that ship as you can." He turned without pause and walked towards where Amonar was waving at him.

"Grunhilde says we can rest in here," Amonar said, peeking in. "It looks comfy, too bad you don't sleep huh?"

"I still like to rest and meditate Amonar, It rejuvenates me."

"Hey elf," a voice barked from behind them.

Seltemver turned to see the runt of the orcs standing with his chest puffed out, glaring at him. *Oh gods above he's going to try something*, Seltemver thought, making a point to keep his hand away from his sword. "Yes?"

"You say you're no slave master but what's the catch then? You're an elf, am I supposed to believe that you're going to just let us go afterward?" The orc stepped even closer and snorted.

Seltemver had no time to dance around this. They needed to know that he was in charge, or the whole plan could backfire. Not that he had much of a plan, mostly like a running thought he was stitching together as he went. Seltemver hauled off and punched the orc square in the face, right at the bridge of the nose, and watched his head snap back. The orc stumbled and let out a cry of surprise and shock, then swung wild with his fist. Seltemver ducked and then stood back up with his right fist connecting under the orc's chin, taking him clean off of his feet. When the orc hit the ground the elf placed his foot on the orc's chest and leaned in. "What's your name?"

"Crak."

"? Well, Crak, the answer is simple. I am going to get you all off of this island, then we can figure out what's going to happen after you are all free. Is that all right with you?" Seltemver asked.

"All right. Can I ask you something?" Crak asked, clearly subdued.

"Sure."

"Could you teach me that move?"

"I sure can. Let's get out of here first, though." The elf took his foot off and helped the orc up, dusting him off. "Now get some rest, you guys have a ship to fix."

CAVE OF DESPAIR

Seltemver shook his head as he stared at the trail before him, paved with skulls, and edged with stone spikes. They had traveled for a day and a half to get to the ravine that held this trail, knowing that it was called the *Trail of Skulls,* but hadn't expected it to be actually paved with the skulls of humanoids.

"Of course, it's paved with bones, that's not creepy at all," Amonar said, hovering over the trail as he looked down.

Seltemver couldn't disagree. "Well let's keep going. The cave is supposedly at the end of this trail." He walked carefully over the skulls, his footing precarious at best on the rounded objects. Amonar flew next to him, a smirk on his face at the trouble the elf was having. If it wasn't for his agility he would be making far worse time.

"Hey look on the bright side, Seltemver," Amonar said as they reached the halfway mark. "At least it doesn't have a guardian."

"Why would you even tempt the gods like that Amonar?" Seltemver asked, slipping on a rather large skull and catching his balance. As if in answer, the ground trembled and skulls started to rattle together. Near the cave mouth, skulls were moving on their own accord, shifting as if something were coming up from underneath. Seltemver drew his sword and found a good place where his footing was stable and waited, eyeing Amonar with a hardened look.

"What?"

"You know what."

First, an arm burst through, then a shoulder. It was a huge skeleton with a skull resembling a massive orc. The tusks sticking out of its face gave it a fearsome look along with the enchanted emerald glow of malign power.

"Oh, that," Amonar said as he flew the other way down the trail.

An imp that hates violence, Seltemver thought to himself as the skeleton creature continued to crawl its way to the surface. *Of all the creatures I could get cursed with.* He stood his ground, waiting for the abomination to come to him. Finally, it started to stride towards him, its lumbering steps crushing the skulls underneath with every step; three more steps and it raised its foot high to crush the elf.

"Thanks for the clear path," Seltemver said, then slashed the leg it was standing on as he rushed under it, dancing along the skulls underfoot. He jumped for the crushed skull path and spun as the skeleton came crumpling down in a heap, already reforming. "Oh no you don't," he yelled, swinging his enchanted blade with two hands. The razor edge on its magical blade sliced through the thick bones with ease. Within a minute the creature was back to its component parts, the emerald glow fleeing its cold eye sockets. He looked back at the trail, the footsteps the creature had taken giving him a clear alternating path to his goal. "Let's go scardy imp," he called as he walked on.

"Not funny," Amonar said, flying next to Seltemver.

They stopped at the cave mouth, reflecting on the name they were given. *The Cave of Despair.* After seeing the skull path they took this name to heart and steeled themselves before going through the opening. It was a long tunnel with no light at all. Thankfully they could both see in darkness, Seltemver's elven vision, and Amonar's demonic sight.

"Am I going to feel anything?" Amonar asked, looking back and forth every few feet.

"I have no idea Amonar, I've never been here before."

"Oh, well I'll let you know if I start to feel weird."

"You do that."

Fifty feet in the tunnel came to a wide cave with four other tunnels branching off of it. The air was dank and stagnant this deep in, and the sound of dripping water was all they could hear. Amonar flew to each opening, staring down the dark passages one at a time and then flying back to Seltemver. Though the elf could see in the dark as well, Amonar's vision was three times as good as his.

"Nothing. It looks like each of them curves so I can't see from here," the imp sighed.

"It doesn't matter anyway," Seltemver stated, pointing back the way they came. He was pointing to a wall, with no evidence of the tunnel they came here through. "Just pick one and we'll see where it leads."

"This is part of the despair isn't it?" Amonar asked, his voice sounding worried already.

"More than likely."

They walked down a random tunnel and repeated this process twice more, with Amonar getting antsy every time the tunnel they exited disappeared.

"I feel weird," Amonar said at another junction.

"You're just afraid," Seltemver said as he closed his eyes and listened at each tunnel this time. Their eyes weren't helping so maybe hearing would help? Sure enough, Seltemver could hear faint dripping coming from one of the tunnels and nothing from the others. "Don't worry so much."

"You say that all the time."

"Fine stay here then."

"Coming Seltemver," Amonar said flying after him with a sigh

Finally, they came to the end of a tunnel, torches lit on either side of a single golden door. The door itself was engraved with the symbol of Dava, god of protection and honor, and seemed solid.

Seltemver inspected the door but saw no obvious locks or traps; the key-word was obvious.

"You're just going to open that door aren't you?" Amonar asked, backing up a little from the door just in case.

"Well, I don't see any other way in do you?" Seltemver turned the handle, opened the door slowly, and stepped in.

Conundrums

Seltemver stepped into a room that was a light golden color like the door, the floor covered in a thick coating of dust that said no one had set foot in it for a very long time. Torches burning in all four corners of the room made him arch an eyebrow. *I'll think about why those are still burning after all this time another day*, Seltemver thought as he walked carefully into the ancient room. The only other thing in the room was a pedestal holding a golden statue of a waterfall scene, with real running water falling endlessly. The statue radiated such a sense of evil that it was physically hard to approach it, making Seltemver take one forced step at a time.

"What?" Amonar asked, looking past Seltemver at the statue. "Oh yes I remember you," he said, flying right towards the statue like it was nothing.

Right, Seltemver thought. *Amonar is used to this feeling of evil, being from the deep hells and all.* "Amonar, what is it?"

"It's an imprisoned demon. Yngilithol, by name," Amonar answered, then flinched as if he had been whipped. "I'm sorry! I know...well he asked and I *had* to tell him because I'm bonded to him," The imp lied, then turned towards Seltemver and held a clawed finger to his lips as if to shush the elf from intervening. "So what are you doing in there?" Amonar asked the statue of the waterfall, once more turning to face the pedestal. "Ah, yes that would make sense. I'll tell him, hold on." Amonar flew back towards the door beckoning Seltemver after him.

They left the room and Amonar closed the door behind them gently. "All right Amonar, what is going on?"

"So it seems that the demon, Yngilithol, is imprisoned in that replica of a waterfall and one of the things holding him in it is the life force of the only human on the island. Since there are only orcs on the island and one human, it must be the sea witch." Amonar kept looking back at the closed door like he was worried that something would be bursting through it any minute. "Unless the witch is an elf..."

"She wouldn't have needed my help if that were the case. No, I'm fairly certain that Helarna is the sea witch," Seltemver said, finally putting the pieces together. "It's why the orcs have never seen the witch; keep the power mysterious and hidden to stave off rebellion."

"Yeah I was afraid of that," Amonar said, then he frowned. "Oh and the demon wants us to free him—I'm not telling him no, he's also quite peeved at me for telling you his name."

"Why?"

"Names have power against creatures like this and if he could, he would flay the red skin right off of me," Amonar said, rubbing his arm with his clawed hand absently.

"Well, that is good to know. Wait, one of the things holding him? What's the other?" Seltemver asked, not liking where this was going. The sea witch, Helarna, had lied to him, and now he wasn't sure what was going on.

"If I were to guess, I would say the water is," Amonar said, hovering nervously. "All demons have a weakness; like stone, wood, or water, so whatever imprisoned him also tied the spell to her soul. If she dies it weakens and he could try and break free...eventually. It would take him a while to overcome the water."

"So why did she want us to break this seal?" Seltemver asked rhetorically, knowing that Amonar wouldn't know. He thought over the conversation again and tried to see what she would get out of this. Then it hit him. If the demon was set free her soul would be free as well, her part of the prison moot. "Amonar, is that safe to hold?"

"It *should* be," the imp said, looking at him curiously. "What do you have in mind?"

"I'm going to make sure that she can never find another poor soul to break this, then I'm going to find her and thrash her within an inch of her life; after all, if she doesn't die, then it's fine right?"

"You're a twisted one aren't you?" Amonar asked, smiling now at the plan.

"I never said I was a good guy, Amonar." They opened up the door once more and retrieved the statue, carrying it out of the cave and down the path.

Days later they were back at the orc camp, a plan finally falling into place. All they had to do now was to confront the sea witch. "Toth, How goes the ship?" Seltemver asked, a slight bounce to his step.

"Good, the hull is patched and should keep us going for a bit, as long as we don't hit any storms," the orc said, nodding to others as they went by. They all seemed busy packing what they could so they were ready to leave in a hurry.

"Toth, I've got to talk with you about the plan," Seltemver said, guiding him away from the other orcs, lest they hear his crazy scheme.

"What's up?"

"So we found out that the sea witch wanted me to break that seal because she has been guarding it."

"That makes no sense."

"Tell me about it. Turns out it is a captive demon and she's part of the prison keeping it locked away."

"And you broke the seal on a captive demon?!" Toth asked a little louder than he should've. He saw the other orcs looking and cursed quietly, leaning in towards Seltemver. "Tell me we don't have to fight this thing?"

"No, I didn't break it. I have another plan."

Misled and Betrayed

Helarna heard the elf whistling up the path and frowned. As far as she knew he hadn't completed the task, so why was he back? She stood and sauntered out, keeping the rouse of being the *mouth of the sea witch* going... for now. She ripped her skirt a little up the side to show more leg and smiled as the handsome elf walked through the gate. "Well, my friend, I see you're back. Did everything go as planned?" she asked, noticing that he was without an orc escort.

"Well, to tell you the truth, it didn't go well at all," the elf said, coming to a stop with that ridiculous imp trailing behind him.

The imp was the only thing that was standing in her way. If it weren't for him, she would've overwhelmed the elf's magic and enslaved him as well, but that little creature's demonic ties could get through her defenses. "How so?" She walked closer as she asked, making sure to swing her hips seductively as she did, noting the elf's eyes following her movements.

"Oh it was awful!" the imp started, interrupting his elven master and babbling away. "A huge skeleton rose out of the ground and smashed the skulls. Then Seltemver cut its legs and it fell on him!" the imp howled with laughter, holding his sides as he hovered in mid-air.

"All right, Amonar, that's enough," the elf commanded, then turned towards her once more. "It took me another day to traverse the caves, getting turned around at least twice."

"Those caves can be tricky, or so I've heard," she added hastily, almost forgetting who she was supposed to be. She had played the role of *Mouth of the sea witch* for the last five years, both for the ling that were here, and for the orcs that came after their demise. No one on this island knew that she was the sea witch except Yngilithol—curse his name for eternity. If it weren't for him she could leave this accursed island and spread her fear and hatred to the mainland. She should've never attempted to enslave him to fight that holy warrior of Dava. How was she to know that he was that powerful?

"Yes, well, Once I finally got to the room, I couldn't open the door."

"What now?"

"The door, my magic couldn't open it. It was like it was sealed against elven magic."

She clenched her fists and tried to keep her calm, but underneath she was seething with anger. *Who could've locked the door? It was open the last time I visited it ten years ago,* she thought, as she started to pace. "Are you sure?" Helarna asked, panic starting to set in. She was almost free! This couldn't be happening.

"Positive, but I thought I would try again. All I need is some seaweed to help me erode the door hinges and rust them," Seltemver said, looking out over the cliffs towards the ocean.

"You can take any amount you need," Helarna said, turning away and stomping off. "I will contact the sea witch and have her meet you at the door to lend her power to yours," she said absently.

"Truly?" Seltemver asked.

"Well yes," she answered, thinking maybe she had given herself away. "She desires this as much as you do after all." With that, he seemed content and walked away down the path, while she went and started the ritual of relocation to take her right to the door.

"You were right, Seltemver," Amonar said as they walked down the path. "She bought it."

"Yes, now we have a reason to be by the water and some time to get the orcs on board before she realizes what we've done," Seltemver said, quickening his pace. They reached the camp and saw the orcs filing out towards the cove where the ship was waiting, with Toth standing guard to make sure no one was left behind.

"Ho there, Seltemver. Did she buy it?" the burly orc asked

"She seemed to. If my plan works, she should be coming for me any minute so let's get you all on board quickly," Seltemver said smiling at the thought of her finding out he had lied.

They were just getting to the beach where the ship was moored in the surf when a hideous scream echoed throughout the trees. "Hey, she *might* know that you pulled one over on her, Seltemver," Amonar said sarcastically.

Seltemver ignored him with practiced ease. "Toth, get them on board and push off, I'll give you time to get clear," he said, drawing his enchanted blade. Toth nodded and ran off, shouting orders and carrying those that couldn't go fast enough.

"Seltemver I thought you said you couldn't kill her?" Amonar asked, getting that sound in his voice he always did when he thought violence was imminent.

"There are a whole lot of ways to cut someone without killing them, friend," Seltemver said, as a crimson glow appeared on the black sands not far away. Seltemver thought quickly of what he could do to stall her, then it came to him...she didn't *know* he couldn't cast magic! He stood straighter, with an air of confidence and as she came into view he shouted the words he had said for decades to no avail. "Ash'anti ethir, sran ea dosit em'rem!" he called, begging the ether to shield him against her. Of course, nothing happened, but she wouldn't expect that.

Helarna stopped, stomping the sand in frustration and looked at them both with murder in her eyes. "Where is it, elf?"

"Amonar, do you know what this woman is talking about?" Seltemver asked, breathing an inward sigh of relief. Helarna—or the sea witch—seemed to have bought the fake spell act...for now. He walked toward her slowly, trying to close the gap so he could start this beating he so vehemently owed her.

"I sure do, Seltemver," Amonar said seeking cover from the coming confrontation. He flitted around a rock buried in the black sand and ducked down. "Just tell her and get on with it."

"You think so?" Seltemver asked nonchalantly, then shrugged.

Helarna stopped and looked at Seltemver with her piercing eyes narrowed in suspicion. The powerful witch knew something was up. "Tell me what exactly?"

Escape Plan

Seltemver was almost close enough to the sea witch...he just needed a couple more feet. "Where I put the seal of course." Seltemver inclined his head to her before continuing; stalling for time. "You tried to put one over on us, Helarna, or should I just call you the sea witch?" he asked, watching surprise creep across her face. "Yes, I figured out who you were when we found the trapped demon. He only mentioned one human on the island and you're it; you don't serve anyone but yourself."

"How could you have spoken..."

"The demon is a friend of mine," Amonar bragged from behind the rock.

"Not now, Amonar."

"Sorry."

"Enough!" Helarna yelled, taking out a small rod made from a tree branch. It was white wood—not bark like some of the northern trees from his homeland, but the very wood seemed bleached—and was topped with a tiny animal skull of some sort. Her other hand pulled out a small knife with no handle and closed it in her fist, squeezing it tight as it cut her pale skin. "Tell me where it is or suffer the loss of both that ship and the pathetic orcs you're protecting," she said, starting to cast some sort of blood magic. The blood from her cut hand was dripping down onto the black sand but then lifted back up slowly towards the rod.

Seltemver didn't anticipate her attacking the ship, never mind the orcs on board. He wasn't sure why he cared, they were only orcs after all, yet he had promised them salvation and he was damned to the hells if he wasn't going to come through on his word at least once this tenday. "Fine. You win Helarna," he said, taking two more steps towards her and holding his arms out wide. "I'll tell you where I put the seal." He was within five feet of her now, and she still felt confident; he could see it on her face. She must know he couldn't kill her, yet hadn't guessed what he had planned.

"Well? Where is it?" Helarna asked, rage twisting her once beautiful features.

"Oh, I tossed it out into the deep sea by the reefs," Seltemver said with a lazy gesture toward the ocean. "It will probably get pulled out deeper, washing in and out with the tides, until it eventually gets buried in the silt for centuries," he said as he watched the rage grow in her visage. "You know, surrounded by water and untraceable."

"Insolent fool!" she screamed, pointing the wand at the ship as it drifted slowly into the surf.

Before she could cast whatever foul spell she was trying to call forth, Seltemver leapt the rest of the distance and brought his enchanted sword down on her right arm, the one holding the wand, with everything he had. It cut clean through her flesh and bone, severing the arm up high, and causing her to falter in her spell. You needed some level of concentration to cast any type of magic, and that much pain and shock would stop an elven archmage in their tracks, never mind a blood mage. Helarna screamed her sanity away as he picked up the severed arm and tossed it towards Amonar's rock. As he turned back to her, he punched her in the face, followed up with a solid kick to her stomach, knocking the wind out of her and folding her up into a ball on the black sand. "Let's go, Amonar," he said, running towards the drifting ship as the sea witch was left gasping for air, her blood mingling with the black sand around her knees. Seltemver was hoping that the pain would keep her from casting until the ship was far enough out to sea...and it was almost there.

Amonar flew after him holding the witch's severed arm, concern on his tiny face. "Won't she die from all the blood she's losing?" the imp asked, constantly looking back to make sure she was still down.

"She's a witch Amonar, she'll be fine. Once she gets a little focus she can heal her wound and go back to her sad little hut." Seltemver waded into the coming waves, knowing that he would have to swim the rest of the way to the drifting ship. He hadn't gone far when he heard the sea witch start screaming again, yet something was different.

"Curse you, elf!" Helarna screamed in pain and agony, blood still dripping from her wound as she struggled to stand. "You are doomed! Doomed to sail those distant waters until you *all* find a home," she said, flinging her blood with her good arm at them and moving her mouth in a spell he couldn't quite make out. When she was done, she fell to her knees crying.

Seltemver felt it, like a tingling up his spine, and swam faster. She had used her blood to hurl that curse and gods above knew what else she would do if they didn't hurry. Hopefully, she used most of her power to cast that one and needed to rest. *And heal that wound,* he thought to himself as they neared the ship. Toth was lowering a rope down to him as the tattered sails unfurled in the breeze.

Amonar flew over the waves, still holding the arm, then he went up and over the side of the ship, landing near Toth. "Need a hand big guy?" the imp asked holding up the severed appendage.

Toth pulled Seltemver up, hand over hand, and looked down at the imp with a sly grin. "I like your humor, little one," the big orc said as the others blanched at the grim joke.

"Try listening to it for a year," Seltemver said as he climbed over the rail. He was soaking wet, his longcoat dripping and covered in seaweed. He looked up at Toth and smiled. "Toth, for now, you're my first mate. Once we get out of here and find Larishan Cove, you can have this ship as captain."

"What's in Larishan Cove?"

"An old friend that knows about spells and curses," Seltemver answered as the crew gathered around them.

"So we truly are free?" the small orc named Crak asked as the ship caught the wind and sailed out of the cove towards the open sea.

"Yes. You all are, but first, we have to get there, and for that, I need a loyal crew," he said, walking up to the wheelhouse and looking out over them all. Their tusked faces all stared at him with something like admiration. *Orcs...who would've ever thought to see that from them,* he thought as he turned the wheel, getting the feel for the new ragged ship. "Can you all do that?"

'Aye Captain!" they all shouted at once, their voices full of hope for the first time in a long time it seemed.

THE STORM

Toth came walking over as the others went about getting the ship rigged and tied up. It wasn't seaworthy, but it would have to do. "Just so you know, Seltemver, we all heard that crazy witch scream that curse. You saved us all from a fate worse than death, and were with you until the end."

"Well that shouldn't be long," Seltemver said, looking out over the waves as they fled the island. "It's just three days to Larishan Cove then you're all free." He was going to head there after the treasure on this lost island and find out about this curse, but he would have to try without the money for now. Once he was there he could always find another ship and head north again. Novrantir may hold some answers as well.

Three days in this wreck?" Grunhilde asked as she passed them and headed below. As she said that a storm came over the horizon, bearing down on them with ferocious speed and menace.

"Toth?"

"Yes, Captain?"

"Didn't you say we'd be fine unless we hit a storm?"

"Aye, I did indeed."

"Crap," Seltemver said as the thundering clouds converged upon the rickety ship. "Well, someone come up with a name for her before we go under," Seltemver said as he spun the wheel, trying to get away from the oncoming disaster. If he could cut eat fast enough he might skirt the edge and scrape by.

"Oh, I know!" Amonar said, flying over still holding the severed arm. "How about the *Seahaven*?" he asked, smiling proudly.

"Any particular reason?" Seltemver asked, grabbing the arm from him and tossing it overboard. He had just wanted to keep it from her so she couldn't put it back on with magic.

"Yeah, we're going to need someplace safe out here with that storm coming. A haven is supposed to be a safe place right?" Amonar beamed at the ingenuity of his wit.

Seltemver looked at Toth and they both laughed. "I like it," Seltemver said, turning towards the crew once more, seeing that he couldn't outrun the storm. The rickety ship just would turn that quick. "Welcome aboard the *Seahaven,* crew, now grab onto something and pray to whatever gods you hold dear...this is going to get rough!"

A cry of challenge went up from the orcs as they scrambled to get the ship ready for the rough beating it was going to take. The first winds hit and tore the flimsy sails clean away, sending the ship on a listless course. Tossed and thrown around like a ling in a hurricane, the ship fractured and cracked in more places than should be possible, yet somehow it kept going. Standing at the wheel, shouting defiant curses into the rain, Seltemver felt that familiar pull of adventure once more. He felt alive here, defying nature and trying to tame the wild seas. *Though I admit this storm is unlike anything I've ever seen,* he thought as the winds buffeted them from all sides. He looked at the orcs, keeping their footing amidst the pounding waves and cracking beams, and smiled. A finer crew he couldn't have asked for. The elven pirate smiled as Amonar landed on his shoulder again, despite saying he wouldn't anymore, and laughed at his diminutive friend. "Ready to get some answers, Amonar?"

Amonar held on as a wave came clean over the side and drenched them both, then shook his horns out. "As long as we get far away from that demon, I'm happy," the imp said, shivering at the memory.

Seltemver laughed and looked for the edge of the storm. He would get this ship out of here if it killed them. He spun the wheel again, the ship protesting with a moan felt deep under their feet, and headed right towards a massive wave. "Once more into the dark..." he said as the ship started climbing up the cresting wave.

JAIL BREAK

What would happen if the crew were all arrested? Funny you should ask that question. This one is one of the funniest stories and one of my personal favorites. The entire crew had been taken into custody, except Crak and myself. It was up to the two of us to somehow break Seltemver and the gang out of a stone prison guarded by elven wizards.

We had help, don't get me wrong. Met a cool woman named Janna who came to the rescue and helped us and boy did we have some fun times on this one. The crew doesn't like to bring this up too often, but Crak was the real hero of this story. So sit back and grab a pint and hear some wild antics and laugh as we pull one over on some stuffy elven guards.

—Amonar

Sailing Calm Seas

He spun the wheel and angled out of the fierce storm once more, his crew ready for whatever came at them this time. They had been doing this for a long time now and were almost used to the magical curse that sent them to different worlds every time they came out of this horrendous storm. They had just come from a world with almost no wind and very small islands. Being becalmed on the open sea with very little life for miles around was a sailor's nightmare, so for once the storm was appreciated by all.

Seltemver Ashblade looked out as the storm dissipated and saw the sun shining brightly, a cool wind blowing strong bringing a chill that could only be from the far north. The elf tossed his short white hair out of his eyes, let go of the wheel, and spun around; his worn long coat fanned out around him as he did. Slender but calloused hands gripped the wheel once more and spun, getting the wind into the *Seahaven's* sails for the first time in a very long time.

"Captain!" a large orc called out as the crew whopped and hollered at the pleasant change.

"I feel it too, Kona," Seltemver answered. Kona was one of the new orcs they had picked up on an orcish slave world and had fit in so seamlessly that the elf couldn't tell he was new.

Small-clawed feet landed on the elf's shoulder, a tail wrapping gently around one arm to steady the little creature. "I don't see any land yet though," Amonar said with a hint of worry.

"Don't worry Amonar, with this wind I'm sure we can find something," Seltemver said patting the tiny imp on the feet.

Amonar was an imp, bonded to Seltemver due to a curse placed on the elven pirate captain over three years ago. The imp was three feet tall with red skin, small bat wings, and a two-foot tail. Tiny horns protruded out of the top of his head and his eyes were usually black. Usually because when he channeled the power of the deep hells they turned blood red. "I'll try, but you know how I like to worry."

Seltemver laughed and nodded his head. It was one of the weirdest things about Amonar. The imp hated violence and was a scaredy imp most of the time. In all of his hundreds of years, Seltemver had never heard of an imp acting like this.

"Captain, I think I see a coast!" a voice called from the Crak's nest. It was aptly named for the small orc currently sitting in it. Crak was small for an orc, with the typical umber skin, but being only five feet tall compared to the six or taller orcs. His physique was a bit on the skinny side as well, and he often felt like he wasn't good enough, though the crew loved him. He kept his jet-black hair long and pulled back in a ponytail and his tusks barely protruded from his mouth.

"Nice work Crak," Seltemver answered, looking out over the beautiful sea with his own elven eyes. He could see it now, a dark line on the horizon. They needed a port soon or more would starve.

The last trip had been brutal, not just because they couldn't sail properly, but mainly from lack of food and water. With little wind and scarce land, they had to ration their stores. Normally that wouldn't have been an issue, but the world before that they had taken on extra passengers and slaves at that. The elves they had rescued from that slave world were already bone thin from starvation, so the rationing hit them hard. They lost over ten people in just under six months.

"We've seen a lot of worlds, Seltemver, but that last one was brutal," Toth said coming up to the helm. Toth was a burly orc and the *Seahaven's* first mate. The orc's long hair fell across broad shoulders and his heavily muscled arms bore tattoos of various weapons.

"I know, Toth," Seltemver said sullenly. "How many elves do we still have hanging on?"

"Grunhilde has five elves and an orc that can't get up but they are still breathing. They need food and water soon; hells we all do."

"Tell Grunhilde that we see a coast and to hold on," Seltemver said with a growing smile. "And inform Bernice to fire up the fire in the galley."

"Do I have to?" Toth asked wincing. Bernice was an orc they brought with them from the slave world; one that was tired of living with slavery in her life. She had taken a shine to the first mate, despite her husband, Hammond, being right there next to her. Bernice was now the Ships cook and with the lack of food, she had been more of a bother to Toth.

"Yes, you do. Just bring Hammond with you for reinforcement," Seltemver said with a laugh.

WRONG PLACE...

It took only another two hours to reach the coast and find a port city, the cold wind buffering the sails like an old lover blowing into town. The city was situated by the mouth of a river, so there were plenty of docks and ships, but that also meant that the crew may have to stay hidden. In most places they went the orcs weren't liked, even being cursed at sometimes because of their race's past violence. Seltemver usually liked to drop anchor a ways out and take the longboat in, but this time they needed to bring the ship into dock.

"Going in this time?" Grunhilde asked coming up and clapping him on the shoulder. Grunhilde was a huge, grey-skinned orc with long braids and a fierce smile. The best healer Seltemver had ever seen, the female orc had a good eye and a bedside manner that could level a mountain. She got the job done though, and it still amazed him that she could channel the healing power of the gods, even a little.

"Yeah, though I don't want to," Seltemver said with a scowl. "We only have one long boat left and it would take too many trips to resupply."

"And whose fault is that?" Grunhilde said with a tusky grin.

"You lose one longboat..."

"Two."

"I didn't lose the last one, we had to leave it behind," Seltemver reminded her.

"Because you got us into trouble again."

"Hey at least we didn't have to save him like when he lost the first longboat," Toth said from the deck.

"For the last time, she was a shapeshifter! I didn't know!"

"Trouble coming, Captain," Kona called as they eased into the port.

Seltemver swore and spun, pulling out the nifty tube they found in the empty land. That place had tons of buildings and stuff lying around, but with no people; anywhere. They were calling it a Spyglass, as it let you see very far with clarity, beyond even elven sight. "Yeah, looks like the guard is on the docks and pointing at the ship." Seltemver turned and called down to Toth. "Get the crew below deck and I'll try and figure out how they feel about you first."

"On it, Captain," Toth replied.

"Humans," Grunhilde swore as she walked away shaking her head. She hated that people couldn't take her on her merits and skill; her only weak spot was her heart on her sleeve, but he would never say that to her face.

"You ready, Amonar?" Seltemver asked the imp as the ship grated against the hardwood of the large docks. The elves on board tossed over ropes for the dock workers, their quiet eerie in the cool breeze.

"I'm never ready for you to get into trouble, though I should be used to it at least," the imp quipped.

Seltemver ignored his old friend with practiced ease and kicked the plank into place so he could go down to the docks and talk to whoever was in charge; he never got the chance.

A large man wearing armor and a heavy cloak strode up the plank the minute it touched. he had short blond hair, piercing blue eyes, and a small tattoo of a wing on his cheek. His armor had a symbol of a sword and shield, with silver and blue etched around it.

"Amonar, why don't you go up to the Crak's nest. I have a bad feeling about this," Seltemver said as he watched the man come.

"Got it, Seltemver," Amonar said and flew up, making noises like a parrot the whole way up. Seltemver shook his head and smiled at the approaching human, who was holding the hilt of his sword and narrowing his eyes. Seltemver made it a point to stand right in the man's way.

The man stepped up to the deck of the ship without introduction, looking Seltemver dead in the eyes. "My name is Guard Captain Rosen. By the order of King Daniver, all ships must be searched," the man said loudly.

"Is there trouble in these waters Guard Captain?" Seltemver asked, still standing in the man's way. This was not going well at all, and faster than usual.

"Warlords have been attempting to regain control by smuggling mercenaries into coastal towns and attacking at night." Rosen looked at the elves and scowled deeply. "What is wrong with your crew?" he asked as they moved about quietly.

Seltemver winced inwardly. How could he explain that they were all mute slaves taken from another world? "They keep to themselves in strange ports. Listen, we're new to these parts, can we just grab some supplies under watch and we'll be gone." Seltemver was trying his best, but he could see the man wasn't going to buy it. *I just hope these people don't know what orcs are,* Seltemver thought.

Rosen waved his hand and four more men came dressed similarly, but without the cloaks. Behind them came two elves wearing white leathers, their hands holding carved staves.

Seltemver knew they were in trouble when he saw the elves and was about to ask where they were from when the guard's shout came from below.

"Oran!"

I haven't even left the ship yet, Seltemver swore to himself as he drew his enchanted blade. He was going to just wound the elves, keeping them alive so they could heal later, but they were quicker than he was. They whispered to the air and strong winds bound Seltemver's arms to his sides, his blade clattering uselessly to the deck of the ship. "Wait, I can..." Pain exploded in his temple as Rosin hit him with the pommel of his sword and darkness took him before he could get anything else out.

...WRONG TIME

Amonar flew up to the Crak's nest and was shocked to see the small orc still there. "Hey, aren't you supposed to be in the basement?" the imp asked in hushed tones.

"It's below decks, and there wasn't time. Besides, they won't see me up here," Crak answered smiling.

"Oran!" someone shouted from below.

Amonar leaned over and heard the elves cast magic and knew the jig was up. Then he saw Seltemver go down in a heap and swore to himself. He didn't want to do this again. Before he could call upon the dark forces of the deep hells, he heard the guard captain call out to his men.

"Don't harm any of them, let the king's judgment pass before that. Bring them all to Stonecell." the man said as the guards led the orcs up from the hold. Most of the crew was still weak from starvation and with the magic of the elves in white, they didn't have a chance. Only two were fighting back, and Amonar knew who they were before they came into view.

"By the gods, you will regret laying your hands upon me, elf," Grunhilde said, her hands glowing a soft golden color.

Amonar had never seen her use magic other than to heal and was entranced by what she was doing.

"Oran shaman," one elf called out to his partner and they both converged upon the orc healer.

"Shaman? Nay, elf. I am a healer of Dava, and you will not take me so easily with your magic," Grunhilde said, assuming a stance and brandishing her hands like weapons.

The two elves circled her and it was then that Amonar saw what Grunhilde was doing. She was distracting them.

Toth roared and came charging up from below, his huge axe coming down on one of the guards and cutting into his armor easily. Engaged with Grunhilde, the two elves turned in horror as the burly orc threw one of them over the side of the ship and kicked the other back ten feet. "Run Grun..." Toth started, but his words were cut short when the Guard Captain lunged with his blade and took Toth clean through the side, his blade coming out the other side of the orc's chest.

"Toth!" Grunhilde cried out as she dropped down and laid her already glowing hands on his wounds. "You're not leaving me to deal with that damned elf alone," she swore as she closed her eyes. The last elf on the ship came towards her in wonder and cast quickly once she had finished, subduing her with magic and shaking his head.

Amonar couldn't believe what was happening and was torn with what to do. Even though Toth had attacked them outright, the guards were taking care not to harm anyone and were treating them well.

"Are you going to burn them all, Amonar?" Crak asked with a quiver in his voice.

Amonar closed his eyes and took a slow breath. He knew some of the crew was still afraid of him for his displays of infernal power and it never got easier. "No, Crak. They aren't hurting them and I can't use it unless Seltemver is in mortal danger," Amonar said slowly. They both sunk down out of view and sighed. "I'm sorry I scared you, Crak," the imp said after a minute of tortured silence. "I'd never hurt you guys, you know that right?"

"Oh I know, Amonar. It's just..."

"I know."

"So what do we do now?" Crak asked changing the subject. "And what does Oran mean?"

"I've heard Seltemver talk about it before. It's another name for orc in the far north. They must have them here too," Amonar said, his mind racing. They were alone now, just him and the smallest orc on the ship. No Toth, no Seltemver...no Grunhilde. *Oh my gods above,* Amonar thought with sudden realization and horror. *I'm in charge!*

"Are you all right, Amonar?" Crak asked, feeling the imp's head. "You looked pale there for a second.

Getting Started

They stayed for hours in the Crak's nest until it was quiet, only peaking over once in a while to see what was going on. The guard had taken everyone, even Morn, the dwarf. They had remarked about not knowing what he was, but Amonar was used to things like that; visiting different worlds and all. The guard had even taken the elves, as they were harboring oran. Amonar wouldn't want to be there when they found out why the elves on the Seahaven were so quiet. They had rescued them from a horrific world where they were disfigured at birth, their tongues cut out to prevent them from casting magic.

Once all was still Amonar flew down to make sure there was no one waiting and then signaled to Crak. He whistled softly and waited...nothing. The imp whistled once more, then finally flew back up. "I gave the signal," he shispered—the phrase Seltemver used to explain how Amonar could whisper while yelling.

"Oh I thought it was going to be a bird call," Crak said, then shrugged his shoulders and smiled. The small orc climbed down and they snuck down to the cabins, grabbing what they could. Crak took one of the extra long coats Seltemver had found as well as a pair of daggers and a small hand axe. These weapons could be readily hidden under a long coat so he didn't draw attention.

"You need a hood of some kind too," Amonar said flying around the small orc. "You stick out like a sore foot."

"Thumb," Crak corrected.

"Don't do that. I get enough of that from Seltemver," Amonar admonished. The imp found a hooded cloak and tossed it to Crak. "Put that on, it will hide your face."

"What 's wrong with my face?"

"You look like an orc."

"Oh, yeah."

They went back up as the sun started setting and froze as a guard came up the plank, turning and standing watch with his back to them. Amonar held up his hand to Crak then flew over quietly to the side. The imp picked up a small hook and tossed it into the water near the plank, drawing the guards' attention.

"Who's there?" the guard asked, leaning over the plank to look at the ripples in the water.

With a gentle shove, Amonar had the man off balance and tumbling into the salty water. The imp waved his arms excitedly and Crak ran for the docks, taking to the shadows once off the ship. They stopped in an alley to catch their breath.

"What now?" Crak asked, clearly excited.

"I'm not sure. I'm never the one to make these kinds of decisions," Amonar admitted.

"What would Seltemver do?" Crak asked as he peaked around the corner to make sure they weren't being followed.

"Find a bar and start trouble..." Amonar thought about it and for once it sounded like it might be a good idea; the bar, not the trouble part.

"How about that one?" Crak asked, "The Lashed Girl." The small orc pointed to a dark-walled tavern. It had a faded sign that hung on one hinge and consisted of a gagged woman with her hands tied behind her back.

"Could be worse," Amonar admitted, then shrugged his little shoulders and flew over to Crak. "But I have to hide inside your coat."

"Will you fit?"

"Not sure. I've never tried." Amonar snuggled in and clung to a pocket on the inside of the longcoat, the dark swallowing him as Crak closed it up around him. "Just be casual and don't draw attention to yourself," Amonar hissed at him.

The woman sat back in her chair and drained her mug, her eyes never leaving the door to the tavern. Her ears picked out several conversations, all of them nothing but gossip, and she entertained herself by listening in while waiting. It helped that most of them were talking about her.

She was beautiful and she knew it, with long, brown hair tied up in twin ponytails, and piercing green eyes. She was small and thin, cresting a little over five feet, with clothes that were cut high to show more skin than fabric. She had a harp on the table and a sword on her lap, ready for anything in this dive. As a bard, she had seen her share of filthy taverns, but this place had to take the prize.

Janna Suris waited patiently for her contact to arrive, the only thing she knew about him was that he would be in a hooded cloak. That was what she got for hiring lowlifes near the docks, but she was out of options if she needed this done by the end of the tenday. Everyone else that could help her was busy, and besides, she needed this to be discreet. She had made quite a name for herself in Sirr—being a heroine and all—and it was things like this that she had to keep quiet; some people just wouldn't understand. Just when she thought the man wasn't going to show, a mysterious figure entered the tavern; it had to be her guy.

The man was wearing a long coat with a hooded cloak, covering his face and keeping to the shadows. He clearly had something hidden under the coat and looked extremely nervous. Thank the gods above everyone else was too busy drinking and gossiping to notice the stranger. Janna stood and motioned for the man to join her and, after an awkward moment of the man turning in circles, he headed over to her. *I wonder if he is going to try and cross me?* she wondered, knowing that she had a secret up her sleeve; Janna was more than just a normal bard, after all.

WE NEED A PLAN

Crak walked into the Lashed Girl with the shakes. He had always been the runt of the ship, even before they were on the ship. They always chided him, saying it was all just fun, but he knew they meant it deep down. As such, he was always striving to show that he could handle things just like any orc...only problem now was that he *had* to.

He was the only one left, besides Amonar, and it was up to them to find the crew and figure out what to do. He had to admit it, he was in a little over his head. Before he could even whisper to Amonar inside his longcoat, a beautiful woman stood and beckoned him to her table. Not wanting to draw attention by refusing, he angled his way there and sat.

"The moose moves at midnight," the woman whispered, taking a sip of her empty mug.

Crak looked around and wrung his hands nervously. "Because he wasn't tired?" the small orc answered back. He wasn't sure what was going on, but he thought maybe it was a riddle; he liked riddles.

The woman frowned and looked around, then leaned in closer. "I'm assuming you are here for help?" she asked. "Maybe with a job?"

Crak was kind of hopeful. "Actually yes, we were looking for help. He winced as Amonar elbowed him in the ribs and he cleared his throat. "I mean, *I* was looking for help." He turned and looked at the table next to them and couldn't help but stare. The food smelled so good! His stomach rumbled at the sight and he turned to look at the woman with a shrug.

"Would you feel better with a full stomach before a job?" she asked, signaling for the woman in a small apron. "Two meat plates," Janna said, tossing a small bag of jingling coins at the woman.

Crak nodded enthusiastically and tried to keep his hood from falling back when he did so. He pulled it down firmly and bowed his head. He didn't want to screw this up at the start.

"My name is Janna Suris, mayhap you've heard of me?" the woman said as she sat back and folded her arms.

"Ah, no. I'm not from around these parts," the small orc replied, watching her crestfallen look appear on her gorgeous face. *If she had tusks I'd be all over that*, he thought.

"You haven't? Well, never mind. Let's just say I'm good at what I do and that the payment will be worth it." Janna sat up as the food came, tore off a leg of something, and started eating.

Crak started at the food, wondering how he was going to eat it while keeping his tusks hidden. He tore off some with his hands and ate it, then saw her eyes narrow. Crap, his hands. He looked at them in the tavern light and saw that they were indeed a different color than most people; a dark umber to be precise.

"Uh, sorry, I'm from down south," Amonar spoke up from inside the coat. The imp had used a deep voice to sound like Crak and did a pretty good job.

Crak just nodded and tore off another piece when she nodded.

Janna stopped and looked at him again, a broad smile appearing on her face. "You're not my contact, are you?" Her hand slipped under the table and she backed her chair up slowly.

"Wait. No, I mean. Damn the gods, why can't I do anything right!" Crak swore, smashing the table with his fist. The wood creaked with the hit and everyone in the place stopped to stare at them. He took a deep breath and let it out. "Listen. We aren't from anywhere around here and we desperately need help to find our friends."

Janna stopped and looked around. She sighed deeply and stood with a resigned look on her face. "Gods above I am going to regret this, but follow me."

Once they had stood and started walking towards the door, the tavern went back to its regular chatting and drinking, forgetting all about the outburst. Crak followed the woman out.

"Be careful, Crak," Amonar whispered from inside the longcoat.

Crak slapped the coat and followed Janna to the alley and once there she spun. "You think I'm buying that line about needing help? I can tell you have something under that coat to attack me with, so let's get it over with," Janna said as she lunged with her sword and stabbed the longcoat. Crak dodged to the side at the last minute, but the blade hit Amonar squarely.

"Ow!" the imp screamed, startling the woman and revealing the tiny demonic creature, He flew out dripping blood, his wound already closing. "I may be immortal, but it still hurts!" he cried.

Qvestion and Answer Time

Amonar's side throbbed as it closed up, yet he could spare no time to complain; the woman was dangerous and he didn't have Seltemver. He turned to see how Crak was doing and saw that his long coat was open and his hood had fallen back. *Oh great...trouble already,* he thought

"What, in the name of Ollian's tits, are you?" Janna asked backing up with a wary eye on Crak. "And you're an oran?" The woman started chanting softly, elvish words like the elves on the ship had used to subdue Toth.

Crak stepped forward and punched the woman square in the face, right at the bridge of the nose and her head snapped back. Janna stumbled and let out a cry of surprise and shock, then swung with her sword to back the orc up. Crak ducked low, then stood back up with his right fist connecting under the woman's chin, taking her clean off of her feet. When she hit the ground, Crak placed his foot on her chest and leaned in. "We don't want to hurt you...we seriously *do* need help."

"Well for someone that doesn't want to hurt me, you're doing a *very* good job at it," Janna lamented, holding her head. "Mind stepping off my chest, big boy?" Janna took Crak's offered hand and got to her feet a little unsteady. "Nice hit by the way."

Amonar flew in and sniffed the woman as she stood. Janna wasn't half-elven, but she had the smell of someone who had elven blood somewhere in her past; it was so faint that he almost missed it. That wasn't what worried him though. More troubling was that this close, he could feel the power coming off of her like she was a bonfire. "I'll tell you what I am if you tell us what in the deep hells you are?" Amonar said, crossing his tiny arms over his chest.

"You can tell by smell?" Janna asked, shaking her head.

"No, that was to see if you had elven blood. I can feel the power coming off of you though. It's like a heat wave this close."

"Damn. Good to know for the future," Janna started, straightening her clothes. "Well, I'm a bard by profession, but I'm also the Incarnation of Beauty and Song, serving the goddess Ollian," Janna said but held up her hand to forestall any other questions. "Just do me a favor and keep that between us, all right?"

Amonar nodded and whistled. He had heard of Incarnations back when he was bonded to his old master, Nor'alrin, but he had never met one. They were supposed to be vessels for their god and to work their will on the mortal plane. Not something to mess with, never mind punch in the face. *It would also explain the magic,* he thought. *Bards have their own magic that anyone can cast.* "Nice to meet you. I'm Amonar, an imp from the deep hells."

"Well, Amonar, you certainly fit the description, now that I can put it together," Janna said eyeing Crak again. "What are you doing with an oran though?"

" I don't know why you keep calling me that," Crak said. "I'm an orc."

"It's what they call orc's in this world I think, Crak," Amonar answered turning towards the small orc. "Seltemver once said that in his world, in the far north, they called them oran too."

"His world?" Janna asked tilting her head to the side. "I'm going to need a drink, or five, aren't I?"

"It would probably help you to swallow half of what we have to tell you," Amonar admitted, flying up and landing on Crak's shoulder. "But we should get off the streets."

"Sounds like a good idea," Janna said, sheathing her sword. "Besides, my contact was late to begin with. I'm pretty sure he stood me up, so my plans are scrapped."

"Sorry if we ruined your plans," Crak said as they walked down the alley following Janna.

"No worries, you may even be able to help me with them anyways, so it all works out." Janna smiled over her shoulder and kept going.

"Nice moves back there, by the way," Amonar said to Crak as they followed. "Where did you learn to do that?"

"Seltemver did that to me back on the isle of the sea witch. I asked him to show me and once we had some time he taught me some moves," Crak said stuffing his hands in his pockets.

"What made you think to even do that? And to a woman at that?" Amonar wasn't mad at the choice, but he wasn't used to violence from the small orc.

"She was talking like those elves on the ship. Seltemver always said to hit wizards fast and hard so they couldn't get their magic off,"

"You're smarter than you give yourself credit for, Crak," Amonar said, patting him on the head as they went. "I'm glad you're here with me."

You Scratch My Back

Amonar settled into a wicker chair and kicked a wet blanket to the dirty floor. "Nice place you have here," he said to Janna as Crak tried to sit on a crate. The small orc promptly fell over when one side gave way and spilled lemons all over the grime-covered boards.

"It's my bolt hole for when I need to get away," Janna said with a smile. She shook her head at Crak as he tried to get up and fell again, slipping on a lemon. "You all right there fella?"

"No, I am not," Crak muttered as he kicked a lemon out of his way. The fruit bounced off the wall and came flying back at him. When he tried to move out of the way, his foot caught another one and down he went.

Janna burst into a fit of laughter that seemed to be genuine, falling to her knees and holding her stomach.

"You know what they say when life gives you lemons? Right, Crak?" Amonar asked, laughing himself now.

"You slip on them over and over again?" Janna asked with tears rolling down her face now.

Crak just sat there, scowling...then started laughing himself. He grabbed a lemon and tossed it at the female bard, catching her right in the chest and making her laugh even harder.

Once everyone calmed down—and Crak had finally gotten comfortable—Amonar began his tale. He told her of the curse on the ship and how they traveled different worlds, a new one every time they sailed out to sea. He went into some detail about the crew, sharing Seltemver's curse as well, and watched her take it all in with stride. "You're taking this well," Amonar remarked when he had caught her up to the orcs being taken as prisoners.

"Well I am a vessel for the Goddess of Beauty and have seen some pretty scary things the past couple of months," Janna said, crossing her legs and showing more skin than usual. "In fact, I just helped the king with a Lith problem, so cursed ships are kind of just another day to me now."

"What's a Lith?" Crak asked, biting into a lemon. He scrunched his face up and tossed the bitter fruit away, spitting out what he could.

"It's a type of undead elven wizard...very bad and very angry," Janna said.

"So you'll help us get our friends out?" Amonar asked, batting his eyes at her. Not that it would work, but maybe she would find it funny; humor seemed to be her weak spot.

"If they were taken to Stonecell, then I may be able to help with that. However, I need something from you guys first." It was her turn to bat her eyes, leaning forward as she did.

Crak eyed her as she leaned forward. 'Why do you both keep doing that with your eyes?" he asked, clearly confused.

"Never mind, Crak. I will explain it to you later," Amonar said, patting the orc on the head. "So what can we do for you?"

"During the fight with the Lith, several ships were scuttled off the northern coast near the Noron Reefs. One of those ships was carrying something very valuable and I need it for something." Janna sat back again and crossed her arms. "Get that for me and I will help you free your friends."

"You can't swim?" Crak asked

"Yes, I can *swim*. The water, even the depth, isn't a problem for me with my magic," Janna said with a snort. "What *is* the problem is the pile of timber on top of the chest it is in."

"And you need someone big and strong to help clear it off," Amonar reasoned.

"Spot on."

"Your magic couldn't lift it?" Crak was trying to understand, but magic just wasn't something they had to deal with a whole lot.

"It could, but I need to speak to cast it, and if I'm underwater..." Janna left the sentence unfinished and watched Crak take it all in. "He's almost got it," she joked.

Amonar chuckled at Crak's brow as it furled in thought. "She just can't underwater, Crak." Amonar turned to the bard and flapped his wings. "It's a deal, but we also need supplies for the ship before we break them out."

"That's fine, We can get that stuff once we're back from the north. It should only take us two days to get there, depending on patrols." Janna stood and walked to an iron-bound chest, kicking it open. "Before we go though, you will need a better disguise than a hooded cloak."

Trouble with Time

He paced the cell with a scowl, knowing full well that no one cared in the slightest that he was unhappy. Seltemver kicked the bars once more and refused to cry out at the pain in his foot; he wouldn't give Toth, or Silence, the satisfaction.

"Those bars taking their beating well, Captain?" Toth asked with restrained mirth.

"Shut it," Seltemver said and pointed at the mute elf that shared his cell as well.

The mute elf, Silence, made a locking key gesture near her mouth and laughed quietly.

The elven pirate captain sat down on his hay pile and scuffed his feet. They had been locked up for three days and no one had come to even talk with them yet. Not the guard captain, the warden, or even the lord of wherever this was. They were served food and water quietly by tight-lipped humans and that was it.

The orcs were crowded together two or three in a cell, with Toth sharing one with Beatrice and Hammond in the cell directly next to Seltemver and Silence. They had briefly talked about breaking out, but with the elves' magic, it seemed bleak.

"I still say Am will get us out," Toth said, using his nickname for the little imp while cracking his knuckles for the hundredth time. "And he has Crak to help him."

"I know. It's the one thing keeping my hopes up," Seltemver admitted with a nod.

"Oh great. Our lives depend on an inexperienced orc and a mischievous imp to break us out of an elven prison in a strange world," Grunhilde said her voice dripping with sarcasm. "What could *possibly* go wrong?"

"Prison doesn't suit you," Toth replied, smiling at her with his tusks up.

"No shit."

"Children," Seltemver said raising his voice a bit. "There is nothing to do now but rest, eat, and wait to see what those two can do."

"Can't the little guy magic us out like he does to save you?" Kona asked from the cell he shared with Grunhilde, his tone sounding wary of what it implied. He was just one of the orcs who was petrified of what Amonar could do, making the sign of Dava every time the imp came near.

Seltemver couldn't blame him, yet he wished the crew would get over their fear. It made the imp self-conscious. "Sadly, no. My life isn't in danger," Seltemver said. "Look on the bright side. We have plenty of food, water, and no one is trying to kill us."

"Yet," Toth and Grunhilde said at the exact same time.

"All right. Actively trying to kill us," Seltemver rectified. "I'm sure they've got this."

"I don't think he's got this," Amonar said as he watched Crak swim for the ruined ships. "Does he even know which one is the right one?"

"We told him four times, I should hope he does," Janna answered.

Amonar hovered back and forth, worried that he might lose another friend if this went wrong. "I hope so too."

They had traveled north for three days, going slow because of increased patrols. The apprehension of oran at the docks had made quite the stir in the guard and they were scouring the countryside to make sure it was isolated. Janna had dressed Crak up as an elderly woman and it had fooled every guard that had stopped them; no one wanted to bother an old woman.

Amonar looked at the reefs and admired the scenery. The powerful waves crashing upon the exposed rocks as the tide came in was mesmerizing and he must've lost track of time because Janna was swearing. "What's wrong?"

"He's taking too long," Janna said, taking off her cloak, then her shirt. "And I can't see him with my *sight,* he's kicked up too much silt."

"Wait!" Amonar said, peering into the murky waters with his demonic sight. "I can see something coming up."

Crak broke the surface of the turbulent waves with a deep intake of breath, his chest heaving with the effort. He struggled to the shore and threw the chest on the shore, crawling after it. He lay on his back with his eyes closed and took another breath. "I...got...it."

"We see that," Janna said, her fingers working at the lock with skill. She still had no shirt on and her pants were half off. The chest opened and Janna squealed, holding aloft a small harp of gold. "Yes!"

"A harp?" Amonar asked tilting his head to the side.

"Not just any harp, but Galrien's Harp," Janna said as if that would clear things up...which it didn't. When she noticed the blank stare she sighed. "This is a payment to a certain elf who is going to help train me in magic. I do have some elven blood, though it is thin."

"Ah, makes sense."

"It does?" Crak asked, sitting up. "Well, I'm glad it does to someone I suppose."

"You did great, Crak," Janna said, hugging him from behind.

"Thanks, but I almost dropped it. Twice."

"You are too hard on yourself, you know that?" Janna said

"Well I'm the smallest orc on the ship," Crak admitted with a frown.

"And?"

"And everyone else is strong, competent, and brave."

"Crak..." Amonar started but Janna held up her hand to forestall the imp.

"Crak, you just need the right time to be brave. You can't be brave all the time, there has to be a reason. So, the next time the situation calls for you to be strong and brave-take it," Janna said, helping him stand. "You took out an Incarnation with a punch and just dove down into three shipwrecks to drag up a water-logged chest; you're pretty damned heroic to me."

"Well, when you put it that way," Crak said puffing up his chest.

"Now can we get back and restock the ship?" Amonar asked, impatient to get going. The sooner he got his friends out the sooner they could get out of this world.

"About that, Janna said with a smirk. "It may take a little longer than anticipated, but I've got a plan, then I can help get your friends out."

"Why are you helping us?" Crak asked as he shook his hair out.

"Well, you helped me get this," Janna said holding up the harp. The sides of the beautiful instrument were gleaming in the sunlight. "Plus, do you know the stories I can sing about all of this? An imp and an oran?" Janna laughed as she placed the harp in her satchel and patted it like a small child. "Now let's get back, We've got a lot of work to do."

The Old Woman and the Ship

It was the fifth trip this month and he still got nervous doing it. Crak shambled towards the plank with the cart and tried to keep his head down as Janna said. At the base of the plank, he stopped and shook his cane at the guard like he always did.

"Yeah, I know Mabel, I'm moving," The guard said with a chuckle. He stepped aside and another came up slapping the man on the shoulder.

"How long is it going to take this time?" the new guard asked.

Crak hid his own smile beneath his wig and hood, the white curls of the fake hair tickling his face. Once again the small orc was dressed as an old woman, delivering goods to the newly acquired *Seahaven* bought from the city of Anar. It had been over a month since they went north and Janna had put down a good sum of money—their payment as it were—for the ship. Since it was a city auction, she only had to put down some of the gold, the rest paid when she picked up the ship once its former owners had been executed. The trick was that if anything happened to the ship before that, her money would be returned to her by the city.

"I'm going to guess at least an hour with her back," the first guard said.

Crak shambled up the plank at a slow pace, playing the part of a feeble old woman rather well. They did this every week he came, betting each other how long it would take 'Mabel' to drop off the supplies and return down to the docks; they had nothing better to do. It served as a great distraction so that Amonar could fly up over the other side and meet in the hold.

They had been doing this every tenday, for five tens, just to get enough food and water for the crew once they were back on board. Then they would sit in the hold for a bit and talk about how they were going to break the crew out of a stone prison built with magic.

Crak went down the wooden steps, disappearing from the view of the guards, and stood straight; bent over like that was killing his back. He saw Amonar sitting at Seltemver's desk and pulled off his wig. "Did you hear from the crew?" Crak asked the imp as he sat down.

"Yes, Janna helped get a message in and out so Seltemver is aware of the so-called plan, though I still think it won't work," Amonar said with a huff.

"I still can't believe they haven't executed them yet," Crak said taking a bite from a loaf of bread. They had heard that the Lord of Anar had called for death to the oran and their conspirators, yet the king had called for judgment. Janna had said that it meant they had to wait for King Daniver himself to come and review the prisoners, which she stalled perfectly. It seems she knew the King's Blade—an elf called, Myst—personally and he owed her a favor, no questions asked.

"We'll that was the last trip for supplies so we're ready," Amonar said, a big smile on his dark red face. "I just hope this works."

"It will, Amonar," Janna said coming into the room. The bard was allowed to come and go on her ship, but still had to make sure she seemed inconspicuous; never staying too long. "I helped design that prison with the king himself, once we overthrew the warlords. I know it like the back of my hand."

"Famous last words," Amonar said crossing his arms and pouting.

"You're just miffed that we're not using your plan," Janna said with a smile, walking over and petting the little imp on the head. "Tell you what. If our plan goes south, yours can be the plan B."

"Great! I'll go find us a goat or a sheep," Amonar said and flew off out the portcullis.

"You'll let him do this?" Crak asked with a sideways glance at the Incarnation. He had seen how powerful she was over the last month and he was sure she could pull this off.

"If my plan goes sideways—and I've heard that happens to your Captain a lot—I want a backup plan," Janna said, taking a swig of water and turning with a flair.

"Fair point," Crak said with a smile.

Janna walked out but stopped at the door. "Besides, part of me would love to see the elves' faces when he pulls that stunt, even though I don't think it would work."

The Breakout

Seltemver paced in his cell like he had for the last month and cursed the elves once more. They had refused to even speak with him at all, on the grounds that they believed that *he* was the one that had mutilated the elves on his ship. Silence had tried to tell them the truth, but no one spoke her silent language among the wizards stationed here.

The elven wizards had even tried to fix the mute elves with their best healers, but you can't re-grow tissue with magic, only fix what is there. In the end, they had isolated the mute elves from the orcs and their captain, splitting up the crew. Now he was alone in his cell, and his thoughts; he just hoped that wouldn't mess up the escape plan.

"Is today the day?" Toth asked as he continued his daily regimen of workouts. The burly orc was in the best shape of his life, due to the confinement and Seltemver would never want to fight that one barehanded.

"The last note said that it was close, so best to be ready every day from now on," Seltemver said looking over at Bernice. The orc cook hadn't spoken in over a tenday, and he couldn't blame her.

They had only lost one orc—Her husband, Hammond—due to massive dehydration and starvation. Hammond had given his shares to Bernice when they first were captured and never recovered in time. Had Grunhilde been able to get to him she could've saved him, but she couldn't reach him through the bars. The elven wizards came personally to remove the body, holding Toth and Bernice with their magic and he could see the smoldering rage in her eyes. Now the orcs understood why they couldn't break out easily.

"Well I for one and ready for some payback," Grunhilde said punching the floor while she was doing push-ups. She had seen Toth working out and taken it as a challenge to keep up with him; everyone needed something to keep them occupied while incarcerated.

Seltemver was about to say something very clever when shouts of alarm went up and the human guards scattered. About time, Amonar, he thought, then he saw what had caused the calamity and couldn't keep his jaw from hitting the floor.

Crak shambled towards the *Seahaven* once more, this time just two days later, which made the guards tilt their heads.

"Well, well, well. If it isn't Mabel," the guard said pulling out a small purse of coins. The other guard came over with his fist full of coin and made way for the elderly woman.

Crak had been waiting for this day, yet now that it was here, his stomach was a mess. Familiar doubts came creeping in and he almost fumbled, yet Janna's voice kept repeating in his head; the day was here. As the small orc passed the two guards he lashed out with a punch to one's face as he kicked the other as hard as he could. His wig went flying off and his shawl flew into the wind, all traces of 'Mabel' gone.

The first guard cried out and fell back, while the other went sailing off the dock and into the water. Crak followed up with an elbow to the first guard's chin and a punch to the gut, taking him out. He slashed the ropes tying the ship to the dock and ran for the plank, the now drifting ship pulling the board away. He only had a few minutes before more guards would be here.

Getting to the ship he kicked the plank away then ran for the anchor winch. The small orc pulled as hard as he could, moving the gears that had been inert for so long. Thank the gods above they had this new winch installed in that gear city, it would've taken two orcs to pull this up before. With the anchor loose, he reached into his pocket and pulled out the small bag, releasing it into the breeze. Red powder flew into the sky, signaling his friends and setting the plan into motion; it was too late to turn back now. Sprinting to the helm, Crak only hoped he could guide the *Seahaven* as well as Seltemver or Toth.

Janna saw the red dust sail off the ship and smiled; she knew he could do it. "Ash'anti, fra, gli tow ea!" she called out, asking the wind to blow in her direction. She had put enough emphasis behind it to make the elements strong and she could see the ship list heavily towards her with the wind fully in the three sails. *I must remember to thank Myst for teaching me that one,* she thought as she saw the ship's sails fill. With the commotion at the docks, most of the guards were on their way there and not looking at the cliffs behind the prison. The bard turned towards the wall and looked over the cliff to the spout that usually poured out ashes. It was the run-off for the incinerator and Amonar had flown in to turn it off.

A small stone came rolling out the opening, made of hewn rock, and splashed into the surf thirty feet below, the sign that it was ready. Janna stopped concentrating on the wind and took out her harp, playing a little tune and casting another spell. This one made the heat pull out of the ground, cooling off the tunnel that she would crawl through to get inside. Thankfully the imp was impervious to the heat in the first place. Swinging down she looked back at the ship as it neared the cliffs and saw two more ships after it. This was going to be close. The Incarnation of Beauty hurried through the short tunnel and came out to see the imp over two bodies.

"They're not dead, just fainted," Amonar said smiling. He was still holding that ridiculous bag over his shoulder for his 'plan B.'

"Well, let's get your friends out of here. The *Seahaven* is almost here," Janna said, opening the door and jogging down the hall. She knew the layout well, having supervised the magic made to construct it. These back halls were only for the servants to take out bodies and dispose of them, the prison was a harsh life for anyone who was connected to a warlord after what the people of Sirr had gone through because of those tyrants. She just prayed that the orcs were treated better, or this little imp wouldn't have a lot of friends left.

Janna turned a corner and stopped at a heavy, iron-bound, door.

"What's this door to?" Amonar asked, looking over his shoulder nervously.

"It's the armory and your crew's weapons and armor would be stored in here, if I remember correctly." Janna whispered a little tune and the door unlocked, swinging open on its hinges. "All right, almost there," Janna said as she took off once more.

Amonar followed dropping green dust as they went, leaving a trail the orcs could follow to find the way out. "This is going well," Amonar said absently. "It certainly feels weird."

Janna turned the last corner and ran right into a man, the plates of food he was carrying splattering on the ground. "Damn it to the hells, Amonar, you had to say something," Janna swore, as the man screamed.

"Stonecell Breach!" he called before her punch could silence him.

Janna knew that there was magic in place to listen for that phrase and now the elves would be alerted to their presence. Right on cue, alarms blazed down every hallway. "That's it, time for the exit door," Janna said, playing a violent tune on her harp. It was one of the most powerful spells she knew as a bard and opened a door in anything. The wall crumbled in a door-shaped pattern instantly and she stepped through, seeing an elf with his mouth hanging wide open. "You must be Seltemver," Janna said, curtsying and flashing him her best smile. *Pity they have to leave, he looks like he would be fun in the sheets,* she thought as she whispered to the ether to snap all the locks in the cell area. She was getting tired already, casting this much, but she was an Incarnation and her endurance was better than most.

Change of Plans

"Seltemver!" Amonar cried out, flying over to the elf and settling on his shoulder. "Wait, where are the elves?" the imp asked looking around. He just knew something was going to go wrong; it was like he was cursed...well more than the other two curses at least.

"They were sectioned away from us days ago," Seltemver said, looking at Janna with a raised eyebrow.

"Well, that is not good," Janna said, looking toward Amonar and shrugging her shoulders. "I guess we'll need your plan, after all, Amonar."

"Oh that can't be good," A female orc said coming out and punching her fist into her other hand.

"Janna is a friend and a powerful wizard," Amonar said, keeping her secret to himself. He had sworn in the beginning to keep what she was safe and he owed her big time. "The *Seahaven* is on the way here, just follow the green dust trail and you'll see the way out. The Armory is on the way and it's already open. Amonar loved this colored dust Janna had bought and wished he had thought to grab some to take with them.

"I'm going to get the rest of my crew," Seltemver said, then turned to Toth. "Take them and get to the ship." The big orc nodded and took off, followed by the rest of the crew. "So what's the plan?" Seltemver asked, looking at the door that the elves were going to be coming through any minute.

"You're not going to like it," Janna said coming up next to him.

"I never do," Seltemver said winking at her.

"Just follow my lead and pray," Amonar said as he dropped the bag he was holding and grabbed the dead goat inside.

Four elves, dressed in white leather strode into the room and raised their hands, but stopped when they saw the spectacle that greeted them.

"Hear me, elves!" Amonar called out in a deep voice. It wasn't his infernal tone, but it was as close as he could get without the power. He sunk his arms into the dead goat, coming up covered in blood. "I have been summoned to take your souls to the deep..." he never got to finish the massive speech as the elves fled back the way they came, all thoughts of magic forgotten. Amonar knew demons scared the wits out of people and he was counting that even wizards would blanch at the prospect of dealing with one unprepared.

"You've got to be kidding me," Janna said shaking her head. "That actually worked?"

"*That* was your plan?" Seltemver asked incredulously.

"Part of it, yeah."

"Oh wait until you hear this next part," Janna said drawing her sword and getting ready.

"Amonar..."

The imp shrugged and puffed his chest out, flapping his wings. "Come back here, elves, and face the demon that has come for you!" Amonar screamed, flying after them.

"By all the gods above us, he's chasing them," Seltemver whispered as he ran after the imp.

"Crazy, I know, but you have to admit it kind of worked," Janna said running along beside him, her brown pony tails flying out behind her.

"It hasn't worked yet…"

"I can hear both of you and you're distracting me," Amonar shispered.

They rounded a corner and the elves were banging on a door, desperate to be let out. Amonar shouted in his infernal language for effect and they all thought he was casting some sort of demonic spell. While the elves were panicking, Seltemver and Janna hit them hard from behind, taking the four out easily and gagging them just in case.

"Which way to the other cells?" Seltemver asked Janna as he took an elven sword and made a few passes with it.

"Right through that door, actually," Janna said as she stepped up and sang a little spell under her breath. The door clicked and opened slowly as did all of the cells at the same time. "Now let's hurry, those weren't the only wizards in the prison."

Time to Go

Seltemver raced down the hallways after the incredibly gorgeous woman and tried to keep his mind on the escape. It was hard while watching her run though. His elven crew had gone ahead of them with Amonar and he was taking rear guard with the beautiful woman. "You wouldn't want to escape with us, would you?" Seltemver asked as they came skidding into the incinerator room, slamming the door behind them and jamming a rock under the door to help secure it.

"It's tempting, but I've heard of your curse and I have to bow out for now," Janna said waving her arm and letting Seltemver lead the way down the tunnel.

Seltemver smiled weakly and crawled as fast as he could, praying that they had found his sword at least, if not his favorite coat. He had reached the end of the short tunnel just as the last of his elven crew had leaped soundlessly into the sea below. The elven pirate captain could see his ship racing towards them and the two other ships chasing it. "Who's at the helm?" Seltemver asked, fearing the answer.

"Crak is, he is the one that stole it out of the dock, with a little help from some magic," Janna said slyly. "He is something special you know."

"I know, but he doesn't think so," Seltemver said, as he waited for the elves to swim clear. He could see the line of orcs thrashing in the waves towards the ship and hoped Crak could maneuver around them well enough.

"Yeah, well that poor orc doesn't think so," Janna replied, a note of fondness in her voice.

"Have you seen the size of the orcs in my crew?" Seltemver asked. "He feels like he isn't good enough because his society is based on size and strength. I've been trying to change his mind, but it's hard to retrain someone's upbringing."

"Can't be too hard, you're an elf with an orc crew," Janna fired back with a friendly smile. "Now go get your ship and get out of my world, handsome."

Seltemver felt her kick and he tucked into a ball as he flew out of the tunnel, ending in a dive as he hit the surf. He swam as hard as he could, seeing that the longboat was being lowered for the fleeing orcs as well as the two rope ladders on either side of the fleeing ship. This was still going to hurt. By the time he had reached the oncoming ship, It seemed they had almost everyone on board, but the other ships were gaining on the *Seahaven* fast.

I need to find a way to slow those ships down, Seltemver thought as he reached for a ladder. He grabbed the rope as he went by and almost screamed as his shoulder pulled, but he held on. Halfway up the ladder, he saw one of the ships pulling alongside the *Seahaven*, two elves getting ready to cast. *If I kick off I might be able to land on their deck and take them by surprise,* he thought, getting ready to risk it all. He wouldn't be able to get back to the Seahaven if he did, but his crew would be safe.

Before he could a cry went up from above him and a body sailed over the edge, landing just how he wanted to and barreling into the elves. It was Bernice.

The female orc was screaming curses at the elves and humans aboard as she rushed the helm, pushing two more of the crew over the side. "For Hammond!" Bernice called out as she climbed the short stairs and punched another in the face. The enraged orc cook grabbed the helmsman and tossed him with everything she had, then spun the wheel. The ship lurched and headed for the second ship, ramming it hard and blocking their path to the *Seahaven*.

Seltemver hit the deck of his ship and spun to watch Bernice shrink as they sped away. "For Hammond!" he called back, only to see her go down with two spears in her side.

"That was one brave orc," Grunhilde said quietly as she came to make sure Seltemver was all right.

"Why did you let her do that?" Seltemver asked, knowing that no one let any of these orcs do anything. It's why they were the best crew he ever had.

"She had been lost ever since Hammond died, Seltemver. It was her way of following him." Grunhilde snapped his shoulder back into place and nodded. "If I ever want to die, you better let me."

"Not on your death, dear orc," Seltemver said with a wink. "Besides you're too ornery to die."

"He's not wrong," Toth said coming over.

"Hey, who's sailing the ship?"

"Crak is, until you relieve him that is," Toth said with a tusky grin. "Kid's doing all right too."

Seltemver was going to say something profound when the rumbles of a storm echoed in the distance. "Well, then I better hurry. Here comes our ride." He rushed to the helm, nodding to Crak and taking the wheel. He saw the small orc smile and turn to leave but grabbed his arm. "Hey, Crak. I just want to say that you did great back there. Maybe once we're out of this storm I'll let you take the wheel for a bit."

"That'd be great, Captain. Oh, and I used that move you showed me," Crak said, clearly excited.

"Well, we'll have to sit down and hear all about it once we're clear. Now go hang onto something and try not to break a leg," Seltemver chided, with a grin.

Amonar came over and settled down on Seltemver's shoulder once Crak was gone. "He did do pretty well through all that," Amonar admitted, "But I never want to do that again."

"Same here, now hold on, here comes the storm." Seltemver spun the wheel to face the oncoming clouds head-on, as he always did, and smiled at the sea spray hitting his face. It was good to be free.

Interlude: The Storyteller

Karsis sat up rigidly and let the parchment fall from his fingers, his mind racing. "Brinn, Braelyn, I'll be right back, I have to see about a problem," the bard said and got up quickly, grabbing the pages and tucking them into his longcoat.

"Can't you just use magic to fix it from here?" Brinn asked, clearly not wanting the story to end.

Karsis sighed and realized it was his own fault. He had urged Rhoe and Liss to tell the twins his secret when they were old enough—that he was actually an elven wizard in disguise—and now they knew how powerful he was. It also didn't help that, as a bard, he was drawing them into the story deeper than anyone just listening to it; to them, it felt like they were there. "Not without knowing what I'm dealing with, no."

"But you just got here?" Braelyn said, pouting and crossing her arms over her chest.

How did Gareth do this? Karsis thought as he walked to the door. *And gods above does Braelyn look just like Liss when she does that.* "I'm not leaving, just taking a walk. I'll be right back." Karsis needed some time alone with this book after what he just read and he needed it now.

"Well you better hurry, I want to know what happens," Brinn said as he kicked his sister for no good reason.

Karsis left them to squabble, fighting now with pillows and blankets as he closed the door behind him. He let out a deep sigh and tried to focus on what he just read. The story *Jail Break* wasn't ever one of his favorites when he was a young elf, but when he read Janna's name and figured out where it truly did take place, his world fell out from beneath him. He remembered the name now but never put the pieces together when he met Janna in Everknight...just eight years ago.

How is it possible that this story is about the Janna I met? Karsis thought, trying to work through the problem rationally. *Is it true then? Are these stories real?* Oh sure he had told the kids that, but it was just something a storyteller does...but this!

Karsis shook his head as he walked down the dirt road and tried to grasp what he had seen in those pages—what those stories implied. This story was written *hundreds* of years ago, yet Sirr was a real nation, formed after the Lith War and the fall of the warlords not more than forty-five years ago. Janna was the Incarnation of Beauty and Song, but she had said she had only been doing it for fifty years...

"So, the ship truly does visit other worlds and travel through time..." Karsis said aloud, talking now to himself as he circled around to the house once more, nodding to some of the townsfolk in the dwindling light. "That means that the elf, Seltemver, truly did come from Novrantir and came home without knowing it." Karsis smiled at the irony and had to know more. After all, he had read these as a young elf but some of the places and names didn't ring any bells back then. Now, hearing about the water-trapped demon, he knew that it was accurate. *And possibly why Ill'lyth stole the only remaining copy.*

Karsis stopped at the door to the house and collected his thoughts, wrapping them up around him like a cloak against the cold. "Well, time to find out how the second half of the story fits into the world I know now," Karsis said opening the door.

"He's back!" Braelyn called out, covered in small white feathers.

"I can see that, nitwit. Get back in bed," Brinn demanded, covering up with the blanket he grabbed from the floor.

"Who are you calling nitwit, Ogrann face!"

Karsis laughed, feeling a little better but still overwhelmed. "Easy, children. Settle down now and stop calling each other names Now where were we? Oh yes, the Shattered Sea."

THE SHATTERED SEA

What can I say about this one? If Ximn was the weirdest, then this one was the scariest world I've ever been to. We had just spent sixty-seven days at sea in a world with no land in sight and tensions were high. I've never been so thankful for that storm to come and whisk us away...until I saw where it had dumped us this time. We came out of the storm and slammed right into another one...just not magical like ours. This one seemed to go on forever, days at least while we were there. The world was strange and alien to us, with strange towers amid the never-ending ocean and rainstorm.

Whatever the people of this world had done, they had done it to themselves...and it was terrifying. Grab your hooded cloak and get ready to get wet on this one folks, it's a wild ride.

—Amonar

In the Dark Water

He held on to the stone chimney, struggling to keep Grunhilde's head above the ocean that was bashing them relentlessly against the roof. Another wave slammed them against the structure and he almost lost his grip, tenuous as it was. His longcoat was heavy in the water and his short white hair was in his eyes. This was not his best day.

"Just let me go, Seltemver," the female orc said, spitting the seawater out as she tried to breathe. "I know how bad this is. Save yourself." Grunhilde was a huge, grey-skinned orc with long braids who served as the healer aboard his ship, the *Seahaven*. She had a bedside manner that could level a mountain but could channel the healing power of the gods, so it evened out.

"Shut up, Grunhilde. Toth will find us," Seltemver said, closing his eyes and praying that his first mate swung the battered ship around and saw them this time. Seltemver tried futilely to get his footing on the submerged building and kicked off more of the brine-soaked shingles. He daren't shift his arm to get a better grip, lest he lose it altogether, and Grunhilde couldn't help him. She had fallen overboard and hit something in the water—which they now knew was a building—with her back, and now she couldn't feel her arms or legs.

"That orc? He couldn't find his own mouth with a spoon," Grunhilde said, laughing and choking on seawater at the same time.

"I'm not losing you."

"Seltemver…"

"I'm. Not. Losing. You."

"Fine. Drown then, you stupid elf," Grunhilde closed her eyes and tried to turn her head, yet he could still hear her sobs.

Come on Toth, we're right here, Seltemver thought to himself as he opened his eyes to scan the dark sea for any signs. It was pitch black, during a horrible storm, yet he had to have some faith. Besides, Amonar was extremely motivated to save his life; for if he died, the imp would be dragged down into the pits of the deep hells forever, burning endlessly in torment until time ended. Such was the bond that they were cursed with. Amonar was an imp he had saved from a wizard that kept him as a slave, and one of his best friends through this crazy adventure. Unfortunately, the wizard had cursed them both as he died, and now they were stuck with each other. *Times like this I wish I could call the little pest with my mind,* he thought, then laughed. *Never mind, I would hate that within a tenday.*

A tug brought Seltemver back to reality as Grunhilde was almost pulled from his grasp. "Stop trying to save me, Grunhilde, I'm not letting go," he yelled above the crashing waves.

"That wasn't me, Captain; something rammed my leg!" she screamed back, a level of panic in her voice he had never heard before.

"Seriously? Gods above, I swear this day wouldn't go well if I bribed it," he said as he tried to see what was in the water. It was no use; the dark water was impenetrable to even his elven sight. *What sea creature would hunt for food in a storm like this anyway?* Seltemver thought as he shifted his weight to try and get feeling in his shoulder once more. *The extreme weather of a storm usually sends them swimming for calmer water...or at least deeper.*

They had been hanging like this for what seemed like forever, and he knew he couldn't stay much longer. He felt another tug and decided to kick out. His foot connected with something solid, and that's when he saw a white fin break water. "Of course, it's a shark. Why wouldn't it be?" Seltemver screamed into the storm, but then he had an idea. *What's the worst that can happen if it doesn't work?* he thought as he waited for the telltale tug of the limp body in his grip. It was probably seeing if she was dead, and might only ram her another time or two before biting into her. This was his only shot before he would have to figure a way to drive it away.

"Just let him have me and be done with it...I'm broken, Captain."

"Shh. Hold still, I've got this." Seltemver waited for the telltale tug and kicked out—gently this time—and when he felt the body, he used it as a step. He propelled himself closer to the stone chimney, swinging around and straddling the slippery structure with his legs instead of his arm. With his other hand, he pulled Grunhilde with him, dragging her across the submerged roof. Now that she wasn't floating, her weight threatened to drag him down, and he screamed with an effort to bring her up. Once she was secure in one hand he drew his sword, waiting for the fin to break water again. His sword was enspelled to cut through almost anything, and when he stabbed down he scored a wicked cut into the tough hide. Seltemver was still in about three feet of water, but he saw the shadow of the beast now. Then a tentacle came roaring out of the water and tried to grab him. *What kind of world have we ended up in now?* he thought as he kept his sword up to deflect the tentacles.

"What kind of shark has those?" Grunhilde screamed, thrashing her head back and forth trying to keep her mouth out of the waves.

"Clearly one that is angry that I stabbed it."

"You're not funny."

"Yes, I am, you're just not in the position to laugh," Seltemver said, keeping his eye out for the shadow of the monstrous beast.

"No wonder you're still single."

It came at them again, swimming in the shallow water above the submerged roof and lashing out at the helpless orc with its tentacles. "I don't think so," Seltemver said, slashing the tentacle, almost severing it. His legs slipped then, almost sending him tumbling, and his grip broke on Grunhilde. "No!" he yelled as he lunged for her slowly sliding body as it sunk. He grabbed her collar and saw her eyes, eyes that were filled with something he had never seen in them before...pure fear.

"I've got you, don't worry," Seltemver said as he pulled her back towards him, his muscles burning. *Come on Toth, I'm losing here,* he thought as he looked up once more to the never-ending storm clouds that kept pelting them with rain and wind.

Searching in the Storm

Toth spun the wheel to angle the ship into the waves and frowned, his tusks protruding out past his lip. He was the first mate of the *Seahaven,* and, as such, had assumed command since his captain had leapt overboard. They had come out of the magical storm that always sent them to strange worlds, but instead of leaving the rocky seas and rain behind like they usually did, they were thrust right into another storm. This one however wasn't magical and behaved more like he was used to, so it wasn't as bad. Unfortunately, they had run aground on something and they had lost a crew member overboard, prompting his captain to leap after her. Now, both she and the captain were out in this mess. "Any sign of them!?" Toth called out over the sounds of the wind and rain howling around him. Most of the crew wouldn't have heard him, but he knew that Amonar would.

The imp looked over at him and shook his head, "Not yet, Toth, but they're alive, I know it," the imp said as he kept scanning the stormy seas.

Toth looked up at what they called the Crak's Nest—named after the small orc that used to be their lookout—and tried to shake the grief that had crawled up his chest. The small orc had died saving him, and it was taking a long time to get over. The elven woman up there now was slight, and her elven sight could see almost as far as Amonar with his demonic eyes. They had taken her aboard when they freed her from a world full of slavery, and she had taken to this life like an orc to an axe. Silence was mute, having her tongue cut out as a baby, but had her own form of elven sign that she was teaching the orcs. Toth reached over and rang a bell, designed to get her attention, and saw her look down at him.

Lights to the starboard side, she signed, moving her hand in the motions to indicate what she saw.

Toth smiled and spun the wheel once more, yelling orders to the tired orcs that kept up with the rigging and sails in this never-ending storm. "Am!" Toth called out to the imp, using his nickname for the little guy. "Come here a minute."

Amonar flew over, landing on the burly orc's massive shoulders. "What is it now Toth? Did you hit another roof?"

"You're not funny. Any ideas why this storm won't end?" They had been sailing around in it for almost a day and while they were very good at what they did, in these conditions, the ship couldn't get battered like this for eternity. Especially with the threat of buildings under them as well.

"Well, yes, but you're not going to like it."

"Just give it to me so I can make some sort of decision I will regret," Toth said, knowing that he may have to leave his captain if they couldn't find him.

"It's the moon," Amonar said with a note of awe in his voice.

Toth knew that tone and already regretted asking. "What about it?"

"Well...it's shattered."

"Say again?"

"I saw it through a break in the clouds a while back, it's in pieces..."

Toth didn't even have a snappy comeback for that. As most people who sail the sea know, the moon is part of the controlling force on the tides and waves. If it were broken—and he had absolutely no idea how that could even be possible—then that would account for the devastation they were sailing through. "Is that why all the buildings are under the ocean?"

"Probably. I've never heard, nor seen, anything like this, Toth," Amonar said as he looked up to the sky, "It's like the entire world is *broken*."

Another bell rang out across the ship and Toth looked up sharply as Silence was gesturing with her slim fingers. *There. A shark is attacking something*, she signed quickly.

Toth looked to where she was pointing and indeed saw a commotion in the storm as the ship sailed past. He had told her to report anything out of the ordinary, and that was indeed strange. Sea creatures usually didn't surface in a storm for anything; it had to be them. "How did I know Seltemver would get something to attack him way out here?"

"Cause it happens all the time?" Amonar said with a smile.

"You're not wrong," Toth said, smiling himself for the first time since they had lost Grunhilde overboard. "All hands! Trouble to port, get lines ready." He turned to Sombra who had come up from amidships, "Take the wheel, I'm going to see what this is."

"You can't go without me!" Amonar said, jumping onto Toth's shoulder.

"You're coming with, don't worry," Toth said to the little imp. "Sombra, drop anchor when you're clear of buildings, but if you guys start to get too battered pull it and swing around. Let's go, Am." Toth ran for the port side and grabbed one of the heavy ropes, slinging the coil around his chest and looking before he leapt in. With the surprise of finding buildings under the waves, he had to be careful now, especially after seeing Grunhilde hit that roof as hard as she did and scream.

Toth closed his eyes to block out the gruesome image, and when he opened them he saw a dark spot. Taking his cue, he jumped feet first and plunged deep into the swirling mass of waves towards the thrashing creature. When he came up and got his bearings, he saw Amonar land on a stone chimney and Seltemver swinging his enchanted blade against...tentacles? *Where the deep hells did we end up this time*, he thought as he swam with everything he had, holding onto the heavy rope.

To the Rescue

Amonar flew into the driving wind and rain with a fervor. He could feel Seltemver now, the curse directing him towards his friend. The imp saw them, resting on a stone structure, fending off some sort of monstrous beast. Amonar landed and grabbed hold of Seltemver's coat to steady himself as the elf lunged with his blade, slashing at the tentacle-fish-thing. The water around the beast turned dark red as its insides spilled out and the body slowly washed away in the storm. "Hey guys!" Amonar yelled, patting the elf on the back. "Good job with that...thing."

"Are we glad to see you, old friend", Seltemver said as he pulled Grunhilde out of the water and into his arms.

Amonar saw that Seltemver's legs were wrapped around the stone edifice as he pulled the orc healer up. Grunhilde wasn't moving. "Is she..."

"No, but she's hurt pretty bad. Is Toth bringing the ship around? I can't even see it in the swells and rain."

"He's right behind me. He left Sombra with the boat," Amonar said, flying over to Grunhilde and holding her head up, trying to feel useful. She was trying her best not to look petrified and failing miserably; it was killing him to see her like this. Amonar looked up as Toth came into view, fighting the waves and swimming towards them. "Toth's here, Grunhilde. We'll get you back to the *Seahaven* and everything will be all right."

"I'm scared Amonar," Grunhilde whispered so that only he could hear her.

"I know. We're here now, hold on," Amonar said trying not to tear up.

Toth came up and clasped arms with Seltemver, then they started tying the rope around the stone chimney. The burly orc turned towards Amonar and smiled that tusky grin. "Good job, Am, now go back and tell them to come and get us with the longboat."

Amonar looked from him to Grunhilde, then at Seltemver. "You sure?"

"It's fine, Amonar, we'll get her home, just go tell them to come," Seltemver said, beckoning the imp to his shoulder.

Amonar flew up and hovered, the rain pelting his red skin. "I'll get them, just don't go and get anything else angry at you until we get aboard, all right?"

"Deal."

Amonar flew off into the storm and left them, knowing that his friends were going to be safe soon.

Seltemver watched his friend fly off and breathed a sigh of relief. The crew had found them, and just in time too. He wasn't sure he could hold on any longer. "Any sign of land or somewhere to dock?" Seltemver asked his first mate as they waited.

Toth shook his head, leaning in to get a better grip on the rope as they took turns holding Grunhilde. "All we saw was more structures here and there in the water. We hit at least three of them, but they didn't give much resistance on contact; probably destroyed them when we hit, especially if they are what we think they are."

"Looks like they're buildings," Seltemver said as he tried to think of how that could be possible.

"Yeah, and Amonar thinks he knows why the storm won't stop too."

"I'm not going to like this one bit, am I?"

"Nope; still want to know?"

"Oh, why not."

"Amonar says the moon is in pieces."

"Oh, dear Syll..." Seltemver closed his eyes and tried not to panic. If this world's moon had been somehow broken, then that would also account for the buildings as well. "This world has been flooded, the oceans rose and swallowed most of everything. It makes sense now."

"Dava watch us," Grunhilde said, trying to look at them. "We have to get out of here Seltemver."

"The boat is coming, don't worry," Seltemver said, brushing her hair out of her face as the waves crashed over them endlessly. He was bruised and battered from slamming against this chimney and couldn't wait to get aboard his ship once more.

"No. I mean this whole place. I can't feel Dava anymore," Grunhilde said, a note of panic in her voice again.

"You mean the gods have gone?" Toth asked

"I won't be able to even *try* and heal unless I can feel him and hear his voice. That must be why I feel so...empty."

Seltemver looked up as he heard something on the wind and saw the longboat coming up over the waves. They were having a hard time, but the orcs were getting to them. Toth braced his feet and threw the rope with one hand while he held onto the chimney. The rope missed, but a tiny red figure flew out and grabbed it out of the water. *Good job, Amonar,* Seltemver thought as they pulled the boat towards them. In a short time, they had Grunhilde in the boat and were rowing back to the *Seahaven.* "See Grunhilde, Toth found us."

"Still can't use a spoon without missing his mouth," she replied, her body wrapped in heavy blankets.

"I heard that."

"I didn't whisper."

"Some things never change," Amonar said, curling up next to the orc healer and riding out the waves with her.

Light in the Distance

Once on board the *Seahaven,* Sombra took Grunhilde below deck as the crew worked to batten down the ship once more. They lifted anchor and set course north, hoping to break free of the submerged city beneath them. Seltemver took the wheel and looked out over his crew. They looked exhausted and worn, but at least this was something they knew; It was familiar. The *Seahaven* could weather any natural storm with these orcs guiding her, it was the cursed storm that usually did them in.

It was part of the curse that the old witch had thrown at them; doomed to sail distant waters until they found a home. So now, every time they left a port of call and sailed out into the sea, a storm would hit them, sucking them out of the world they were in and throwing them somewhere else...or even somewhen else on occasion if Amonar was to be believed. They had never found anyone who knew anything about the curse in any of the worlds they went to, nor visited the same world twice—that they knew of at least—and now it seems they had found a completely broken world, void of gods and men. A sharp ring of a bell drew Seltemver's stoic gaze to the Crak's nest where the elf, Silence waved her fingers in warning.

Light in the distance, port side, Silence gestured, moving her hands in her silent language.

Seltemver looked and saw something faint, but couldn't tell. His elven sight was good, but the storm was obscuring everything down here at sea level. Thank god it was still daytime, or at least he thought it was since they could still see somewhat in the ongoing storm. "Amonar, can you see any kind of light to port with that demonic sight of yours?" Seltemver asked.

Amonar looked the wrong way and squinted into the driving rain and wind. "Nothing, Seltemver."

"Other way, Amonar."

"I knew that." The imp turned and looked again, then drew back and whooped loudly. "Lights!"

"All right, all hands, let's get ready for contact," Seltemver called, spinning the wheel into the waves and trying to gauge the best way there in this chaotic seascape. Soon they had a visual they could all witness without elven or demonic sight. It was a large structure, mostly submerged but sticking out of the ocean like a beacon. It reached up towards the sky like a plea to the gods, full of glass windows with bright lights shining out of at least ten of them towards the top. It was almost perfectly square and showed no sign of how far down it went. How the building stood without a stone framework was anyone's guess.

"I've never seen anything like that," Toth said coming up to Seltemver as they pulled alongside at a safe distance. The gruff orc's voice was laced with awe and wonder; definitely out of place for Toth.

"Nor have I," Seltemver admitted as he gave the silent signal to drop anchor. "Go get Morn, maybe the dwarf has seen something like this from his world," the elf said as he watched his crew tighten lines and bring down the sails in the downpour that just wouldn't let up. Toth went down to get the dwarf and Seltemver called over Sombra. The orc was fast proving himself to be a capable helmsman and more importantly, had made peace with the hellish imp on board. "Sombra, I'm taking Toth, Morn, and Amonar, with me to that building, you watch the ship and if she starts taking a beating…"

"Pull anchor and sail away without you?"

"Gods above no. Pull anchor and come get us," Seltemver said with a laugh.

"Aye aye, Captain," the orc said, adjusting his scabbard and taking the wheel.

"How is Grunhilde?" Seltemver asked before the orc could leave. He hadn't been able to get away from the helm to check on her yet.

"She's keeping quiet and berating anyone that comes within ten feet of her."

"Well, that sounds promising at least," Seltemver said as Sombra turned with a smile. Seltemver walked away, the wind whipping his longcoat around despite being soaking wet. There was no time to rest or dry off below, they needed to find someone who could heal Grunhilde.

Amonar landed on his shoulder and coiled his tail around the elf's neck lightly to hold on. "Think there will be some sort of healer in that tower?" the imp asked as they walked towards the bow of the ship. Morn was waiting with Toth near the boat and looked like a drowned rat.

"Well it's high enough that it's out of the sea, and there are lights, so I'm hoping they have a wizard or something that could help us."

"You don't play well with wizards, though," Amonar said mischievously.

"I do when they aren't trying to kill me."

"Someone is always trying to kill you."

"You always say that."

"It's always happening!"

"Guys!" Toth yelled, breaking them up and handing Seltemver a small pack. "We're ready when you are, Capt'n. Longboat is in the water."

Amonar smiled and winked at Toth. "Why are we bringing this guy? Do we want to scare the people?"

"Do you want to row the boat?" Seltemver asked, knowing the answer.

"You always have a snide remark, don't you?" Amonar asked.

"I get it from watching you."

"I'm traveling with a couple of children," Toth said, chuckling to himself as they lowered down into the longboat.

"And you love it," Seltemver said as they rowed away from the *Seahaven* and towards the mysterious tower.

The dwarf settled into a seat, looking severely displeased at how wet he was. "Anyone else tired o' this rain?" Morn asked, wringing his beard out as the wind whipped his red hair around. "I'm fer turnin this tub around and headin out o' this storm."

"Well for one. No. Two, that won't work as we have no idea how far this storm reaches. Amonar says the moon is broken so..."

"Great Dava's beard!"

"Well that's one way to put it," Toth said, clapping the dwarf on the shoulder.

"Just settle down. Morn have you ever seen a tower like that?" Seltemver asked, anxious to get over there.

"Not one like tha'," the dwarf said, staring at the tower with eyes wide. "How that hasn't fallen down is anyone's guess."

"Well as long as it doesn't collapse with us inside, I don't care how it stays up," Amonar said with a huff.

Seltemver sighed. "Let's just hope that the people inside are friendly..."

Ell8 Far Tower

Seltemver watched the tower get closer and closer as Toth struggled with the longboat in the storm. Both he and Morn had tried to help with the rowing, but they couldn't maintain the right timing. Toth, in his frustration, pushed them aside and just did it himself. As the glass tower came into view, Seltemver could see that some of the windows near the water weren't just glass. Some of them seemed made of a weird type of wood, but no wood he had ever seen. It was a very light color and seemed cut very thin; possibly with magic. Near the middle of these wooden pieces was a large green sign with a small blue shield at the top with the number 15 in white. The green sign had "Alt Lak" written on it, and he could only assume that was the name of the strange tower they had found. Under the sign was what could be taken for some sort of dock, more like a ramp, though it would be hard to bring the boat up in these waves. Before he could relay this information to his first mate, Amonar shouted over the din of rain and wind.

"Look. People!"

Seltemver saw two figures dressed in ragged clothes opening double doors near the water's edge. They looked like they were attempting to throw some sort of rope to them, yet it was like no rope he had ever seen. They whipped it at the longboat and Amonar caught it, handing it to Seltemver. He took it and tied it to the front mooring pin, astonished at the smooth feel of the rope. It was deceptively strong, almost like pliable steel. *Well, this place just keeps getting stranger by the moment,* Seltemver thought as they pulled the longboat up the ramp. Amazingly, they kept pulling right through the opening and all the way into the tower.

Toth stood when they were in and put out his hand, "Thank you for the...." his words died on his tusks as they backed up in alarm, clearly frightened of the burly orc.

"What in the name of Salt is that?" one of them asked, pulling out a crude, thin, metal club. It was bent near the top with a tiny flare at the end.

Seltemver slowly drew his sword, but kept it pointed at the ground as he climbed out of the longboat. "He is an orc. We mean no harm, just looking for information and a healer," he said carefully. This was why they usually left Toth aboard the ship, just in case.

"An orc? Like in the books?" the other asked, a flash of wonder crossing his visage. He tugged on the weird robes of the other and almost giggled. "Like the books, man! Look!"

"I can see, but those are just stories the Librar tells us. They cannot be real."

"Well I, for one, am feeling very real," Amonar said, flying up out of the boat and landing on Seltemver's shoulder.

"Demon!" the strange men shouted as one and turned, fleeing down an odd hallway.

"Look on the bright side, Amonar," Seltemver said, patting his friend on the head, "At least they didn't call you a thing."

"Well, we best git ready for a fight," Morn said, getting out of the boat as well and standing next to them. He pulled an axe and smiled, his hair and beard matted with seawater.

"This isn't going to go well is it, Capt'n?" Toth asked, pulling his axe out and taking up a stance as the sound of running feet approached rapidly.

"Does it ever?" Seltemver answered as five men with blue shield badges came into the room brandishing crude swords and clubs of metal. All of the badges had the same number on them, 15, and they didn't look at all frightened, though their clothes looked ragged as well. "Listen, I think there has been some confusion here. Is there a leader or high elder we could speak to?" Seltemver asked in his most calming voice.

"The Librar?"

"Sure, him."

"The demon and dwarf stay here though, as well as the…"

"Orc," Toth said spitting on the floor as he said it.

"Orc."

"Fine, lead the way," Seltemver agreed, knowing that Toth would be seething that he was going alone. He wasn't worried though, the way these men stood showed that they weren't nearly as trained as he was, and with his enchanted sword, he had the upper hand in any close-quarters fight. "Amonar, Morn, stay here and guard the boat. Toth, try to keep out of trouble huh?"

"Shouldn't we be telling him that?" Amonar asked Toth as he landed on the orc's shoulder while looking at the men.

"Would he listen?" Toth asked with a wry smile

"You're right."

"You two are just as bad as he is," Morn said with a hearty laugh.

Seltemver shook his head and followed the men, all of whom seemed nervous in his company. *Stories? Books? Could they truly not know what an elf, dwarf, or orc was?* he thought as he walked the cramped hallways. They came to a flight of stairs made of a strange stone—with metal rails—and walked upwards for what seemed like forever. The odd stone had deep red water stains all over the place, like something was bleeding through, and the stone itself looked ravaged by time. Every time they reached a sort of landing, a number was written on the metal doors, like they had to keep track of where they were. Finally, they came to a door marked 25 and went through and into a torch-lit area. The room was surrounded with shelves—all lined with books— and the massive windows in the back showed the ravaging storm. Sitting in the center of the room was what could only be their leader.

The Librar

Seltemver looked at the man and almost laughed. He was an old man, dressed like some sort of scholar and surrounded by books—stacks of them— and other scroll-like bundles. The man wore spectacles that hung on his long nose and his messy grey hair hung down to his shoulders. The man sat cross-legged while reading some sort of flat scroll and a small sign on his robe-like clothing had the faded words Librar on it, but looked ripped at one end, like it might have had more letters.

"This is the stranger from the stories, Librar," the head guard said, bowing reverently.

"Oh, most holy Librar," Seltemver began, bowing at the waist and coming up, keeping eye contact the entire time. "I am Seltemver, and I come seeking knowledge of healing."

The old man stood in a flurry of books and flying pages, noticing the elf for the first time it seemed. "Holy Salt! You're an elf!"

"Yes, most holy Librar, that I am."

"Where did you come from? There is nothing out there but the mountain cities and the raiders," the old man asked, stomping over and looking at Seltemver with curiosity; poking and prodding various parts of the elf's anatomy.

"My ship, the *Seahaven*, came to this world through a magical storm..."

"You came from another world?" The Librar interrupted, his eyes wide with astonishment.

"Yes. Does that not happen in this world?"

"Hasn't ever happened here in Alt Lak that I know of."

"Is that the name of this grand tower?" Seltemver asked, trying to keep the conversation going while he studied the man.

"Oh no, the tower is called Ells Far, the land surrounding it is Alt Lak, though we have all but stripped the underwaves of anything valuable. You said you had injured?"

"Yes. Our healer, Grunhilde, fell overboard and hurt her back; now she can't move her arms or legs."

"Oh, that is most inconvenient.

"Quite. Do you have a priest or healer in Ells Far?"

"We have a doctor, though it's usually for the little things, not paralysis."

"Doctor? Parali-what?" Seltemver was lost to some of the words, but the concern on the man's face was plain to read.

"Never mind. I'll send word to Doctor Hendricks and tell her she may have a patient. Though you probably don't have the type of payment we would be looking for," the Librar said, looking down his nose through his spectacles.

Seltemver winced inwardly but looked around, getting an idea. "Well, I can see that you like knowledge, and we have traveled many worlds..."

"That you have. Would you be willing to trade that knowledge for treatment?" the old man asked, a greedy look in his eye.

Seltemver knew he had him hooked. "Why I *do* think I could do that. We even have a talkative imp that could tell you some tales."

"Truly? Oh, that must be what the guards thought was a demon."

Seltemver laughed and nodded. "I'll head back down and tell Toth and Morn to bring Grunhilde over and let Amonar know you would like to talk with him."

"Is he able to be separated from you? You would allow him to be apart from you?" the old man asked, curiosity etched across his face.

"Amonar is my friend, not a slave. And yes, he can stay with you for a bit. We are bonded, like a curse if you will, but distance does not hurt that."

"Very well, I look forward to hearing about these stories," the Librar said, smiling like he was making out in this bargain.

"Done." Seltemver went back down the stairs, accompanied by only two of the men now. After two flights he grew curious about the world he had found himself in. "So, what happened to flood the buildings with sea water?" he asked.

"As far as the Librar can find in the books, the moon was broken during some sort of mining catastrophe," one of the men said.

"Yeah, then the tides and everything went nuts, melting the ice caps and making the oceans rise. The books say we used to be in the middle of a great dry land," his companion added.

"So, *all* of this used to be land?" Seltemver asked, horror creeping into his spine. He knew it had to be flooded, but for all of this to be land was unthinkable. To have the seas rise that much must've been catastrophic to every living thing.

"From the old maps we've scavenged, it seems so. We've been living this way for over two hundred years, so none of us remember that time."

"What do you do for food? Most of the sea life must be driven down deep with the storms." Seltemver asked, getting a bad feeling all of a sudden. Maybe he had misjudged these people. Just because they weren't warlike didn't mean they weren't bad.

"Oh, the rains only last for about two months, then move on. Once they do, the fish almost jump into our nets. We've modified the bottom of the tower into a kind of trap for sea creatures."

"Yeah, we go down in suits to trap the smaller fish, and occasionally nab a shark when we can," the other guard said.

"You trap that tentacled thing? You are braver than I gave you credit for," Seltemver said, impressed at their bravery.

The first guard laughed. "Not all of them have grown tentacles, just those that lived near Blue Cas in the Southeast," the man said as they neared the bottom of the tower. "They migrate north from time to time, as the storms don't hinder them at all"

"What's Blue Cas?" Seltemver asked, not knowing if he wanted to know.

"Some sort of site where the old world got most of its power from; at least as far as the Librar can tell.

Seltemver was going to ask more, but the door with the number 10 came into view and the rest of the stairs seemed underwater.

THE GOOD DOCTOR

Getting Grunhilde back to Ells Far tower took a while, but Seltemver kept himself busy with more questions about this strange land. It seemed that they had only one god, a being that had no name and only went by the title of God. This powerful being ignored the people most of the time, yet was credited with adding salt to the water all around them. This was a blessing because they could distill the salt and use it to trade with the other colonies that weren't submerged as a type of spice in exchange for vegetables and other foods they couldn't normally grow in the tower. Raiders were always a problem, as most of the people were scavengers in this devastated world, but with the pockets of people banding together, they fended them off the best they could. The good news was that they rarely went out during the rains.

Water was another question that Seltemver was curious about. It seems the abundance of rain, filtered through the flat roof, kept them going for all these years and also kept them clean as they could bathe with it as well. Huge, square collection vats were stationed near the top floor under small holes and strange tubes led to the lower floors, funneling the water down with levers to shut certain ones off and on. It reminded him of that gear city they had visited many trips back when their ship had to be repaired. Strange contraptions that seemed like magic until you understood the way they worked.

The tower had a ship, a trading vessel, but they usually went out during the rains as the raiders were scarce. It wouldn't be back for at least another week, and by the description they gave, Seltemver wasn't sure he wanted to see this metal nightmare. By the time Toth and Grunhilde came back to Ells Far, he was more than ready to get this over with and take his chances with the storms once more; magical or not.

"Glad you made it back safely," Seltemver said as they were pulled into the building.

"Aye, though I wouldn't call it a safe trip," Morn said, his accent echoing in the closed space. The two guards that hadn't seen the newcomers yet stood with mouths agape at the dwarf and after a couple of seconds, ran over to touch his hair and beard.

"Get off a me!" Morn yelled, backing up and fighting them off, "I'm not a playthin, you pair of dobs!"

"It's all right Morn, they've never seen one of your kind that's all," Seltemver said, trying not to laugh and failing miserably.

"Except in the stories that is," one of the men said.

"Yeah that one long story with all of those dwarves and that little guy, that went on the adventure," the other said. They both eased off and helped carry Grunhilde up the stairs, grunting with the effort.

"How are you doing Grunhilde?" Seltemver asked as they went up and up, around and around.

"Oh, I'm doing just peachy, Captain," Grunhilde replied, heavy sarcasm dripping from her voice. "This doctor, whatever that is, better know how to channel the gods or I'm doomed."

"Oh, she doesn't channel anything, she usually cuts into us and sews things up," one of the guards said in passing.

"That's it, take me back to the ship."

"Now, Grunhilde, I won't let anything happen…"

"You're right because I'm going back to the ship!" She threw her head back and forth, but that was all she could do. That and curse up a storm.

They reached the door that said 20 soon after and went through to a white hallway. This was the cleanest place in the entire tower so far and even had a pleasant smell. A woman wearing a white, thin, longcoat approached them quickly, her long blond hair cascading over her shoulders.

"Hello, I'm Doctor Hendricks, but you can call me Sam," the woman said, offering her hand to Seltemver.

He shook it hesitantly and looked at her coat with curiosity. It wasn't meant for weather or even combat. It was too thin and had a tiny pocket on the outside breast. She had a strange rope around her neck that ended in a metal clasp that seemed to intertwine. "Hello, Sam, this is Grunhilde, my healer, and she fell overboard and hit something in the water."

Ignoring the obvious difference in race, the woman directed them back towards more doors. "Bring her in here and let's take a look," Sam said, walking back the way she came and pushing through the twin doors that swung each way.

Seltemver and Toth carried Grunhilde in, being careful not to overly move her more than they had to. Any excess damage was already done being battered in the sea while they clung for their lives, so

Seltemver wasn't too worried that they would hurt her more than she was already, but you never knew. They laid her on a weird bed, supported by metal and with tiny black wheels. "What is that thing?" Seltemver asked, looking at the bottom of the bed again.

"Sam looked up and smiled, understanding blossoming on her face. "You're truly not of this world," she said, almost to herself. She pulled a small dart out of a drawer and flicked it with her finger as it spurted some sort of liquid.

"And that?" Toth asked as the woman walked towards Grunhilde with it.

"It's only something to ease her pain, I promise," the woman said as she jabbed Grunhilde in her arm with the dart. "Supplies like this are in abundance ever since we found the sunken building with the red cross on it."

"It's all right, Capt'n, not like I can feel it," Grunhilde said.

Sam looked up as she finished probing the orc's back, her face a mask of concern. "This bump here feels like a slipped disc. No, don't ask, it would take too long to explain," Sam said, holding up her hand to forestall their questions. "I will have to open her up and see if I can remove part of the disc that is causing the pressure, making it so she can't move. It is a lengthy procedure, but I'll try my best." She walked over and laid her hand on Toth's shoulder like she knew he would be argumentative to her next words. "That being said, I'll have to have you two wait upstairs until someone comes and gets you."

"We understand, Doctor, just come and get us," Seltemver said, pulling Toth out with him. The big orc wasn't saying anything, but his eyes were glued to Grunhilde. "She's in good hands Toth, let's go see what trouble Amonar got himself into."

A Deal's a Deal

Seltemver and Toth went upstairs, walking into a very deep conversation that they had never been privy to. Hearing Amonar speak on his life in the hells was rare, so both Seltemver and Toth stopped just inside the door, fearing to interrupt their friend before they, too, learned something.

"No, Librar. Demons are tricky, and not at all like the stories make them out to be. You probably think demons are horned creatures with tails and wings—like me—summoned with magic into chalk outlines. Rubbish, all of it. Demons are beings of immense power that dwell in between the worlds and can only reach out through magic conduits, like certain rituals. They come in varied shapes and sizes, and they only want one thing. Souls. Once they get inside your mind, they attack your soul and devour it, then leave you an empty husk, fleeing back to the space between worlds." Amonar hovered in mid-air as he talked.

"But if they are in-between worlds, who dwells in the hells then?" the Librar asked.

"Well, they used to. See, at one time they ran the place, torturing souls and such, but then they grew overconfident and decided to rise up and overpower Krist, the God of Death. He broke their forms and threw them back into the hells, this time as occupants instead of rulers. The God appointed us, the imps, to watch over them and keep them shackled, but they eventually escaped—through no fault of our own, mind you—and now they live in the spaces between places, hiding from the dark one and waiting for hapless mortals to be, well, stupid." Amonar finished, puffing out his chest.

"That...that's horrifying," the Librar said, fear evident on his face. "Now you imps torture souls that go there?"

"Well...yes, though I don't *like* doing it," Amonar said in a quiet voice. "Imps used to be carefree tricksters that were malevolent at times, but only if you deserved it. Now...now we hurt people and it sickens me."

"It does?" the Librar asked, his voice softening at the regret in the imp's voice.

"Yeah, but that's all behind me now. I've got a great new family, and they don't ask me to do things like that."

Seltemver couldn't keep quiet any longer. "Well, that's not exactly true, old friend; and for that, I am truly sorry." He had heard some of that story awhile back when the ship needed repairs in that gear city, but not all of it.

"Seltemver, you're back!" Amonar flew over and punched him in the arm. "And don't worry about it, those things you asked, well, you asked them because you had to. Down there I had to do it for no other reason than to hurt people for things that they felt guilty for."

"Amonar has been a font of knowledge, especially on your adventures across the many worlds you have seen," the Librar said, standing up amid his stacks of books. "He has even named our world for your records. The Shattered Sea, he calls it."

"Well that's certainly an apt name for it," Toth said, sitting down next to a couple of guards and smiling, showing them his tusks just to put them off. If I may though, how are you taking what he says so easily? Toth asked, genuinely curious by his expression. "How can you believe him?"

"Hey!"

"Easy, Am, I'm just wondering is all," Toth reassured the imp, turning back to the Librar.

"I have always been a good judge of character and when someone is lying or not. Your friend here is quite an open book, speaking with his heart more than his mind," the Librar said with a nod to the burly orc.

"I'm glad he was helpful, Holy Librar. I assume it was payment enough?" Seltemver asked, while he sat and took off his longcoat so it could dry in the warm room.

"More than enough," the Librar said, "But please call me Erik."

"Erik it is, then."

They spent the next hour or so talking about things like challenges they've faced, things they've overcome, and of course people they've lost. Toth got up and walked over to one of the huge glass windows, staring out over the stormy sea when they mentioned Crak; something he still working through. Soon after a guard came to get them; Grunhilde was out of surgery. They all went up the stairs this time, but Amonar landed on Seltemver's shoulder and whispered to him as they climbed.

"He asked a lot of questions about the ship Seltemver. Questions that made me get that bad feeling," Amonar said, a tone of warning in his voice.

"You think they want the ship?" Seltemver asked in a hushed tone.

"I just get the feeling that we won't be able to just leave when we want...I hope I'm wrong."

"I won't ask you to hurt them."

"I know, but I may have to anyway, and that makes me feel even worse."

"Well let's not worry about the water until we sink," Seltemver said using an old proverb he learned when he first started sailing the seas.

They came to the floor and walked in, the imp flying off and ahead of them. Amonar was the first one through the double doors, his wings flapping wildly as he searched for Grunhilde. Sam was there, her weariness plain for all to see. Her arms were covered in blood, but she looked happy. "Don't worry, everything went well. Grunhilde can feel her legs and arms again, and even move them a little. In time she will recover fully but until then she has to rest."

"Can she make it back to the ship?" Seltemver asked, leading them into the question to see if Amonar was on to something.

"I think if we move her in one of *our* boats, she could be transferred there, yes," the doctor said, nodding to one of the guards. "Barry will go see if he can call one back from salvage so that we can get here there a bit easier. I can't imagine that what you came in has cushions?"

"What is a cushy on?" Toth asked, walking over to hold Grunhilde's hand and ignoring the doctor's order to let the orc healer rest.

Seltemver saw the big orc's concern on his rugged face and knew that Toth had lost one person he cared about recently and that this probably opened up old wounds; opened and poured salt in them. "Whatever it is, I think you would know best, Sam. You're the healer here after all."

Trouble in the Boats

As they walked out and back upstairs to say their goodbyes, Amonar tugged on one of the guards' sleeves and pointed to the weird club most of them carried. "So, what is that thing called?" the imp asked, his curiosity piqued ever since the exchange of stories upstairs.

"This? It's called a crowbar. It used to be a tool of some kind, but when everything flooded, there were a lot of them lying around so we just kind of use them to defend ourselves."

"It's used to hit crows?"

"No, nothing to do with birds. Wait; you have crows on other worlds?" the man stopped intrigued.

"Oh yeah! They're like thirty feet tall with flaming eyes," Amonar said kiddingly.

"They are?"

"No! Of course not. Do you not have sarcasm in this world?"

Seltemver laughed the rest of the way upstairs, trying to tell himself that they were just curious, but the imp's words caught in his cynical mind and wouldn't let go. *Maybe this world isn't so different than ours, after all*, he thought.

The next day they were on a boat made of steel and soft seats, cutting through the waves like it was nothing, towing their own longboat with Morn and Toth behind them. The four men that rowed seemed like experts and they got back to the *Seahaven* in record time. The men were in awe of the ship, having never seen anything like it except in books.

"So, I thought your ship was out for at least a week?" Seltemver asked, noticing that their ship had mooring like their own. It was meant to be kept on a larger vessel, not indoors, and he had seen that it was wet when they pulled it out of storage.

"It is, we keep this just in case of raiders," one man said as he tied his ship to the *Seahaven.*

"I thought raiders didn't go out in the rains?" Seltemver asked, using the sign language that Silence had taught him to signal Toth that something was up.

"Oh yeah, we will have a good couple of weeks left to get ready for their attacks," another man said as he untied the longboat with Toth in it, pulling the dwarf and orc around closer.

Seltemver inched closer to Grunhilde, who was still stiff and trying not to move. "Why don't two of you go up and then you can haul Grunhilde up while we keep her steady," he said, luring them into his own trap.

To his surprise, they agreed, but sent three up and left one man down to watch both boats. The minute the three climbed over, the fourth kicked the longboat away, sending Toth and Morn back out into the storm. "All right, elf, keep your hands away from that sword unless you want my men to kill the rest of your crew."

"You're kidding, right?" Amonar asked with a laugh.

"What?"

"Your men are going to get trounced, you know that?" Seltemver asked, already hearing the sounds of battle up above.

Amonar laughed, landing on the seat next to Seltemver. "Oh, I forgot to tell you Seltemver. I told them the crew we left behind didn't know how to fight."

"Wait..." the man started, finally realizing the rouse.

Seltemver laughed as three bodies came crashing down into the roiling waves, their passage marked by dark blood that washed away as the waves rolled over them. He grabbed the line up and saw that Toth was rowing back steadily. "All right, what is going on?" Seltemver asked the last remaining man.

"We need your ship. The tower is eroding and won't last another two years; if we're lucky," he said.

"Then why heal Grunhilde?"

"If we didn't at least try, it would look suspicious. The doctor knew that if we helped you, then it might go easier."

"Well, that didn't work, now did it?" Seltemver said dryly.

"Ahh, didn't work," Amonar echoed like a parrot, landing again on Seltemver's shoulder and smiling at the man.

"If I were you, I would jump," Seltemver said as he looked over the man's shoulder to see Toth coming in fast. The man did just that. Seltemver didn't even look to see if the man made it, instead, he worked getting Grunhilde up into the *Seahaven*. It didn't take long after that to get the orc healer into her cabin, then they were on their way.

"They were the raiders, weren't they?" Toth asked coming over to the wheelhouse after they had set sail.

"More than likely," Seltemver said, gauging the winds. "There was no way that tower could have repulsed a group of raiders. They had no defenses." Seltemver spun the wheel as Toth went to make sure everyone was ready. He was looking for the telltale storm clouds, knowing that the ones he needed would be a bit more violent than the ones they had been sailing in for their stay here. Grunhilde was below decks, resting and Silence had climbed down from the Crak's nest. Then he saw it. The black clouds rolled in and seemed to almost shove the normal clouds out of the way, hungry for his ship and crew. Seltemver grinned like a man seeing an old enemy, turning the wheel to meet it face to face like an old-fashioned duel; drawing swords at thirty paces if you will.

The *Seahaven* hit the storm head-on at speed, knowing there was no way to traverse this cursed weather safely. After a solid two minutes of battering wind and waves taller than the ship itself, a familiar voice carried out over the tumult.

"Now, Seltemver, please tell this storm to take us to a pleasant world for once?" Grunhilde shouted, seeming like her old self once more. The crew could be heard, barely, whooping and hollering at her as she passed them.

"I thought you needed rest?" Seltemver called out, seeing the rest of the crew racing to their positions as the storm gathered its animosity to batter them.

"I felt Dava the minute we entered the storm and healed myself," the orc healer said, grabbing the rail of the deck as a wave cascaded over them.

"Good. Now please try and stay *on* the ship this time, would you?"

"Aye aye, Captain!" Whatever else she was going to say was lost as Toth hit her from behind in a hug that stole the wind out of her.

It's going to be all right, Seltemver thought as he spun the wheel in response to another wave rising on the horizon, *as long I can keep bringing them out of the storm.*

THE WIZARD'S TOWER

This one is truly the very start of it all. I know I've said that before, but I mean between Seltemver and I. You see, a wizard—archmage—had summoned me decades ago and made me do some pretty awful things. I served him for years carrying out his wishes and it made me sick to do so after a while. That's when Seltemver happened upon the island and turned both of our lives upside-down.

Need to stretch your legs before getting into these stories? Grab another pint? Maybe hit the privy real quick? Go on, I can wait...you won't want to miss this one.

—Amonar

THE HIDDEN COVE

The *Ravencrest* sailed quietly into the dark cove, dropping anchor a ways out and waiting for any sign of welcome; or more precisely, a welcoming party. It was a sleek ship, with two masts sporting three sails each and a thin bow running into a figurehead of a female with a spear held in two hands. Elves ran across the deck as they tied off lines and tightened heavy ropes, with one particular elf at the helm.

He had brought his ship to this place for one reason only, as it was not high on the list of vacation spots, but this hidden cove *was* on the list of places with lots of treasure. A powerful rogue wizard—archmage—was known to live here, his tower filled with gold, and treasure he had taken when he fled the land of Xesh almost a century ago. A well-paid informant had told the captain that the archmage was going to be in Tanaril for the next tenday; He couldn't pass this one up.

The *Ravencrest* was an elven pirate ship—one of the fastest ships to sail away from the secret isle of Novrantir—and its captain was both known for the trouble he would get in and his expert swordsmanship in getting out of said trouble. Seltemver Ashblade blew the short white hair out of his eyes and motioned for his first mate, Branil, to come up to the wheelhouse.

"Yes Seltemver?" Branil asked, forgetting to use the title that was afforded to the man. He had never called him captain and wasn't going to start any day soon. The elf was a rather short man with a long scar down his cheek and his long white hair tied back with black silk. It didn't help that Seltemver had given him that scar in the first place.

"Branil, do you sense any magic nearby?" Seltemver asked, hoping that the answer was a simple one. Knowing this elf, it wouldn't be.

The first mate closed his eyes and whispered to the ether, asking the element to show him trails of magic. "Nothing close, Seltemver, but that doesn't mean that creatures summoned by magic won't be on guard or even that..."

"I got it, Branil. Thank you," Seltemver said as he looked to his crew. He nodded and they lowered the first boat, getting the scout crew in first. The scout group would secure the landing, then Seltemver would go over and lead the expedition. The cove was also rumored to have the archmage's pets living around it, waiting for trespassers to wander into the dense woods. "Maybe we will have some good luck this time, Branil," Seltemver said, his hopes dashed when the elven wizard started laughing at him.

"With your luck?" Branil asked, still chortling. "You'll be lucky to make it to the tower without bloodshed. This is an archmage, Seltemver."

Seltemver closed his eyes and counted to five; he hated magic. To be fair, he only hated it because he couldn't cast it. All elves had the innate ability to ask the elements to do the things they wanted. From causing fire to moving the ground itself, the elements encompassed everything around them. It was all for the asking; except for Seltemver. He tried when he was young, going through the schools and classes like every other elf, but the elements just didn't—or wouldn't—hear him. Branded an abomination in society's eyes, he took to the blade with enthusiasm and learned from the best, striking off on his own and leaving his family behind. He stole the *Ravencrest* and fled with a small crew to the southern lands and became a pirate; he never looked back. "All right, let's get going and hope that we can get into the tower without too many surprises.

"That will be a first." Branil stomped off towards the second boat, his robes swirling in the ocean breeze coming into the cove. He stepped off the edge and floated down into the boat as it was being lowered, just to show off.

Surprise Guests

"Gri, Amonar," the archmage ordered, using the word for *bring* and pointing at the shelf lined with black jars. He hated using this infernal language, but to his knowledge, the creature understood nothing else. *Next time I'm summoning a faerie, they're less trouble,* he thought as he tied his long white hair back with a small leather strap. *Or even a purple squirrel.* Nor'alrin Aeslyn was an elven archmage, and the current master of this troublesome imp called Amonar and gods above did he regret it.

He had been branded a rogue by the council of Xesh over his studies into demons and to a lesser extent, imps. They could never appreciate his vision.

The imp flew over, grabbed one of the black jars, and then brought it to the desk. The two-foot-tall creature placed it carefully with his clawed hands. "Ut meh zar," Amonar said as he flew back to his pedestal. Amonar was only three feet tall with deep red skin and bat-like wings. The small infernal creature had a tail that stretched out another two feet in length and he had tiny horns on the top of his head that stuck up about three inches high.

"Thank you Amonar," the archmage said, sliding the ink towards him. When he didn't hear anything he sighed and turned in his chair, eyeing the little creature. "Gorn Wok," Nor'alrin said carefully, trying to remember the words for good work. He had been studying this language of the infernal races for the last two years and wasn't any closer to speaking it consistently without looking at his notes. Elven and Infernal were so close that he had a hard time memorizing the different meanings of the same word, even though he was one of the smartest wizards in all of the southern lands. It should've been easy, but the words were so far from each other in definition, that it wasn't easy. His notes were extensive, but now he was trying to do it without looking. *It's like I'm back in mage school,* he thought, turning back to his work with an audible sigh.

A loud screeching noise permeated the entire tower—all three floors—forcing the archmage to scratch his scrollwork as he jumped in alarm. The hours-long work translating this scroll was gone as the entire thing was ruined. Throwing the ruined parchment aside, Nor'alrin turned and whispered to the ether, stopping the magic alarm that he had set up decades ago when he came here from the southern lands. Someone had opened his front door, even though it was magically locked. Nor'alrin strode off, waving for Amonar to follow, which the sad little creature did obediently, but not happily.

Seltemver looked at the four bodies of his men on the ground, burned despite their magical wards, and thought twice about going through that doorway. The seven of them had made it through the forest relatively easily, only encountering three trolls which the elves dealt with well enough. Trolls had tough skin but magic took them out nicely; especially fire.

"I thought you said you got rid of the magic?" Seltemver asked Branil, who was staring at the door in horror. Seltemver walked to the side of the doorway and peered in, not wanting to be in front of this death trap.

"I did...It shouldn't have done that Seltemver." Branil whispered once more and cast a spell at the doorway, flinching despite his skill; nothing happened this time. "Now it doesn't register magic at all, it..." Then his head shot up, his eyes going wide with barely contained fear. "Oh gods above,

Seltemver...he's home!" Branil turned and started running, barely getting three feet before a bolt of white-hot lightning slammed into him from behind. Branil was dead before he hit the tree in front of him, shattering what was left of his face.

Seltemver backed up even more into the shadows and held his breath as Haerlin, the only other elf still up, hissed words of magic at the doorway as fast as he could.

"Ash'anti fir, yanel dost halven ent wal," Haerlin said, trying to increase the heat around the frame into a wall of fire; It worked, building slowly into a sheet of pure flame.

"Not sure how long that will hold against an archmage," Haerlin said, drawing his slim blade and looking for cover. Suddenly the flames snapped off immediately as an elf came striding through them unscathed. Haerlin backed up but heard the elf casting already so he lunged with his sword, hoping to catch the elf off guard and wound him enough to disrupt his spell. His sword bounced off an invisible shield and was torn from his hand by an unseen force.

The Imp

Seltemver watched the elf stride through the wall of fire and frowned at the sheer power this archmage was displaying. Branil was one of the most powerful wizards he had found and Haerlin wasn't that far behind him. Seltemver knew that they were all in trouble. He saw Haerlin's lunge and subsequent failure but noticed a key mistake that the archmage had, The shield flared when it was struck, showing it for a second to the naked eye; there was no such shield in the back of the elf.

"Ash'anti fra, tur dosit ston haryen!" the archmage yelled as he cleared the fire and smiled. The wind around them tuned into a funnel, picking up small rocks on the ground and flaying Haerlin to the bone. The whirlwind was spinning the tiny stone shards so fast that they were taking the elf's skin off faster than he could try and counter the magic. "That will teach these fo..." the archmage's sentence ended abruptly, as a sword came out of his chest, spraying blood everywhere.

"Never leave an elf behind you, wizard," Seltemver said, pulling his blade out sideways, tearing the man's back and sides apart. He kicked the wizard to the ground, confident that the elf was dead. Seltemver heard a strange noise then, and turned to see a small creature, skin the color of blood, staring at him aghast. It was an imp!

"Zat dos col?" the imp asked in a strange tongue.

Seltemver thought it might be a dialect of elven, as some of the words were close. *Here the cold?* he thought, then tried elven. "Dost col?"

"Esh?" the imp asked, clearly surprised and pointing at himself.

Seltemver was going to try again, but the murmuring of the not-so-dead wizard brought his head spinning around.

"I should have...had the imp protect me...never thought I would need it," The archmage said, coughing up blood as he crawled to sit up. "He will *have* to kill for you though, forever. I'll make sure of it... because he hates it." The archmage whispered and clapped his bloody hands together as a spell of concussive force exploded out from him in an invisible wave. As the dust settled, The archmage's head dropped...he was gone.

Seltemver felt the wave hit him and fell against the tower. His sword broke into pieces as the wave hit and fell among the bloody leaves at his feet. The elven pirate looked over at the imp, feeling a bond he couldn't explain, and knew that the imp was his for some ungodly reason. He tried to smile but shivered as the spell crawled up his spine. *The wizard must've cursed me with this thing,* Seltemver thought as he stood on shaky legs. *I'll deal with that later. I suppose I should see what's worth taking from inside at least.*

Amonar looked upon the wizard that had tormented him for decades and tried to feel bad, but he couldn't; Nor'alrin had made him do such terrible things to people. Torturing, killing, and even siphoning their life essence—something the wizard needed—were the daily rituals for Amonar, so much so that after all of the killing he had done, he could barely even stand to see blood, never mind cause it. He had tortured souls in the hells before, but at least there they were already dead. Here, they were alive and vibrant, full of such life that he could almost smell it if he was close enough. It almost broke him to do the things he had been commanded to do.

The imp's attention was pulled to the new elf that had slain his master, then he too took the hit from the invisible wave. His little wings flapped to keep him from flying off, but he still spun in a lazy circle for a good hot minute. *That was weird,* Amonar thought as he saw the new elf stand straight and walk into the tower, eyeing the imp with a curious glance. "Zat?" Amonar asked him in infernal. He wished he knew how to speak elven.

"Zat?" the elf asked, confusion written on his face as he started walking over towards the imp.

Communication is Hard

"Zat dos giv?" Amonar asked the elf, backing up by beating his wings. He wasn't sure if the elf was going to try and kill him—he was technically immortal—but he didn't want to find out; he hated violence. "Gol fer!" Amonar said, pointing to the tower doorway. He hoped letting the elf know there was treasure inside would calm him down and make him go away; not that it would do any good. He had felt the archmage's binding curse and knew he was stuck with this new elf forever now.

I just hope he is a little less ruthless than the archmage, Amonar thought to himself.

It worked, the elf walked in shaking his head, and Amonar breathed a sigh of relief. He flew over to the archmage and searched Nor'alrin's pockets, hoping that he could find something to help with this new curse. When the archmage had first summoned him it was for personal gain—the old elf wanted something to kill people for him—but it wasn't a protective binding. This new curse...It was just cruel! To watch over an elf forever, knowing that if the imp let him die he would be dragged down to the deep hells for eternity; it was horrible! Amonar didn't care about this elf's soul...the elf would be dragged down regardless now that he had been cursed, but to get pulled along with him!

Amonar found nothing in the pockets of the archmage's robe, so he decided to go in and see if Nor'alrin had any notes that he could translate someday...and to see what his new master was doing.

Seltemver walked carefully into the wizard's tower, hoping the imp was right this time. It was plain that their communication was a bit off, but money inside was pretty easy to understand. He passed by the rooms that looked like normal living quarters, even by-passed the library; any important notes and books would be in private holdings anyway. Seltemver did stop at the ornate, iron-bound door, however. The thing that stopped him wasn't the door itself, but the glowing blue runes etched into the very wood. They seemed alive, almost moving on their own accord. Runes of power were known to him, though admittedly he had skipped that class in school.

"Ma in por," the imp said as it flew in, pointing to the door.

Seltemver frowned, not knowing what to do. The imp had said to open the door, yet it was clearly guarded with magic. "Ma in por?" Seltemver asked to make sure.

The imp shook his head in agreement, seeming relieved that he understood. The little thing flapped his wings and alighted on the wall sconce, smiling.

Seltemver shrugged and grabbed the handle. *After all*, he thought, *he has to keep me alive right?* At least that's what he heard the archmage say when he talked about cursing him. Seltemver instantly regretted touching the door; hells, he regretted leaving the ship at this point.

A frigid cold arced up his arm like lightning, burning away his shirt and throwing him back against the wall. Seltemver fought hard to remain conscious as his heart was busy filing a complaint to his brain for letting him do that...his arms weren't even bothering to move, outright refusing to work on general principles, and his head just decided to sit there, and spin for the moment.

Tiny hands grabbed his shirt, shaking him back and forth. "Ya liv?" the imp asked, clearly worried by the frantic tone of his voice.

"Barely!" Seltemver croaked, trying to stand against the better judgment of his entire body. His coat was ruined, his sword was broken and he had been almost killed; not once but twice! This was not his best day. He stomped off into the now open door, which lay on only one hinge, and its wood was frozen solid. He said nothing to the imp as he started rummaging through the things in the room.

?

Seltemver found a black silk bag on a hook and started putting things into it. The room was a mess that only a wizard could love. Scrolls and jars lined every shelf and books were piled haphazardly on every surface. This had to be the archmage's workshop and Seltemver found various items that seemed expensive. Normally he would have one of his crew check for magic curses or traps, but they had all died horribly. So he planned on just taking them all back to the ship and pray. As he rummaged through the various shelves and cabinets in the room, he noticed a very nice-looking longcoat on a peg and smiled. He grabbed it and spun it around him, slipping into it and striking a pose; it fit perfectly. "All right, now all I need is a weapon," Seltemver said, slipping back into the common tongue he used most of the time; he only used elvish with his crew.

"Try that sword," the imp said, speaking plain common as he pointed to a gleaming slim sword sitting on a rack hidden behind some jars that held gods-above-knew-what.

"You can *speak*!?" Seltemver yelled, ready to strangle the tiny creature.

"Well...yes. I just didn't know you spoke common until you just said that. By the way, my name is Amonar," the imp said, smiling innocently and holding out a clawed hand.

Seltemver stared at the imp incredulously...then he broke into a fit of laughter. He was bent over with his hands on his knees just laughing until his sides hurt. "And I'm stuck with you. Forever." He took a minute to breathe and calm down then straightened up and smiled. "Hello Amonar, my name is Seltemver."

"That's a funny name for an elf," Amonar said, then saw the look on Seltemver's face "I mean...a lovely name. Couldn't be more regal."

Seltemver drew the sword out of its scabbard as it lay in the rack and knew that it was special immediately. It was deceptively light and well-balanced, and extremely sharp. "Well then, Amonar, you are now part of my crew, and, as a new member, you get to carry the bag." Seltemver handed the black silk bag to the imp, who took it and fell to the floor with the weight of it. "On second thought, just hold the torch," the elven pirate said, handing him a torch from a wall sconce and taking the bag. "Now, let's grab everything not nailed down," Seltemver said, turning to the stacks of books that he knew he could sell on the market.

"And pry up everything that is?" Amonar asked, his old smile returning for the first time in decades.

"That, my new friend, is the best thing you've said all day."

"That you understood," Amonar quipped.

In a little while they were back on the *Ravencrest*, their fellow pirates in awe at the haul, despite the deaths of the others. The elves that had died would be missed, but the treasure would make up for it; such was the lives of pirates. Seltemver sailed out of the hidden cove feeling pretty good about what would come next.

As the Gears Turn

This is one of my personal favorites, as I got to relax for once in a place that didn't find me frightening. The strange city was alien, even to our standards, and we spent some time getting to know the local customs and people. I always thought that the one constant in our world travels was the gods— even if they had different names they were still the same old gods—but this world changed my perspective and gave me something to think about.

—Amonar

Limping into Port

The ship came out of the storm listing to port and still smoking. Gaping holes, located in the upper part of the ship's side were letting in water every time they hit a large wave and one of the three masts was broken in half. The elf spun the cracked wheel and struggled to get the rudder to listen to him, even though it too was in half; he had no idea how they were still afloat. His short white hair stuck to his face as the wind died down, and his worn longcoat flapped about him like a tattered flag.

Seltemver Ashblade was lucky to be alive and he owed it all to his crew. The problem was that they all knew it and would probably never let him live it down. "Any sign of land, Crak?" Seltemver called out to the small orc in the Crak's Nest. They had renamed it that when they found out that the small orc was the only one that fit comfortably in it, besides Amonar that is.

"I see ships and a lot of smoke, Captain!" Crak called out pointing to the north.

"Amonar?" Seltemver called out to the imp on the railing next to him.

The red-skinned imp flew up and hovered, looking out over the sea. "Yup, there are a lot of ships and smoke, but I can also see buildings and tall towers," Amonar said, smiling up at Crak and sticking his tongue out.

Seltemver smiled and spun the wheel, trying to get the ship to respond. Amonar was bonded to him and had proved to be a pretty good friend on these crazy journeys through the wild storms. Most of the crew was afraid of the demonic little fella, but some of them were warming up to him.

"Capt'n, I don't know if we can make it that far," Toth said from the stern as he held a rope taut in both hands. he was the only reason the boom was steady at this point and any more wind and he may lose his grip. Toth had umber-colored skin, as most orcs did, and curved tusks protruding from his mouth. His long hair fell across broad shoulders and his heavily muscled arms bore tattoos of various weapons. His bulging arms showed his strength as he held on to the fighting boom and the rest of the crew gave him plenty of space; they all knew they wouldn't be able to help. Toth was his first mate and possibly the strongest one on the ship and Seltemver couldn't ask for any better.

"She'll hold, Toth, as long as you do," Seltemver said, knowing that the orc wouldn't fail this ship. The *Seahaven* had been theirs since escaping the sea witch gods above knew how long ago. "We just have to make it to that port and we can fix her."

"Let's try not to have the entire town after us this time," a woman's voice said behind him. "Especially with cannon fire."

Seltemver winced, knowing that this last attack was his fault. "I didn't know she was a shapeshifter," Seltemver said. "I thought we agreed to never bring it up again, Grunhilde?" The elven pirate captain looked over his shoulder at the grey-skinned orc and narrowed his eyes.

"Last time, Captain," Grunhilde said with a smile. She was attractive, for an orc, with long braids and a fierce smile. The best healer he had ever seen, Grunhilde had a good eye and a bedside manner that could level a mountain. She got the job done though, and it still amazed him that she could channel the healing power of the gods, even a little. Why Dava would deign to impart his power to an orc was beyond him, but if he had learned anything throughout their travels was to never look a gift orc in the mouth.

A cheer went up as they limped closer, the rest of the crew now able to see what the demonic eyesight of the little imp could. It looked like a strange city built right on the water, with a big river running right through the town from a port full of wooden docks and weird contraptions. The strange things looked like the pulleys used to unload ships but with iron discs and cranks. Thick smoke lingered over the city like a blanket and the bustling of the people showed promise as he could see both humans and orcs milling about the ships and walkways as they neared.

"No elves," Amonar said as he perched upon Seltemver's shoulder.

"There weren't any in Freeport either," Seltemver countered with a smirk.

"And they tried to kill you."

"Point taken." Seltemver pulled his hood up and tucked his hair under, making sure that his enchanted blade was snug on his waist.

"Technically there weren't any in the last city either," Grunhilde added with a smirk.

"Oh that's right, they all looked elven but it was a rouse," Amonar said

"All right, crew, never mind," Seltemver said with an inward groan. "Let's get this ship into a dock and see if they can help us patch her up."

"And maybe stay away from strange attractive women?" Toth asked as he started to let the rope go slowly, easing the boom across the deck.

Seltemver rolled his eyes and turned towards the city, hoping it was going to go smoothly for once. and knowing it probably wouldn't.

Stranger in a Strange Land

The *Seahaven* came into the busy port with all eyes on her. The ship was a mess with half her sails ripped and torn, as well as water sloshing below decks up to an orc's knees. It truly was a miracle they had made it out of the magical storm that transports them from place to place. Originally they had discussed that the storm might not be transporting them like that, but after the last trip, the entire crew now understood they were visiting different worlds altogether. This led to the all-important thought as they neared the docks: Where in the gods above were they this time?

The first thing that Seltemver noticed as they slowly pulled up to the giant wooden docks was a giant tower to the right of the river that seemed to cut through the middle of the city. This tower was made of stone but had windows at the top as well as a curious dial with numbers and black arms. There were also several water wheels attached to small buildings and varying winches off-loading cargo.

These winches were only manned by one person who didn't seem to be struggling at all with the weight.

"What sorcery is this?" Toth asked as he came up to the helm rubbing his arms.

Seltemver had no idea how to respond, he just shared a look with his first mate and shrugged. The heavy smoke drifted across the city like low-hanging clouds, giving the entire place an ominous feel to it. Small islands with large structures on them held piles of cargo and ships docked, some without visible sails. Seltemver saw small longboats making their way up the river and passing under stone bridges that stretched over the water to link the land masses. This was a strange place indeed, and Amonar was right; there was no sign of any elves. "Let's go find a place to pay for the mooring and maybe eat, then ask around about repairs," Seltemver said pulling his hood over his head lower. "Toth, you have the ship."

Seltemver, Amonar, and Grunhilde walked down the dock and saw a large building with a hanging sign made of iron. The sign had some sort of round symbol that seemed to have bumps all the way around it, reading: *The Bent Gear Inn*

"I have a bad feeling about this Seltemver," Amonar said as he crouched on the elf's shoulder.

"You always have a bad feeling," Grunhilde countered.

"And I'm usually right."

Seltemver stopped and looked around, making sure they still weren't being stared at; it was no good to draw that much attention this early. Thankfully the stares had died down once they tied off the ship. "Look, we need the ship repaired, no matter how bad this place is; we won't make it anywhere else."

Grunhilde nodded and stuck her hands in her belt.

"At least I see some orcs around the docks," Amonar said, changing the subject. "And they seem cheerful."

"They've never met you," Grunhilde said with a tusky grin.

"That hurt," Amonar said clutching his chest in mock pain.

"Children," Seltemver said as they walked under the red awning of the inn. The place was packed with humans, orcs, and—to Seltemver's surprise—dwarves.

Dwarves had disappeared from his world five hundred years before he was born, sailing south in their ships never to be seen again. They were thought of as myths now; stories to be told in dark taverns. Seltemver had never seen one before, but they were unmistakable in their appearance. *It would make sense that they would be in other worlds too,* he thought as they walked towards the bar.

Dwarves were very short, but stocky, only reaching about four to four and a half feet tall. Their appearance was very distinct, however, always having long beards and bushy facial hair in general. The longer the beard, the more prestigious the dwarf, or so the stories told. Even the females of the species had beards, though thinner and more braided.

"Is that what I think it is Seltemver?" Amonar asked, looking at the stocky humanoids sitting at tables all over the inn. They were singing and drinking and even the orcs were joining in with them; a truly odd scene to be sure.

"Yes, it is, Amonar. Dwarves." Seltemver kept his hood low and made his way to the far side of the bar, hoping to talk to the barkeep about who was in charge. "Let's keep a low profile…" he started, but he was too late.

"Well call me Ivan and give me a keg," Grunhilde said striding over and grabbing a stein out of the hands of a dwarf. She drained it in one shot and then slammed the metal mug down on the table. "Nice ale, good froth," she said, winking at the dwarf and slapping him on the back.

The dwarf pitched forward and hit the table, coming back up with wide eyes; eyes that narrowed quickly. "Lass, that was me first drink of the evening and I've been at sea for a tenday,"

Grunhilde laughed and grabbed a chair, spinning it and straddling it. "Then you better order some more and try to keep up with me," the female orc said, setting her axe on the wooden table.

The room went deathly quiet for the span of three heartbeats. The dwarf pushed his chair back and stood, slamming his fist down hard. "I like her!" he called out, the rest of the inn erupting in cheer. "Gilen! Another two rounds here!" the dwarf called to the serving girl who was weaving through the crowd.

"And we lost Grunhilde," Amonar said, pouting. "Now who is going to keep you in line?"

THE WAY THINGS WORK

Seltemver shook his head and walked to the bar. He brought Grunhilde to distract people from looking too closely at him, and now that was gone. *Well she is doing what I asked...no one is looking at me now,* he thought taking in the barkeep standing behind the solid oaken bar.

"You folks the ones that came in that flooded ship?" the barkeep asked as they neared.

"The *Seahaven*, yes," Seltemver answered evenly. "We were hoping to get her fixed up." The barkeep was human and much older than he should be. The man seemed to be in his late seventies, if not older.

"Yer moored at the wrong docks fer that," Another dwarf said passing by. "But I can help ye with that later if ye got the tokens." The dwarf had a long, dark beard thickly braided with metal balls and deep brown eyes.

"My name is Seltemver," the elven pirate said, nodding and keeping his hands inside his cloak. "But we don't have much coin. We were hoping to trade services or something of that nature."

"Me names Gile, and good luck with that," The dwarf said shaking his head and walking away. He was stopped by another female dwarf with a light brown beard braided in three.

"Hold up, Gile. You heard that the Forgemaster is looking fer help right?" she asked, looking Seltemver up and down like he was a plate of meat. "They might be able to help him for the cost."

"Kili, he won't take unknowns fer a job," Gile said. "And you didn't see the ship that they dragged into port."

"He's turned everyone else away."

"Who is the Forgemaster?" Seltemver interrupted, trying not to sound too desperate for information.

"He runs the Forge District and oversees all the production and repairs for Gear City," Gile said, eyeing Seltemver suspiciously.

"Hey at least we know the name of the place now," Amonar said quietly from Seltemver's shoulder.

Gile looked at Amonar like he had just noticed the winged creature and tilted his head. "Fancy parrot you got there."

Amonar sighed dramatically and folded his wings. "Ahh, fancy parrot," he imitated, playing the part. "Why does everyone talk to me like I'm a thing or a pet?"

"Hush, Amonar," Seltemver said softly. "So he is kind of like the lord of the city?

"Nah, that's Lord Paran, but he's just a figurehead for the Emperor. The lord handles the budgets and defense of the outposts, while the Forgemaster keeps the city running."

"Can you take me to this Forgemaster?"

"As I said, he probably won't hire outsiders," Gile said shaking his head.

"Well, I bet he would after talking to me, " Seltemver said noting Kili was still staring at him. He had seen that look before; it was got him in trouble in the last world.

"Yeah...his people skills are great," Amonar said with dripping sarcasm.

"Fine, I'll take you to the Forge District, but it won't be fer two turns of the wheel," Gile said ignoring Amonar. "Listen. You might be able to trade manual labor for the small repairs—the sails and stuff like that—but the other stuff is going to take time and materials and I'm not sure you're gonna be able to convince him of yer worth." Gile took a step away, then sighed heavily, turning back. "But if mah sister has taken to ye, then I won't hear the end of it until yer gon."

"He's not wrong," Kili said with a wink at Seltemver.

"Great. We'll start with the small stuff and you come and get me when we can go see the Forgemaster," Seltemver said with a nod to Kili.

"Oh, you misunderstand," Gile said with a laugh. "In a couple of days, we can go to the Forge District and *ask* to see the Forgemaster, but it may take up to three tens *after* that for an actual audience."

"I thought he needed help?" Seltemver asked, desperation creeping into his normally calm voice.

"He does, but he's got an entire city to repair and keep working, lest the gears break down. We never know where he'll be on any given day." With that Gile nodded and walked off, tugging his sister after him.

"See you in two turns of the wheel, stranger," Kili said as they vanished into the crowd.

"Gears? Turns of the wheel?" Amonar asked as they grabbed a drink and went to find Grunhilde.

"Just different ways to say things, Amonar," Seltemver said with a grin. "Don't worry, I think things will be better this time."

"Yeah, but you always say that."

"No one has tried to kill me yet..."

Amonar scoffed and swished his tail. "Yet is the keyword there."

Learning the Gears

Amonar flew down the dock with an armload of silk, marveling at the ease with which the people of the city had adapted to him. It had been two tendays—or two tens as they say here—since they had transferred the *Seahaven* to the Ship Ward, from the Dock Ward for repairs. They had visited the Forge District and applied for an audience with the Forgemaster and ever since then, Amonar would fly out for errands without worry; no one seemed to know what he was here.

"Morning, Amonar!" a human girl called out as he went by, her arms laden with a box of metal fixings as well. She was waving frantically while holding the box in one arm, desperate to get his attention.

"Morning Soph!" the imp called back, his smile even wider. They had learned that the different wards and districts were for varying things, all laid out like a plan or blueprint. Ship Ward was for repairs and upgrades, while the Dock Ward was for trade; loading and unloading ships of their wares. The crew of the *Seahaven* didn't even have to worry about breaking any regulations, for once, as the rules in the city were very simple. No stealing and no killing; both punishable by varying jail times. Only one thing would incur the death sentence in this world; being elven.

It seemed that in this world's history, the elves had gone to war trying to enslave the other races. It was a very dark time and the elves lost, retreating west across the seas. As such, the people of Gear City would curse one another by using *white hair* as a way to demean others.

"Did you get enough silk, Amonar?" Toth asked as the imp flew over the railing of the ship. It was sad that the people of the city had accepted Amonar better than most of the crew still, but in all fairness, the crew had seen him unleash some pretty horrible things with his power.

"I think so, Toth," Amonar said watching one of the crew, an orc named Kona, walk away making the sign of Dava.

"Don't mind him, Am," Toth said quietly, taking the pile of silk from the imp. "Did you have enough tokens for it?"

Amonar handed four small iron discs back to the first mate with a sad smile. "Yeah, they gave me a break because I ran some parchment over to the guild house." The crew found out fairly quickly that gold coins were useless here. Instead, the city ran on Forge Tokens or just Tokens. Steel, Iron, and Copper tokens respectively. They were hammered flat in the Forge District and used for trade. The good news was that a collector in the Clock District had given them a small fortune in Steel tokens for the gold coins they had on board. It seems they were rare in this world, just not to everyone.

"It's great that you're taking odd jobs to help out, Amonar. The crew will never forget it," Toth reassured the imp.

"Yeah, well, I'm a bit of a commodity since I can fly across to the different islands faster than they can use the boats," Amonar said, patting the burly orc on the shoulder and flying off to find Seltemver. Amonar found the Captain of the *Seahaven*, standing at the helm with his new shadow, Kili, and another small dwarf; this one dressed like one of the messengers of the city.

City Messengers had a distinctive look. All of them had their hair, or beards, braided with tiny gears and wore a cloak with a large gear embroidered on the back of it. These gears, they had learned, were metal wheels with 'teeth' that interlocked to form some sort of magic to make things move easier. The simplest explanation that they had received was that it was like the wagon wheels, but locked together. The entire city was built with these weird gears and they were an integral part of their whole society it seemed.

Weirder than that, was Seltemver's appearance now. Amonar had to chuckle every time he saw the pirate captain now, his short white hair colored with crushed charcoal and his ears tucked under a cornered pirate hat. The hat was Kili's idea; she thought it made him look more dashing than the hood, though she was still kept in the dark as to why he wanted one.

The imp flew up just in time for the messenger to turn and walk away. "What did I miss?" Amonar asked, flying a slow circle around Seltemver, then landing on his shoulder.

"That was a note from the Forgemaster," Seltemver said with a grin. "It's finally time to meet him."

Seltemver walked into the Forge District and not for the first time marveled at how anyone could work in this much smoke. The last time he was here it was quick, with Gile leading him right to where he filled out the forms and then they were gone. Now, Seltemver had a better chance to look around and check things out. "Stay with me, Amonar. No wandering off." It was the first time Seltemver ever had to say that to the normally frightened imp, as here the people liked the small demonic creature and many had befriended him.

"Don't worry," Amonar said with a cheerful smile. "Who else is going to keep an eye on you?"

"You're not funny."

"I'm a little funny."

"You two are a riot," Kili said trailing along with them.

Seltemver sighed at the sound of the love-smitten dwarf. He had tried everything he could think of to make her leave him alone—short of hurting her feelings—and nothing had worked. Not that he wasn't attracted to her, but after the last world he was taking a break from women for a little bit. "So tell us more about this Forgemaster," Seltemver prompted the dwarf, trying to get her mind on something else. "How long had he been called that?"

"He's been Forgemaster ever since he came here. About one hundred years back," Kili said as they wandered through the packed district. "Stories say he was married to an elven wizardress but when they tried to enslave humanity he turned on her and trapped her in a cage for eternity. People say that's why he is always so grumpy and gruff, 'cause he had to turn on his true love, or something like that."

"Little old for being human," Amonar remarked.

"Yeah there are plenty of rumors about that too," Kili said with a laugh.

"Is that why elves are so hated here?" Amonar asked, elbowing Seltemver and smiling. "Because they tried to make slaves of you all?"

"Pretty much. Any elf now is attacked and killed on sight," Kili said in a voice that made it clear she had some history with the subject herself. "But no one has seen an elf for a very long time."

"And everyone works for the Forgemaster in this district?" Seltemver asked, flicking Amonar with his finger for bringing up the elves.

"Yeah, every aspiring smith would love to. We've all applied at one time or another," Kili said with a faraway look. "They say that he is much more intimidating in person. I've never met the Forgemaster, myself, but that's what goes around the gears."

"You've never met him?" Amonar asked.

"Nope. I've put in to be an apprentice. Now it's just waiting for the wheel to turn to see if I'm accepted."

Seltemver would never get used to the slang terms they used here, but hopefully, with this job, he could get the ship repaired and they could sail off once more. He looked at the district more closely as they walked, wonder creeping into his eyes at the chaos of it all.

The buildings were squat and made of dark grey stone with red tiled roofs and seemed more like stone fortifications than habitats. Each one had a small forge of some kind attached to it and heavy smoke poured out of tall stacks from the sides somewhere. Dwarves dominated most of the forges around the large square with some humans and orcs mixed in, hammering weapons, gears, and all sorts of odd things. The crowd swarmed the places looking and yelling their orders in and paid little mind to Seltemver and his company.

People were everywhere, running buckets of water from the well in the middle of the street to the different forges, bustling to and from the piles of crates with raw materials, and shouting their services to all who could hear them. The place wasn't just chaos...it was *organized* chaos. It wasn't long before they stood in front of the largest building in the district, a massive chimney stack blasting a four-foot diameter column of black smoke straight up into the sky. Seltemver knew they were here.

The Forgemaster

They walked up unopposed, nodding to the two dwarven guards who stood at the entrance with axes and shields. They entered into a hall with a massive door at the end and intense heat coming out of it. A distant clang rang continuously throughout the place and it smelled of coal. Smaller forges seemed to be in connecting rooms, with their smoke being directed by long steel tubes to the main room further down the hall.

"I told you they wouldn't stop you if I were with you," Kili said, grabbing Seltemver's arm and walking with him down the hall towards the archway. "Applicants may come and go to find out their progress."

"You two make a cute couple," Amonar whispered into Seltemver's ear as they walked.

"Immortal or not, you still feel pain. Remember that," Seltemver whispered back with a deep growl.

"Hey settle down, grumpy breeches, I was just kidding," Amonar said with a slight chuckle. A deep gong brought them out of their conversation and the two of them turned to see a large man step out of the room, the absence of the clanging almost deafening.

"That's the Forgemaster," Kili said in awe.

"Wow, I never would've guessed that," Amonar said rolling his little black eyes.

The man was massive, almost seven feet tall, and all muscle. He wore no shirt and his barrel chest was covered in fine scars that seemed like cuts. He had long blond hair that was dirty with soot, and his steel grey eyes seemed to see into your very soul. The Forgemaster carried an equally large hammer, blackened by the heat that it worked in, and sweat poured down his chiseled face.

Seltemver nodded his head at the man and spread his arms out wide. "Greetings, Forgemaster, and thank you for meeting with me," Seltemver began, but was cut off by the man's laughter.

"No need for that much formality, Captain. Come, we have much to discuss," the Forgemaster said, turning and walking back into the room.

"Why does it feel like he already knows us?" Amonar said with a slight tremble to his voice.

Seltemver laughed at his friend, knowing that the old Amonar was showing once more. "Because we have been making a name for ourselves these past tendays, Amonar. I told you all to do that, remember?"

"Gorgeous and smart," Kili said with a squeeze of Seltemver's arm.

They followed the man in and stood in the archway, unsure of where to go. The massive room was full of piles of gears and rods, as well as crates of raw materials and other strange pieces. There was a large cage hanging from the ceiling that looked bent, its bars twisted as if something had broken into it. "The dwarf has to wait outside," the Forgemaster said flatly before they went any further.

Kili let go of Seltemver's arm. "I'll be waiting outside, handsome," she said, stomping back out of the building.

"This way," the man said once the dwarf was gone. He walked by all the materials and pressed a panel on the wall in the back. Loud gears whined as the stone wall grated and slowly slid aside, revealing another room. "Please, both of you, make yourself at home."

Seltemver walked into the new room and felt a wave of cool air wash over him. The room was a bit smaller, but with only a small hearth and four comfy chairs, as well as a small bar and drinks on a metal shelf. "Nice secret room," Seltemver said as he sat in a comfy chair and leaned back. He was relieved that Kili was sent away, being able to relax for the first time in a long time without her right there.

"It serves my need for secrecy on occasion," the Forgemaster replied pouring himself a drink. "Anything for you?"

"Do you have mead?" Amonar asked clapping his hands together.

"Not now, Amonar," Seltemver cautioned. The last thing he needed was a tipsy imp when he was negotiating. He looked at the man and smiled, putting the fingers of his hands together and sitting forward. "I understand you are looking for help?" Seltemver asked as Amonar flew off to look around the room. Seltemver watched the Forgemaster eye the imp with curiosity for a minute then focus back on him.

"That I am, and it is the reason I've moved you up the list of people that want work done from me," the Forgemaster said drinking from his huge stein. "Otherwise, you would be in the dock for another five tens, fixing the little things on that ship instead of the things you need to be done."

DEALS AND SECRETS

"This sounds like you need something done quietly," Seltemver said narrowing his eyes. The elven pirate had never claimed to be the good guy and had done his fair share of questionable things in the past; he knew the tone of this conversation all too well.

"Something very dear to me has been taken and I need it back, but I can't trust anyone else with the job," the Forgemaster said, once again looking at Amonar.

"And you can trust someone that just blew into port?" Seltemver asked, knowing that it must have something to do with his winged friend.

"What's this?" Amonar asked, holding up a weird contraption. It had the curved handle of a cane but was attached to a long steel pipe with a cylinder. Small gears and wheels could be seen near the curved handle and it clicked as Amonar played with it.

"Gods above they are all just as curious aren't they?" the Forgemaster whispered to himself as he stood and walked towards Amonar. "That is a Hand Cannon. I'm working on a new prototype now, but can't finish it until what was stolen is returned to me."

"A cannon in your hand?" Seltemver asked incredulously. He saw Amonar drop the thing and fly back to his shoulder, clearly scared of setting it off.

"Yes, the force is too strong for normal steel—it explodes quite nicely—but I'm close to making it viable."

"The force doesn't send you flying?" Seltemver knew that cannons had a massive recoil when fired; it was why you never stood directly behind them when lighting the fuse.

"Not at all. The charge is significantly smaller and propels a tiny steel ball at your enemies," the Forgemaster answered, smiling now.

"You should rename it. Call it a Crossball," Amonar said.

"A what now?"

"Like a mix between a crossbow and a ball...never mind I just heard how dumb that sounds out loud," Amonar said with a frown.

"Ha! It does my spirit good to see another mephit," the Forgemaster admitted, laughing at the face Amonar was making. "Though I have to admit I wasn't sure until now that you truly were one."

"That's why you have been looking at him," Seltemver reasoned, sitting back and folding his arms across his chest. Mephits were another name for imps, but he hadn't met anyone outside of books who mentioned it before—and even those were the oldest tombs he had found in the archmage's tower back when he first found Amonar. Those books had said that there were two kinds of mephits, one for the realms below and one for the realms above, though there was absolutely no information on the latter.

"Aye, I'm accustomed to them, tis true," the Forgemaster said with a bit more emotion than he may have intended. "In fact, that's why you're here."

"Tell him he can't have me, Seltemver," Amonar said sounding worried.

"No, Amonar. I think he wants us to find his friend," Seltemver said slowly. When the Forgemaster nodded it confirmed what the elven pirate had started to think. The man was somehow connected to his as well. "What happened and why the secrecy?"

"Ixiar was my wife's familiar and when she was killed, my wife transferred the bond to me, somehow; Ixiar is a Sidhe from the realms above," the Forgemaster said as he stood now and paced the room

"A sidhe?" Amonar asked, sounding confused. The Forgemaster stopped and looked at Amonar with his head tilted to one side.

Seltemver wasn't sure why Amonar sounded like that, but he would figure that out later. "Go on."

The Forgemaster cleared his throat. "Ixiar was taken seven tens ago by a weapons dealer in the Clock District; a slaver known as Hagan Finesteel. He found out what I've been working on and is trying to stop me from making it and putting his weapon shop out of business."

Slavers, just what I need, Seltemver thought. "Does Ixiar look like Amonar or have the same powers?" Seltemver asked. He knew enough about slavers—in any world—that he didn't need much info on them; the creature though, *that* he needed to know about. *Especially if she can do what Amonar does.*

"No. Sidhe are more bird-like. Ixiar has wings with blue feathers, three eyes, talons of ivory, and a long beak. Sidhe can't channel the power of their realm as imps can—they lost their voice a long time ago—instead, they channel lightning by screeching at their opponents and can heal minor wounds with their birdsong." The Forgemaster stopped and picked up a small book, caressing it softly. "I need her back."

"And if we get Ixiar back you will repair my ship?" Seltemver asked, feeling hopeful despite Amonar's troubled look. There was a lot of damage and they could never hope to pay for it all, even with the small fortune they got in tokens.

"Every last bit and I'll even make some improvements, if you want them." The Forgemaster set down the book and leaned in close. "I know how damaged your ship was—word travels fast in Gear City—and to be honest, it's worse than you think, but Ixiar means everything to me and I will do anything to get her back."

"You still haven't answered why you wanted us?" Seltemver asked, fearing he now knew why.

The Forgemaster eyed him with a stare that spoke volumes. "Because I don't want word to get out that Ixiar is bonded to me like Amonar is bonded to you."

"Why?" Amonar asked, not catching on. Something was throwing the usually quick imp off his game.

Seltemver felt like he had been hit in the stomach with the prow of a ship; the man across from him truly did know who he was; what he was. "The Forgemaster doesn't want anyone to know that an elf cursed him," Seltemver said flatly, concerned that he may have to kill this man since his cover may have been blown. He couldn't risk the city rising up against his crew.

The Forgemaster let his head drop, nodding slowly. "Aye, and they would take her away from me if that came about. So, *elf*, I'll keep your secret and you can keep mine and we can get you and your ship out of Gear City as fast as we can. Agreed?"

"Just give us the details and where this slaver is and I'll get Ixiar back," Seltemver said breathing a sigh of relief. The last thing he wanted was to fight his way out of this city.

Time to Plan

Seltemver remained quiet as they left, knowing that Kili would be waiting for them. He needed to figure out what was bothering Amonar before they dove into this head first. If something was distracting Amonar, things could go sideways quickly. Seltemver saw the dwarf come bouncing towards them and decided to try a new tack with the smitten girl.

"Kili, how would you like to go with me to the Clock District and give me a tour? Just the two of us," Seltemver said with a sincere look.

Whatever questions Kili had for the pair were lost in that moment as she stopped breathing, her eyes widening into twin pools of emerald green. "Just the two of us? Alone together?" Her hands went to her hips sliding over her voluptuous curves as her smile widened.

"Yes, meet me at the *Seahaven* by..." Seltemver struggled to remember how they said sundown here in this strange city. They told the time with a strange circle with black arms that moved by the gears, denoting different phases of the day. The two hands would spin slowly, displayed by the large tower in the aptly named Clock District for the whole city to view. "...Hands down?" Seltemver saw her nod and bounce away.

"You're getting this clock/hands thing down pat, Seltemver," Amonar said without his usual sarcastic tone.

"All right, spill it. What's wrong Amonar?"

Amonar paused, shaking his head. "Seltemver, I haven't seen a sidhe in a very long time; to my knowledge, they were all wiped out."

"Aren't you all immortal?"

"Well, technically, yes. Only up here though," Amonar said, waving to another group of children as they went. "See, at one time demons ran the deep hells, torturing souls and such, but then they grew overconfident and decided to rise up and overpower Krist, the dark god of death. They assaulted the realm of the gods in concert and the sidhe were the first line of defense. The demons slew them all before Krist broke their forms and threw them back into the hells, this time as occupants instead of rulers. The dark god appointed the imps, to watch over the demons and keep them shackled." Amonar sounded sad and wistful at the same time; bad memories of home will do that to you sometimes.

"I'm sorry Amonar," Seltemver said

"No, it's fine, but that's not what's bothering me." Amonar rung his hands together nervously. "I just figured out why no one is bothered by me," the imp said as they walked up the ramp to the *Seahaven.*

"Why, Amonar?" Seltemver asked as he looked at the sun through the smoke-filled city. It was almost highsun, or hands up, and he had to figure this out before he walked into a mess he didn't understand.

"I think in this world my kind died instead," Amonar said as Toth came towards them. "See, I've never heard of a sidhe being called to the mortal plane—let alone bound—by anyone, elf or otherwise. They despised the fact that imps were summoned by mortals and have always hated us for it. Here, it must be switched."

"So, why so worried?" Seltemver asked, patting Amonar on the back. "I'm sure Ixiar will be overwhelmed to see you."

"What if I'm the bad guy in her eyes?" Amonar asked, worry plain in his voice.

"It will be fine."

"Run into an old girlfriend, Amonar?" Toth asked with a laugh.

"No, but we got the job," Seltemver interrupted before the two of them got into an insult match. It's not like he didn't like to hear them, but he had plans to make. He led the way down below to his cabin and some privacy.

"And Seltemver has a date," Amonar said, some of his usual cheer coming back as he flew along behind.

"Ah, must be that little spitfire of a dwarf," Toth said elbowing Seltemver with a wink. "Think we may have a new member of the crew?"

"No. I just need a way into the Clock District that doesn't seem obvious," Seltemver said rolling his eyes. "Now, I'll fill you in, but you're not going to like it," Seltemver said closing his door.

"It's slavers again isn't it?" Toth guessed.

"Yes, and this Forgemaster knows I'm an elf."

"I'll break out the armory," Toth said without missing a beat.

"Not yet, but keep everyone on standby," Seltemver said with a smile. "He has his own secrets he needs kept so we're good for now."

"And some we may not even know about," Amonar added cryptically.

Toth shook his head. "So what's the plan that I know I'm not going to like?"

Seltemver sat on his couch and smiled. "Oh you are most definitely *not* going to like it, but it's a good one this time."

"You always say that, too," Amonar added as he rolled his eyes.

"He's right you know," Toth said and ducked as Seltemver threw a vase at him.

Hide and Sidhe

He walked down the cobblestone street with Amonar on his shoulder and shook his head for the hundredth time. This wasn't just a bad plan, it was the worst one he had ever heard of. Toth Irontusk had been the first mate of the *Seahaven* since its inaugural cast off two years ago, breaking free from the slavery of a dangerous sea witch. Seltemver had rescued, not just him, but all the orcs on the ship from her grip of coercion and slavery. The crew had pledged their loyalty to the elven captain after that, of course, it was only supposed to be for a little while; sadly, this curse had other plans.

"I think this may work, Toth," Amonar said quietly as they both watched Seltemver and Kili walk, arm in arm through the Clock District.

"I doubt it, Am."

The aptly named, Clock District, was a place of merchants, storefronts, and grand villas. Here were the homes of the noble and the wealthy, the movers and shakers of Gear City, and, of course, anyone who made money off of those beneath them. The streets were packed with cobblestone—much smaller than Toth had ever seen—and the buildings all had a strange look to them. Winches, gears, and metal contraptions were everywhere, seemingly working magic doing everyday tasks. Toth had been told that it only seemed like magic because he didn't know how they worked, but it was still strange to see.

Children walked by with boxes that played music, men rode on metal frames like a horse with stirrups that circled around, and men stood on corners with parchment folded neatly with tiny script on them detailing the day's events.

The entire district was dominated by the massive clock tower, which was the only thing that Toth could understand readily. A massive sundial that worked by black iron hands, spinning in very slow circles. *We've seen some strange worlds, but this one takes the cake so far,* Toth thought as he turned the corner and almost ran into two ladies wearing foxes on their shoulders. *Honestly, what wouldn't these rich people wear?*

"Why hello, Amonar," one of the women said as they passed.

"Hello, Madam Bisu," the imp replied with a mock bow.

"Made quite the name for yourself here, haven't you?" Toth asked with a tusky grin.

"It's been nice, Toth, for once."

The giggle of the dwarven girl, Kili, brought Toth back to the very bad plan. The stout, but attractive dwarf was head over beard for Seltemver and it showed to everyone that could see them. He looked over and spotted Sombra, another of his crew, and nodded, setting his captain's horrible plan into action. He picked up his own pace, falling in behind the pair at about ten paces and staying with them.

"This is the place," Kili said pointing to the weapons shop. "Told you I could find it."

The shop had a blue color to the stone walls and the metal sign swinging from thin chains read simply, "The Etched Blade." Toth raised his fist and Sombra burst into action, ramming Seltemver so hard that the captain flew through the air and into the glass window of the shop. The elf in disguise smashed through the glass, shattering it into a thousand pieces, and rolled into the shop amid screams of fear and shock from the people inside.

"Where is my money, pirate?" Sombra yelled, brandishing a huge wooden club.

Seltemver made a grand gesture of placing Kili behind him as he stood and drew his enchanted blade, the gleaming steel shining in the torchlight of the shop for all to see. "You dare attack me, here?" Seltemver said in his best theatrical voice. "Filthy white hair!" The pair made a spectacle of attacking each other and dancing around the shop until armed men came running with a wealthy-looking nobleman at their head; not city guards but paid muscle.

"That's our cue, Amonar," Toth said ducking around the side of the shop and down an alley. They had scouted the area hours before and found the back door, reasoning that it would lead to the storage rooms; It was a start at least. With no time to waste, Toth gripped the handle and, with a grunt and heaving muscles, he ripped the door open, breaking the lock and slipping inside while the commotion of the fight up front had everyone distracted. They didn't have long before the confusion died down. "Look everywhere, Amonar," Toth said as he searched the back office. The orc knew that the slaver would have to have a basement or hidden room for any people he had stashed away.

Slavery wasn't exactly illegal in Gear City, but it was heavily frowned upon; so much so that anyone known to own slaves would lose favor in high society. The money was all too good though it seemed, from what they gathered talking to other sailors. So If this slaver had people, he would keep them well hidden.

"Here, Am," Toth said as he found a door with a heavy lock on it. He was no lock pick, so he went with his strengths. Toth wasted no time in shouldering through the wooden door, and as the frame splintered—and Toth was fairly certain his shoulder did as well—it revealed a steep staircase; a staircase that the orc clearly wasn't ready for. Toth kept running to avoid spilling into a tumble, keeping his balance and gaining momentum down the steep incline. The door at the bottom of the stairs looked to be a problem though.

This door was a thick one bound in iron and seemed a lot tougher than the one that just splintered his shoulder. *Well, when the devil rides...*Toth thought as he squared his other shoulder to the door and lowered his head. The orc hit the door like a thunderbolt, crashing through it with a scream of pain. The hinges on the soft stone gave before the wood did, but it had the same effect; he was in.

All's Well...

"Toth! Are you all right?" Amonar shouted from above.

"Help us!" voices called as the imp flew down the stairs, marveling at the destruction caused by the first mate.

Hells, that one is strong, Amonar thought as he flew into the room.

Toth was struggling to stand on shaky legs while looking around, the orc's mouth dropping in horror at the sight.

There were over a dozen filthy cages in this vast room with up to three people per cage. They were ragged and half-starved, begging to be set free. There was no sign of the sidhe.

"Get them out, Amonar," Toth said cradling his arm. "I'll look for the target."

"Toth, your arm." Amonar saw that the bone was showing and sticking out at an odd angle. He knew Grunhilde could help, but it would take weeks for the bones to heal, even with magic.

"I'll be fine, just get these people free."

Amonar saw a key ring on the wall and flew it over to a man in the first cell. "Free everyone and go," Amonar said. "There are sure to be weapons in the shop upstairs if anyone tries to stop you." The imp flew after Toth and stopped, prevented by going to the far wall by an invisible wall.

"Ixiar isn't here, Am," Toth said, staring at the back of the room.

"I think she is. I can't get to you, Toth," the imp said, struggling against the unseen barrier.

Toth turned and looked at the wall and started punching the stone, sure enough on the second hit a hollow thud rang true. The orc backed up and rammed the section of wall with his good shoulder and the stone pushed in a little bit. Two more hits and it was open.

"Is she there?"

Toth's answer came in a grunt and a metallic dragging sound as he re-emerged with a cage, a blue feathered sidhe inside. The creature was singing loudly, sending golden rays of healing energy into Toth's arm. Just in time too, as booted feet could be heard coming down the steep stairs.

"Toth?!" Amonar called out looking for somewhere to hide.

"Here," Toth said, setting down the cage and flexing his arm. The bones were set and the wound was fully healed. "Watch her while I deal with them."

Amonar swallowed and nodded, turning towards the sidhe that didn't exist in his world. "Nice to meet you, now hold on, things could get messy."

Nice to meet you as well, lost cousin, Ixiar said in Amonar's mind.

For once in he couldn't say how long, Amonar was speechless.

Seltemver strolled back to the *Seahaven* with Kili, her anger simmering like an overdone stew. She wouldn't even hold his arm as they walked, instead just stomping beside him the entire way in silence.

"You all right, Captain?" Sombra asked as they crossed out of the Clock District into the Ship Ward.

"I'm fine, Sombra," Seltemver reassured his crewman. Once the slaves had poured out of the basement and into the shop, grabbing any weapon they could and fighting their way clear, the orc had slipped away in the confusion and Seltemver had backed up with Kili and watched the armed men get trounced. When it had died down and the city guards had arrived, Seltemver had given a wildly different description of the assailant, much to Kili's complaints. In the end, he paid for the broken window and left the owner, one Hagan Finesteel, fuming at the loss of his slaves.

"Is she still mad?" Sombra asked.

"*Yes, I am still mad!*" Kili shouted at the pair as she turned on them in the middle of the cobblestone road.

"We couldn't tell you ahead of time, Kili. I'm sorry," Seltemver said with a frown. He was mildly confused about why he felt as bad as he did. Normally he didn't have any qualms about using people—after all, he never claimed to be a good guy—but for some reason, he felt bad for deceiving her like this; he wasn't used to this feeling. He had tried explaining it to her once they had left, but she just ignored him.

"You said as much," Kili said turning once more and stomping off. "I didn't believe ya then, and I don't, now."

"At least she's still headed for the *Seahaven...*" Sombra said with a half-shrug.

"Shut it, orc," Kili said not even bothering to turn around.

"If I could tell you why, I would," Seltemver started but he stopped when he spied a familiar orc carrying a large buddle in a cloak with an imp on his shoulder. "But if you happen to find out on your own..." Seltemver loosened his belt and took off his sheath. He drew his sword and winked at Sombra, running ahead. Seltemver quickly caught up behind Toth, the darkening shadows of the late evening helping him hide from both the orc's and the imp's scanning eyes. Seltemver tossed his sheath between the orc's legs, tripping him up, and watched the cage spill onto the street, the cloak flying off.

"What in the endless forge?" Kili swore as Seltemver rushed to cover the sidhe back up before anyone else could see.

"Do I want to know why, in all the deep hells, you did that?" Toth asked Seltemver as he climbed to his feet.

"Yeah, you almost gave me a heart attack!" Amonar said with a smile.

"You're immortal," Sombra said gruffly as he joined them.

"It's a figure of speech."

"So *that's* why you couldn't tell me? Because of some magical creature?" Kili asked, still not convinced. Then the dwarf's eyes went wide and she looked around frantically.

"Oh yeah, Seltemver, Ixiar can speak in your head," Amonar said. "Like unicorns could."

Toth picked up the cage covered with the cloak once more and started walking ignoring them all.

"Come, Kili. I think I can explain a bit more on the ship." Seltemver put his arm around the girl and led her away, leaving Sombra and Amonar to follow.

"He's going to get into trouble again, isn't he?" Sombra asked.

"Well, at least this one isn't a shapechanger," Amonar answered with a wry smile.

...That Ends Well

Amonar flew through the Forge District with a box of broken parts; scrap metal for the Forgemaster. Repairs were almost done on the *Seahaven* and soon they would be setting out once more towards that magical storm and be sent gods above knew where. He had been visiting the Forgemaster every day, spending what little time he had with Ixiar before he left this world, and he had learned that he was right; all the imps on this world had died in the demon uprising. In her world, the demons used the imps as fodder to attack the gods.

The sidhe had refused to fight their cousins and stepped aside. Krist slew them all, then punished the demons by locking them in the deep hells. The sidhe were cast out, sent to the world in-between to suffer their disobedience and live among the other races.

"Greetings Amonar!" Kili called out as he flew into the main temple of the forge.

"Hey Kili, are you *seeing* the captain tonight before we sail?" Amonar asked with a wink. The dwarf and Seltemver had been pretty close when they had the chance during the repairs, often taking long walks through the Clock District and disappearing for hours; much to her brother's dismay.

"Amonar!" Kili said, clearly embarrassed as her soot-stained cheeks turned red. "You know very well that we've been helping Gile with the new store."

Amonar rolled his eyes. "Helping with the new store...is that what they call it in this city?" Amonar laughed at her face and flew off towards the main forge. Kili wasn't exactly lying. Seltemver did help Gile take over the weapons shop after that slaver was run out of town. The other nobles found out about his slavery and shunned him, forcing him to close up shop and go north to somewhere called Ravensbrook. Now Kili would make the weapons in her apprenticeship, and Gile would sell them, giving a cut to the Forgemaster to help pay for Kili's smithing costs.

"Ah, here he is," the Forgemaster said walking towards the imp. "You have the scrap from the new cannon mounts?"

"Sure do," Amonar said dropping the box with a heavy thud. "The note said you had something for me to bring back as well?"

"It did. I knew you would want to say goodbye to Ixiar and I wanted to have you make one final delivery for me," the Forgemaster said with an odd look.

"This is going to get me in trouble, isn't it," Amonar said flatly.

"Not at all, but it will be met with skepticism." The Forgemaster pulled out a copper medallion, hanging from a golden chain. The symbol on the worked copper was Dava's, though it differed slightly in some of the etchings. It looked like the one Grunhilde had carved into a round piece of wood.

Amonar narrowed his eyes, still feeling like the man was hiding something. "How did you know about Grunhilde?" the imp asked tilting his head. "She's never talked about her being a healer to you that I know of." Amonar knew that the female orc had spent most of her time in The Bent Gear with her new drinking buddies, or in the ship, helping with the minor repairs; she said she didn't care about seeing the rest of the strange city.

"A mutual friend told me about who she worships and I was told to make this for her," the Forgemaster said with a wink as he pulled a medallion out of his pocket. "He said she had earned it."

"How would you..." Amonar froze, realization flooding him. The man in front of him wasn't just old, he was immortal. "You're an Incarnation, aren't you?"

"Of Dava or Davalar as they call him from the far west where I'm from originally." The Forgemaster stooped down and placed the worked copper medallion in Amonar's hands, folding his massive hands over the imp's red claws. He looked deep into Amonar's eyes and smiled. "Tell her this: *When you prayed at the altar as a child, you were heard but not fully believed. Once you felt your heart grow warm, I knew that your love was mine; now I repay that sacrifice.*"

Amonar was stunned, unable to speak. He nodded numbly and flew off to talk one last time with Ixiar and bid her farewell. He knew what the man was now, and he silently thanked the gods above that Seltemver didn't get this one angry with them.

Seltemver spun the new wheel as they slowly moved out of port and waved to Kili on the dock. The ship was as good as new, if not better considering it had never been new. The sails were fixed, the hull was sound and they had a bunch of upgrades that would give them an edge if it ever came time to use them. Even their cannons had been fixed, the moorings reinforced and the swivels replaced; they would be much easier to aim now.

"Grunhilde is still in her cabin," Toth said, concern etched on his stern face. His tusks were twitching with anxiety, as he searched the horizon for what they both knew was coming.

"I heard. Amonar says she will be all right," Seltemver assured the first mate. Amonar had told him who the Forgemaster was and he agreed that they got lucky. Getting the Incarnation of the God of Protection on your bad side wasn't high on his list of things to do.

"Still not going to say why are you?" Toth asked, clearly irritated with the captain's silence.

"I can just say that it is very personal to her and if she wants to fill you in, she will," Seltemver said with a wry smile. It wasn't every day that you got a message from your god saying you were doing great and from the little context he had, he knew that channeling the god's power had been rough for her in the beginning. This was like a massive pat on the back.

"Storm on the horizon, Captain!" Crak called out from the Crak's nest.

"Well, Toth, go test that new winch and set the sails for the wind. It's going to be a little better rid than the last time, but be ready for anything."

"Aye, Capt'n."

Here we go again, but at least this time things worked out better than usual. Maybe we're almost home...Seltemver thought as the edge of the storm came into view.

The City of Mys'tire

This is one of those stories that we will never let our beloved captain live down. the infamous story of the shapechanger that waylaid Seltemver. It was an awful place with elves who weren't elves and hidden dangers everywhere.

Daring fights, beguiling magic, and hidden dangers abound in this city. We barely made it out of this city and it's one of the few times I truly thought we were done for; more than once.

—Amonar

Strange Indeed

The gold-flecked gravel path that led away from the docks gave way to a solid wooden bridge that spanned the lazy river leading into the small harbor. He walked with a little bounce to his step, feeling good about this place they had ended up in. He and his crew had been on this cursed journey for a little over a year—to his best estimation—and they had seen some fantastic sights, from a turtle the size of an island to an all-out attack from female pirates in swan ships, and even an enchanted lord in impenetrable armor. When they sailed into this strange, stone-walled, harbor they had their reservations, yet they had seen elves from the ship, as well as some humans, and that gave them some hope. When they were waved in, no one seemed to care that an elven pirate captain had a crew of orcs and even after five minutes, no immediate shouts of alarm rang out.

Seltemver Ashblade smiled as a warm breeze came from the north, ruffling his short white hair in his eyes and blowing his worn longcoat out behind him. *It was nice for once not to be attacked the minute we arrive*, Seltemver thought. *Be even better if we could go the entire stay like that.* The elf walked across the bridge with his gaze scanning the weird buildings and sights, getting to know his surroundings just in case. The structures were an odd yellow stone color, all in a weird design that didn't resemble any race that he could name off the top of his head. It wasn't orc or dwarven, nor elven. The gold-flecked gravel seemed to serve as roads leading around the small city and torches stood on tall poles even in the middle of the day. The elves he saw went about their day without so much as a simple spell that he could see but kept to themselves, and they were all dressed in tunics of an odd yellow cloth; it seemed to be the color theme in these parts. In fact he stood out so much that it was a miracle no one had even given him a second glance as he strolled through the odd city. Another first to be sure, especially with his companion on his shoulder.

"At least they're elven this time," Amonar said from his perch on Seltemver's shoulder. "Maybe they won't want to kill you."

Seltemver scowled at the imp, then laughed. His little red companion wasn't wrong. Amonar was an imp from the deep hells, bonded to Seltemver due to a curse placed on the elven sea captain. The imp only stood about three feet tall with red skin, bat wings, and a two-foot-long tail. He had tiny horns on his head and a mischievous grin...until there was violence of any kind.

"Don't worry Amonar, I'm sure this place is going to be better than Freeport," Seltemver said. The last port of call was bad, almost getting killed by a warlord in enchanted armor. Even Seltemver's enchanted blade couldn't cut it, and it could slice through anything.

"Famous last words."

Seltemver sighed and followed a sign towards what he imagined was an inn, the sign swaying in the warm air reading *The Plaza*. Seltemver had left his ship, the *Seahaven*, in the strange stone docks they anchored at in search of answers to where they might be this time and what they could purchase for supplies. The curse that kept transporting them from world to world was a drain on the ship's stores as they never knew how long it would be and he always liked a full hold, just in case.

"How come none of the elves are using magic, Seltemver?" Amonar asked, an uneasy note creeping into his voice. His head darted from side to side now, taking in all the people.

"I don't know, Amonar," Seltemver answered, smiling at his old friend. Amonar was the only imp he had ever read or heard of that hated violence and bloodshed, actually hiding in fear when fights broke out.   Amonar had stepped up when it came time though...the imp couldn't let Seltemver die or he would be dragged back to the deep hells. Of course that would happen even if Seltemver died of old age as well, but he had a good eight hundred more years left before worrying about that. Seltemver spotted an elf coming out of The Plaza and stopped him, stepping in front of him and putting on his best *I'm friendly* face. "Excuse me," Seltemver started, but the elf backed up, bowing and apologizing.

"Sorry, sorry, I have no time," the elf said, hurrying away.

"All right, I am officially freaked out," Amonar said turning to follow the elf as he hurried away.

"I'm sure he was in a hurry," Seltemver said as he walked into the building. He didn't truly believe his own words, but there was no sense in worrying Amonar this early. Besides, he was a damned good blademaster in his own right and could stand against most warriors with his blade. "Now, let's go see what we're in for this time."

"Every time you say that we get into trouble," Amonar replied with a heavy sigh as he folded his tiny arms across his chest

A Tale to Hear

The Plaza was busier than it looked from outside, humans and elves all crowded at stone tables eating and drinking what looked like wine and an odd reddish-colored bread. Of course all conversation died when Seltemver walked in. They quickly went back to their food and drink, but at a much quieter pace, whispering in hushed tones.

"That can't be good," Amonar said quietly in Seltemver's ear as he clung to the elven pirate's shoulder.

"What can I get for you, stranger?" the female barkeep asked. She was a human with long curly red hair and sparkling green eyes; eyes that must've seen barely eighteen summers.

"My name is Seltemver and I'm simply looking for information, if you have any," Seltemver said pouring on his charm. "What do they call this city and who rules here?"

"I'm Pashan Vell and you happen to have come to Mys'tire, Free City of Jal'in Da," she said as she poured two drinks. They both seemed like some sort of wine—oddly colored and with a fruity smell—and she pushed them at Seltemver with a wink... "As for who rules, that would be Lady Dae'ri, Seventeenth Mistress of the Jal'in Da."

"Seventeenth what now?" Amonar asked, clearly confused by the odd title.

"Heh, not from around these parts are you?" Pashan asked, clicking her tongue. "Saw that fancy schooner you sailed in on, not bad."

"No, we're from the far north," Seltemver lied as he looked around at the patrons of the inn as they talked, taking a sip of his drink absently. No one was staring at all, just keeping to themselves. Odd.

"Argin, want to tell the tale?" Pashan asked an older man by the corner table.

The old man stood, a human in his very late years of life. The man had to have seen over eighty summers and could almost not stand without a wooden cane. "Aye, lass. That I would love to do," the man called Argin replied.

"I *do* love a good tale," Amonar said sarcastically.

"Shush, Amonar."

Hobbling over, Argin leaned against the bar and looked Seltemver straight in the eye as Pashan poured him a tall flute of orange-colored wine. "This here is the refuge of the Jal'in Da, an elven wizard that came to this deserted isle centuries ago to start over with his followers." The man took a sip of wine and cleared his throat. "It's said that he came because he was tired of how magic was enthralling his people, crippling them with how dependant they were using it in their everyday lives." Argin spun deceptively fast and slammed the countertop for effect. "They sought to break the ties of the ancient pact with the elements, to finally be free to be themselves...and Jal'in Da had the way to do it." Argin had become something more, almost transforming into a different person, channeling the story to give him power it seemed.

Seltemver knew that the old man was a bard now, only they could channel stories to this effect and he could feel himself being drawn into the very story as if he were there. He closed his eyes and took a deep breath, trying to hold off getting sucked too far in just in case this was a trap.

Argin kept going, animated by his tale now. "Jal'in Da found an ancient power to make a deal with, binding his soul and offering himself to this being in exchange for his followers to be free, but at a great cost. Jal'in Da was kept, bound, and imprisoned within the great Obelisk, forever being the beacon of freedom for our people here in Mys'tire and he rests there to this day, locked behind walls of stone; sleeping forever." Argin took a deep breath and seemed to come back to himself, his exhaustion almost crippling him.

"What power did this elf give himself to?" Amonar asked leaning forward.

"It was a being known only as the Great Ssmar," Argin said trying to catch his breath. "Now if you will pardon an old man, I need to go sit down." The old man bowed and hobbled away, smiling at the other patrons as he went, who silently applauded his tale.

"Well, does that answer your questions traveler?" Pashan asked.

"I think it does, however, it just opened up a few more," Seltemver said, sliding her a few gold coins. "Could you point me in the direction of this Lady Dae'ri?"

"You can't miss it. It's the large temple to the Northeast of the city. Follow the road and you'll get there," Pashan said with a smile as she scooped up the coins.

Seltemver bowed and made his way out of the inn, knowing that things just got a bit sketchier. Religious zealots were unpredictable at best and if that's what they were dealing with, getting supplies and leaving quickly was the only option. He looked at the buildings as they walked and took in the architecture. Not many of the dwellings had more than two stories and all of them used red cloths for covering the various openings. Cloth awnings and open archways dominated the designs and the same yellow stone seemed to be the only material for the buildings. Once again the people avoided getting too close, probably wary of strangers. "Any idea what this Ssmar could be, Amonar?" Seltemver asked as they walked down the gold-flecked road.

"No but I think we're about to find out," the imp said with a quiver to his voice. Amonar was pointing to the patrol coming their way, a gorgeous woman at their head.

"Well, bless Nor, that saved us some steps," Seltemver said as his hand went to the sword at his side.

The Lady in Red

Amonar had a bad feeling about all of this. The lady at the head of the patrol of soldiers didn't seem threatening, yet there was something about her that was making his stomach turn. She was tall—almost six and a half feet—and thin with curves in all the right places. She had very long raven black hair and her eyes resembled twin pools of emeralds; eyes that sparkled with joy as she looked Seltemver up and down. She wore only a long red dress—and not much of one for that matter—with no shoes or weapons on her person. Amonar didn't like her already.

"My my my, what a specimen *you* are," the lady said, her voice dripping with lust. Her hips swayed as she approached, the dress cut up the sides of her legs to reveal more skin than cloth. "And what brings an elf with a crew of orcs to my fair city?"

Seltemver bowed low. "We've only stopped at your fair city for supplies before we head back out," he said, looking at her with eyes that screamed interest. "You must be Lady Dae'ri."

"That I am, and you are?" she asked, stretching her arms above her head to reveal even more of herself. Her breasts were heaving now, her excitement plain to even a dumb ogrann for the gods' sake.

"His name is Seltemver," Amonar answered quickly, knowing that this woman was trouble already. She didn't smell right at all, even though she looked human. "And I'm Amonar."

"Well, Seltemver and Amonar," Lady Dae'ri said, as she subtly licked her red lips. "You both *must* come and dine with me at the temple. We can discuss what supplies your fine ship needs and let you *rest* for the night." The patrol of guards dispersed at a wave of her hand and went along down the road leaving the three alone. "Come." Lady Dae'ri walked away without waiting for an answer.

"Seltemver, I have a bad feeling about this," Amonar said as his friend started following.

"You always have a bad feeling, Amonar. Besides, we need some supplies before we leave in case we're stuck again in that storm," Seltemver said with a shrug. "Besides, she's human, so no magic to speak of, and she is no warrior; you can tell by the way she stands."

Amonar knew there was no arguing the point. Not when it came to his master and the *Seahaven*...or a pretty girl for that matter. Still that name, Ssmar was bothering him. It was there in the back of his mind somehow, like he should know it.

The rest of the walk to the temple was quick as it was right down the road. What bothered Amonar more was the lack of shops along the way. Sure they could just be in a ward or section of the city that didn't have any, but these buildings didn't seem like dwellings either. They all felt empty somehow like they were only shells meant to look like houses. Then there were those strange torches. They were bigger than usual and seemed to radiate heat more than give off light; made sense since they were lit during the daytime. There were also some strange water pumps, that seemed to channel water out of the ground and into buckets when the handle was pushed down again and again. Before Amonar could dwell on his surroundings anymore, the temple loomed up at them, dominating the northeast end of the city like a dragon poised over its horde.

The building was massive, compared to the other structures of the city, and had an enormous open doorway that stood atop a wide set of stone stairs. *What could be so big that they would need a giant door to get in?* Amonar thought as they walked towards the great opening. The stone structure was built in an odd way— being wider at the bottom and getting smaller the higher up it went—and bright yellow stone was built in layers every twenty feet or so, and seemed to radiate the same heat as the large torches around the city. *It's not like it's cold or anything,* Amonar thought as Seltemver climbed the stairs. *Why all the heat?*

"Welcome to the Temple of Jal'in Da," Dae'ri said, spinning slowly as she walked up the steps alongside the elven pirate captain. "Unfortunately, no weapons are allowed inside the temple as it also acts as the living space for the acolytes; no weapons are allowed in any dwelling here in Mys'tire," Dae'ri said with a slight frown. It seemed like she hated saying it to them, yet her eyes shone with a fierceness that belied that feel.

"I can run your sword back to the *Seahaven*, Seltemver," Amonar said, feeling that Toth needed to hear some of this before they went too far. Amonar didn't want to leave Seltemver on his own, yet his friend was right. This woman didn't seem like a warrior.

"An excellent idea," Dae'ri said, still not making eye contact with the imp.

"Yeah, why don't you run this back," Seltemver said, handing over the weapon easily without even a look. Seltemver wouldn't even look away and seemed different out of thin air.

"You want me to tell Crak that he's in charge of the ship?" Amonar asked, knowing that something was wrong. *Weird though,* he thought as he took the sword from his friend. *I can't even feel any influence on Seltemver.* The bond/curse usually helped keep Seltemver's mind safe against charm.

"Great idea," Seltemver answered.

Amonar knew that his friend was lost. Crak was not anyone even close to running the ship in his absence. It would've been the first mate, Toth, above anyone else. "Right away." Amonar turned to fly off as quickly as he could but stopped dead when he felt something bite into his back as he flew off. He cried out as another bite lashed into his other shoulder then everything went black.

Leaders Dilemma

Toth paced the ship as the messenger walked away, the burly orc still holding the crumpled parchment in his fist. His curved tusks, protruding from his mouth, twitched as he thought of what to do about what he just read and he didn't relish telling the rest of the crew; he knew their reaction would be just like his. Toth was the first mate of the *Seahaven* and acting captain until Seltemver came back, which, according to this missive, wasn't going to happen. The orc's long hair fell across broad shoulders as he paced back and forth and it wasn't long before he heard the one voice he was dreading.

"Well, where are they?" Grunhilde asked as the female orc stomped towards him. Her grey skin stood out among the rest of the crew as most of them had a darker, umber tone to their skin. The orc healer had long braids and a fierce smile, her tucks protruding higher up when she was angry; like now. Grunhilde had a fierce heart and a soul filled with compassion, even if she never showed it. It was the reason she could channel the healing power of the gods so well.

Toth handed her the crumpled missive and turned away, not wanting to see her face darken. He knew it was a lie, yet he didn't know what else to do. He listened to her grunt and huff while reading it

"I'm content and happy here?" The orc healer slammed her fist into the side of the railing. "I've found a home where I never thought I would?" Grunhilde took a couple of deep breaths, then laid a hand on Toth's shoulder. "Toth, you know this isn't him, right?" Grunhilde's voice turned uncharacteristically soft as she spoke.

Toth turned with a tusky grin, his dark eyes laced with uncertainty. "Of course, yet do I endanger the entire crew for him?" he asked pointing towards the channel gate. The harbor they had sailed into was walled off, with a massive gate that had been closed once they had docked. It was open now, with the small guard boats moving aside and clearing the way. Cannons rolled out from the top of the wall and leveled down, facing the sea; the message was clear. If the *Seahaven* wanted to leave in one piece, now was the time.

"And no mention of Amonar at all?"

"I know, that's what has me worried the most," Toth said. Unlike most of the crew, Toth liked the curious little imp. Amonar had saved them twice now, using his demonic powers, and most of the crew thought he would bring the dark gaze of Krist upon them. Not Toth though. He knew the little guy was just trying to help using what he was born with and he would level a stern gaze on any of his crew when they insulted the little imp. "I just..."

Grunhilde hauled off and slapped him across the face, spinning his head almost all the way around. "Let me help your tiny, troubled mind, Toth," Grunhilde said, a little more of her anger creeping into her voice. "We're going to go get Seltemver and Amonar back and then smash our way out of this place." The fire in her deep eyes seemed to burn into

Toth's and he smiled despite the blood trickling down his chin.

"Thank you, Grunhilde," Toth said as he stood a little straighter. "I needed that." Toth turned to the crew and whistled, then raised his fist and made a circle gesture. It was the way he called them all in for a meeting of importance and he saw them all grumble and shuffle in towards the helm.

"What is it, Toth?" an orc named Sombra asked, worry lined on his dark face.

"We're going to be leaving soon so I want the ship ready to run those waves within the day," Toth said, keeping his usually loud voice quiet. "The lady of the city is letting Grunhilde and I get some supplies and then depart without resistance."

"What about Seltemver?" the small orc named Crak asked, concern written all over his face. "And Amonar?"

"Well, we're going to have to get them by force," Grunhilde said in hushed tones. "I can't tell you much more, but we need a good plan and we have to be ready to run when it goes south.

"So normal trip, got it," Sombra said with a smile.

WAKING UP

He awoke with a headache and a very sore neck, his mind feeling like it had been hit with a small mountain. Seltemver rolled over and sat up, finding himself on a bed covered in red silk. The room was decorated in reds and gold, from the braided rugs to the tapestries on the yellow stone walls. His clothes were gone and he was in nothing but a long white silk robe. *What did I do last night?* he thought as he found himself naked underneath the robe.

"Oh you're awake," Lady Dae'ri said as she walked into the room. She in turn was wearing absolutely nothing, her breasts covered only by the long hair falling over her shoulders. Somehow it made her even hotter to look at.

Seltemver shook his head, knowing that he had duties to attend to and a crew that needed him, though the temptation was pulling at him like an ogrann. "Well I thank you for a wonderful night, but I must be getting back to my ship," Seltemver started. Not that he remembered the night, but best not to let her know that; women usually hate when men forget that stuff.

"Actually, there is someone here from your ship," Lady Dae'ri said sitting down next to him, her bare skin radiating warmth even this close. "Your second?"

"Must be Toth. He's my First mate," Seltemver corrected, then smiled. *Leave it to Toth to come get me.*

"I'll send him in," Dae'ri said with a smile, then ran her finger across Seltemver's leg as she stood.

Toth strode into the room a minute later, all business and his tusks twitching. "So this is where you ended up," the burly orc said, looking around the room.

"Yeah, did Amonar get my sword to the ship?"

"Yeah and we finished getting supplies this morning," Toth said. "Enough for another month at least."

"You did?" Seltemver was honestly shocked that they finished without him, but he secretly thanked the gods that he didn't have to. "Well, what do you think about staying for a couple of days?" Seltemver asked thinking about that warm goddess of a human that just left. He just couldn't get her out of his head.

"I'll ask the crew. Worst case we take the ship out and see what's around the island while you, uh, have fun," Toth said with an awkward wink.

"Well, don't go out too far, if that storm comes I'm stranded and the gods above know what would happen to Amonar if we were separated that far. The bond may kill us both," Seltemver said quietly so Lady Dae'ri couldn't hear. The last thing he needed was for her to know about the bond between Amonar and himself.

"Don't worry, Capt'n, we won't go too far from shore, just give the men something to look at besides the stone docks," Toth said then turned and strode out.

Seltemver frowned, knowing that something felt off, but a minute later Lady Dae'ri came back in, still absolutely devoid of clothes and staring at him like he was her next meal. All thoughts of the ship and crew flew out of his head as she laid him down and crawled up his body. Yes, it was time for a little vacation.

He awoke with a headache and sore wings, his arms feeling like they were weighed down; mainly because they were. Amonar looked around in a daze to see that he was chained to a damp stone wall, water dripping slowly down over his head. What was even worse was the chains were cold wrought iron, the one substance that could hurt him if used right, so he couldn't even try to struggle or the restraints would cut into him.

"Oh he's awake," a cold voice spoke from the shadows.

"I'd rather not be," Amonar said still trying to figure out what happened. The last thing he remembered was that pain in his back and shoulder.

"What did you do to anger the lady?" another voice asked, this one female. "Did you speak out against Ssmar as well?"

"No, I don't think so. I'm not sure what even happened," Amonar said, that bad feeling creeping up his tiny spine and wrapping cold fingers into his gut. "Is that what you did?"

"All of us in here have," the first voice said, the cold tone even deeper now. An elf stepped forward into the light and smiled, his features shocking. The elf was completely bald with small fangs protruding from his mouth. Scales covered his head, shoulders, and upper arms and even his thighs had some snake-like skin. "Though our numbers are dwindling, people are starting to take a stand."

"You're not an elf," Amonar said backing up against the wall.

"No. Not anymore," the female said as she came closer. She too had no hair and scales, but her fangs were longer. She had one arm that was almost all snake with no hand at the end of it. "We haven't been in a long time."

"And this, Ssmar, did this to you?" Amonar wished he could use his magic to break free, but he couldn't use it for himself...stupid rules.

"Indirectly. It was the bargain that Jal'in Da made with him that did this. Ssmar would take our magic and we would live in peace and harmony, but we were never told about the consequences," the man said, slinking back into the shadows. "Now we live every day in the warmth just to stay awake. We can never rest."

"What happens if you sleep?" Amonar asked, still irritated that Ssmar sounded so familiar. Something about the cold was nagging him again. It all fit, he was sure of it.

"If we fall asleep, we shed and become more monstrous each time, eventually turning into giant snakes for the lady to keep inside the Obelisk," the woman said.

Amonar closed his eyes and tuned it all out, trying to think of why this sounded so familiar. He was sure there was a way out if he could just figure out what was doing this. The cold! "Wait, that Obelisk," Amonar said, remembering that it stood out when they sailed into the closed-off harbor. The tall pillar had a huge stone base with massive fires all around it, burning endlessly throughout the day. He originally thought it was a religious thing and put it out of his mind, but what if it wasn't just a beacon...but a prison? *The demon we found on the isle of the sea witch was imprisoned by its weakness, what if it's the same here,* Amonar thought, *but all the demons I know love fire...Wait. What if it's not a prison?* Amonar knew it had to be Ssmarylix and that knowledge didn't comfort him whatsoever.

Ssmarylix was a demon whose form was a long snake with twin human heads. He preferred to turn humanity snakelike, their souls tasting sweeter somehow, and had a weakness to cold. "Oh gods above, no wonder this place seems empty. You're all being drained slowly." They were doomed.

Breaking In

They left the longboats near the bridge on the southern ward of the city, knowing that the ship would be hard-pressed to leave once the fighting started; and there would be fighting, they knew this now.

Toth had awoken this very morning to find their cannons sabotaged, the iron mountings dissolved and the wood eaten away. It seemed like some sort of acid was used quietly in the dead of night and no one had seen or heard anything. So once the sun dropped below the horizon they took two longboats and four of the crew—including Toth and Grunhilde—and paddled quietly under cover of darkness to the southern bridge.

"Now what?" Grunhilde asked quietly as they moved off the gold-flecked road and into the grass near the buildings.

"That way," Toth said pointing to the large structure that rose in the east. It had to be where the lady resided and his captain was being held. Seltemver had to be held against his will. The elf wouldn't abandon them, not after what they had been through so far. The four of them snuck through the empty buildings, the sounds of chanting in the distance making them anxious. Elves didn't sleep, so darkness wasn't perfect but it helped hide them a little.

"These torches are warm, Toth," one crewman, named Hagain, noted as they moved past one in the shadows. "Far more heat than something like that should."

Toth shook his head, knowing now what Seltemver was always saying about stealth on a mission; these orcs could never keep quiet to save their own lives, never mind someone else's. *I hate when that elf is right,* Toth thought with a grim smile. He would get his captain back if it killed him, he owed that elf far too much not to.

The entrance to the massive temple loomed in the darkness, lit by those weird torches that cast flickering light and radiated warmth. Better yet, there were no guards at the entrance.

"We're either extremely lucky, or we're going to be dead," Grunhilde whispered as they crouched across the road from the huge opening. "And why is it so big?"

"I'm not sure, but let's not find out," Toth said with a frown. He looked both ways down the road and when no one could be seen, he dashed for the other side, leaping into the shadows when he could. He was a big orc and hiding wasn't his specialty. Still, with no one around it seemed like he didn't need to worry about that for once. The four of them snuck into the building and stopped dumbfounded. The entry hall was even bigger than the doorway!

The main hall was easily fifty feet high, with archways almost thirty feet tall. The whole structure seemed built for giants and it made every one of them look at each other with the look that screamed *run.*

"Toth..." Grunhilde started but he cut her off by grabbing her shoulders and looking into her eyes with his own fierce stare.

"I know, but it doesn't matter. That elf saved us and gave us another chance, and I will not leave him without a fight," the burly orc said, determination prevalent in his deep voice. It bolstered the others and even Grunhilde nodded, taking her axe in hand now and gripping the haft with white knuckles. Nothing scared the female healer, but giants were another thing altogether.

Toth looked around and tried to see some door that would lead down to the lower levels, a dungeon if you will. It wasn't a guarantee, but it was where he would keep prisoners. "Fan out and look for a door that seems locked," he said to the others, then moved ahead slowly.

He hadn't gone more than fifty feet when he heard people arguing far away. They were annoyed at something—or someone—and he could guess what it was just by the sheer exasperation in their tone. "Amonar," he swore with a tusky grin. Toth waved to the others and they padded quietly across the floor to the east wall. A large door stood locked and they could hear it now.

Amonar was hurt, his pride mortally wounded by the sheer hate from his cellmates. He had nothing to do but talk since the wrought iron shackles kept him from even trying to get free, but they didn't seem to like it.

"Would you please stop babbling?" the man asked, clearly annoyed.

"I'm just saying that if you guys all stood up to the demon and put out the fires maybe you could break free," Amonar said with a half smile. "Ssmarylix is weakened by cold." Amonar wasn't exactly sure it could work, but leaving a demon free was never a good idea.

Before the man could turn his venomous words on the imp the door to the dungeon shook with a loud crash. Stone dust rained down on them as something hit the door again, and again, finally breaking the hinges out from the soft stone walls. There stood Toth, the burly orc rubbing his shoulder as Grunhilde slipped past him.

"Toth, Grunhilde! It is so good to see you both," Amonar said getting to his feet. He held out his arms to Grunhilde as she came towards him and raised her axe. The weapon came crashing down, severing the chains and freeing the imp from his shackles.

"I see your cellmates are just as annoyed at your talking as we are?" Grunhilde asked, turning and freeing the woman. The orc healer leapt back at the sight of the woman but shook her head to clear it and set about freeing her anyway.

"They're not elves, Toth. There is a demon loose in the city and Seltemver is in trouble." Amonar flew over to Toth's shoulder, sticking his tongue out at the man as he went past.

Shattered Visions

He heard the shouts and cries out his window, but those hands were on him again, caressing his back and neck. Seltemver rolled over and looked into Lady Dae'ri's eyes and smiled, knowing a peace he hadn't felt in a very long time. The deep emerald eyes reflected a trouble that he hadn't noticed before and it started to bring him around to his surroundings a bit more. "What's wrong?" Seltemver asked, sitting up.

"Nothing, my love," Dae'ri said turning away from his gaze. "There is just an argument downstairs that I have to attend to." She slid him another drink then stood and walked to the door, her naked body glistening in the moonlight. Dae'ri stopped at the doorway and looked back, her smile promising exquisite pleasure. "Now just get ready for when I come back, I expect to be worn out again, Seltemver."

Seltemver raised his mug, heard a loud crash, and stopped; that didn't seem like an argument. He set his drink down and stood, looking for his clothes. *Funny, I don't even remember where they are?* he thought as he searched the wardrobe for something to put on. He was about to give up and throw on a robe of teal green when he saw a box at the bottom of the wardrobe and his sword next to it. It was pushed in the back and tucked away neatly. *I gave that to Amonar to bring to the ship.* The shock broke him out of the trance he was in and the fog in his mind seemed to start to burn off. That's when he recognized the shouts.

"Captain!" Toth's voice rang out from the outer hall.

"Your captain is a bit indisposed right now, brute," Dae'ri's voice said coldly, "so you can deal with me now."

Seltemver got dressed quickly, strapping his sword on and running into the hall. He saw four of his crew fighting elves and a monstrosity that could only be Dae'ri. "What are you?" Seltemver asked as he drew his enchanted sword and fell into a fighting stance.

Dae'ri was almost human-looking—her sexy body having all of the curves that he had known for the last couple of days—yet she was definitely *not* human. Her arms seemed like tentacles and her hair was made of long snakes, the forked tongues flickering out at her enemies. Her legs turned into twin tails at the knees and seemed to hold her up as they slithered forward, her body was covered in dark green scales where these snake-like appendages started and her hair was hissing now.

"Seltemver! You're all right!" Amonar shouted, flying behind the orcs from the ship.

Seltemver knew it was grave indeed if that imp wasn't hiding when violence was in progress. *Things must truly be dire,* he thought with a smile. He could always count on his friends it seemed. "I am now," Seltemver said as he saw Dae'ri turn towards him. In a flash she was normal again, sauntering towards him swaying those hips.

"Oh dearest love, why don't you go back and finish that drink," Lady Dae'ri started, but stopped as a sword appeared at her throat in a flash.

"Party's over, Dae'ri," Seltemver said, running past the woman and fighting the other elves to get to his crew. They weren't truly elves but a weird hybrid of snake and elf, all semblance of hair gone as their wigs fell off in combat.

"I knew a woman was at the bottom of all of this," Grunhilde said as she swung her axe into two of the hybrids.

"Fools!" Dae'ri shouted, throwing her hands up. Her monstrous visage was back—no doubt her true form—and she closed her eyes and clenched her her hands into fists. "Ssmarylix, aid me in destroying my ene..." Her strangled plea was cut short by a meaty hand closing around her throat as Toth picked her up off of the floor with one hand.

Toth swung his axe into another snake-elf as he slammed Dae'ri against the wall. "Can we please get out of here now?" the big orc asked, clearly pushing the limits of his endurance. He was covered in cuts, and what looked like bites, but none of them seemed mortal at least. Toth tossed Dae'ri as far as he could and gestured for Grunhilde to lead the way. The female orc healer had bites across her arms and back as well and two other crew seemed like they had very deep cuts on their chest and legs.

Seltemver ran after them with a cloudy head, but it was clearing fast. They burst out of the temple and hit the streets at a run, but slowed as they could hear more people coming from every direction.

"Did she lock you up too?" Amonar asked, rubbing his wrists as he sat perched on Seltemver's shoulder once more.

"No, I think she charmed me. I was quite content to pass the rest of my years in her arms until you all came and broke me out of that daze.

"But you can't be charmed," Amonar said with a troubled look.

How did she manage that? Seltemver wondered as they made their way down the street cautiously, sticking to the shadows now. Speed would only get them surrounded. Then it hit him; the drinks. Elves were very hard to enthrall, and him more than others because of the bond he had with Amonar, yet Dae'ri had him fully under her charms with a natural remedy.

Seltemver had been consuming that weird wine since the Inn and Dae'ri had kept giving it to him as well. He assumed it was a favorite among the inhabitants, but now he could see that it may have been drugged. Elves were susceptible to natural sedatives and toxins, like plants and fungus and he knew of a couple that could also be used to cloud people's minds if taken enough. Dae'ri must've found something similar and made it into wine.

A Little Distraction

Seltemver crept alongside his crew as the night deepened and saw that Amonar was knocking over those weird torches as they went. "Care to fill me in?" Seltemver asked after the third such torch.

"Long or short version?" Amonar asked as he wrapped his tail around another torch and pulled it down.

"Well considering all the time we have..." Toth said with a modicum of sarcasm.

Amonar huffed then landed on Seltemver's shoulder as he pointed to another torch for Grunhilde to take out. "I found out that Ssmar is a demon whose weakness is cold. He has been keeping it warm here so he has more power over his disciples. If they fall asleep, they shed and become more snakelike, eventually being given to him for their souls. It's like he is draining the community slowly of their very souls and they embrace it; well most of them do."

"So not a great place," Seltemver surmised with a crooked grin.

"Oh he's quick," Grunhilde said as she ripped up the massive torch and tossed it down. "Too bad he fell for the wrong girl."

"She was a shapechanger, for Syll's sake," Seltemver fired back as they went on. "How was I supposed to know?"

"Guys, we can belittle our captain once we're away from the murdering psychopaths," Toth said in a hushed voice.

"Speaking of murdering psychopaths," Seltemver said looking around. "Why haven't they attacked us yet?"

"Because there is only one way to the harbor and it's over that bridge," Grunhilde said as she pointed to the mass of people standing in front of said bridge.

Seltemver cursed and stopped, moving towards the shadows. They hadn't seen them yet, but if they kept going it would only be a matter of time before they were spotted. "Any plans?"

"Well, we left the longboats under that bridge so we need a distraction to get to them," Toth said evenly as they all crouched in the shadows of the buildings. "There are two boats and six of us…"

"Seven," Amonar countered.

"You don't count, you can fly," Hagain said.

Before Seltemver could say a word, Toth hit the orc square in the head, rocking the crewman hard. It wasn't a pulled punch by any means.

"You do not speak like that to a member of the crew, understand Hagain?" Toth asked as the orc sat back up and rubbed his head,

"I didn't mean anything…"

Toth raised his fist again and the orc backed down. "Now say you're sorry."

"Toth, it's all right, I'm sure…"

Toth raised his fist to Amonar with a wink that Hagain couldn't see. "You interrupting the first mate?"

Grunhilde chuckled quietly as she stood, brushing the dirt from her knees. "Well, while you boys play, I'm going to go distract those idiots. Get to the boats and be ready to catch me," the healer said as she took off at a dead run before anyone could stop her.

"What did she mean 'catch me'?" Hagain asked, to which everyone there shrugged their shoulders.

Seltemver watched his only healer run at the bridge like a runaway wagon and smiled. They wouldn't know how bad it was going to be until it was too late. "Let's go, she will be worse than an angry dragon if we miss this opportunity," Seltemver said as he ran silently behind the buildings. He watched the bridge through the gaps and saw Grunhilde grab a torch and toss it at them, taunting them to catch her. Once they all rushed her, she ran at them and slid on the ground through them, tripping most of them and getting to her feet quickly amid the confusion. She swung it hard into the rear flank of the group, scattering them and drawing their full attention.

"There," Toth said as he pointed to the boats under the bridge. The burly orc grabbed one with Hagain and Kona, while Seltemver took the other with Amonar.

"I'll get Grunhilde," Seltemver said quietly as he looked up at how the female orc was doing. Grunhilde was sprinting toward the Obelisk now, almost the whole town on her heels.

"That woman knows how to distract all right," Amonar said.

"You guys head to the ship and start getting her ready…" Seltemver said but Toth's laugh cut him off.

"No need, Captain. I instructed the crew to sail the minute there was any fighting. The *Seahaven* is already underway," The first mate said, pointing to the silhouette of the ship as it came closer. "Just hurry and grab that foolish woman." Toth grabbed the oars and heaved the longboat into the harbor, heading right for the ship.

Seltemver grabbed the oars and moved out towards the obelisk, wondering what Grunhilde did mean by *catch me.*"

"There she is," Amonar said pointing at the female figure by the fires. "Oh..that's what she meant."

Seltemver looked and saw immediately what Amonar figured out. Grunhilde was running right for one of the odd water pumps that they had seen. She was going to flood the fires at the obelisk.

Grunhilde took her axe and bashed the pump hard as she ran by, the water gushing out and carrying her along with it as it roared toward the flames. The rushing water took out two of the three flames and washed the healer into the harbor. A scream of pure rage went up from the obelisk and reverberated throughout the city.

"Time to go," Seltemver said as he neared Grunhilde and pulled her into the longboat.

"You think?" Amonar said as he pointed towards the main wall of the city. Cannons were being pulled out and smaller ones were already firing at them and the *Seahaven* as it slowed for them.

Under Fire

Seltemver winced as he saw his ship rock again as more cannon fire hit it, tearing holes in the hull. Thankfully none had hit too low, but the ship would still take on water eventually. Grunhilde was on the oars now, her well-muscled back straining as she gave it everything she had to catch the ship; it seemed like the entire city was mustered against them now.

The ramparts on the great wall surrounding the city teemed with the elf-snake hybrids, leveling cannons and even bows at the ship as well as along the shore firing at the longboat. "Why aren't we returning fire?" Seltemver asked as Grunhilde rowed as hard as she could.

"Because someone, or something, sabotaged the cannon mounts," She answered shortly.

Hells, Seltemver thought. If they fired those canons, they would recoil right off the other end of the ship with that much force not anchored. A loud screech brought him out of his thoughts and gave them all pause as the Obelisk shattered at the top, spilling stone all over the harbor, raining down on them all. Large chunks hit the water with heaving fountains of water and more than a few city dwellers were crushed by the falling debris. Huge snake-like tendrils spread out of the top of the shattered monument and they didn't seem friendly at all.

"This would be a good time to be on that ship," Amonar said with his trembling voice.

"Well now that I know that I can stop rowing in circles," Grunhilde fired back sarcastically. They were almost fifty feet from the fleeing ship when cannon fire hit the side of the longboat, shattering it instantly.

Seltemver came up from the water dizzy, thanking the gods that the steel shot was normal and not magical in nature as some were designed to explode on contact through the enchantments placed on them. Still it left them dead in the water, so to speak. The *Seahaven* had slowed for them, but it could never hope to slow enough for them to swim the rest of the way and still survive intact. Seltemver knew Toth would have to escape the harbor if the crew were to survive.

"That damned stupid orc," Grunhilde sputtered next to him as she tread water.

Seltemver turned his head to see the *Seahaven* turning now, coming around in a sharp spin. They had probably dropped the anchor to make the tight turn, then would cut it loose and slingshot towards them. "Damn it to the hells, Toth," Seltemver swore as he started swimming towards the ship. Amonar had already flown over and was pointing at the Obelisk, no doubt informing Toth of the demon.

"He wouldn't," Grunhilde said as she swam next to Seltemver. A loud boom sounded as the *Seahaven's* cannon fired, followed by an enormous crack.

"He did," Seltemver answered as he saw the cannon recoil back into the mast of the ship. They had set it against the mast for support to try and anchor it, but the force was too much. The mast cracked and fell, decimating the sails and taking out orcs as it fell. The cannon shot hit the Obelisk and shattered the weakened structure, collapsing it almost entirely around whatever was coming out. The responding scream was so loud that everyone in the city had covered their ears, but that meant they weren't firing at the ship.

"All aboard, Captain," Toth called down as they came alongside the ship. Rope ladders were tossed down and they were on board in minutes, attempting to turn once more and flee the city of Mys'tire.

Last Legs

Seltemver spun the cracked wheel and brought the *Seahaven* around as the snake-men regrouped and started firing once more. Whatever was coming out of that obelisk was quiet and, thank the gods above, they were almost free of the stone harbor.

"You would think they would've tried to block the gate," Toth said coming over to the helm as the *Seahaven* came around sluggishly and aimed for the open sea.

Seltemver laughed as he struggled to get the rudder to listen to him. "You know they have more cannons on the outer ramparts right?" Seltemver reminded him. They had seen the two large shelves when they sailed into the sealed stone harbor and they both knew what they were for.

"Yeah, but I've got that covered," Toth said as they passed through the thick stone gate. The burly orc turned and bellowed to his crew as they passed and four orcs opened fire with longbows, taking out the snake-men manning those cannons.

"We made it!" Amonar shouted as they cleared the gate and sailed out into the ocean. Cannon fire echoed from behind them as more men replaced their fallen comrades, but the distance was too great now.

"Yeah but the damage has already been done, Amonar," Seltemver said sullenly as he felt the ship start to list more and more as the waves splashed into the holes in the sides of the ship. A loud snap resounded across the deck as the main boom broke free and smashed into an orc, sending him to the deck like a child's doll.

"Kona!" Grunhilde yelled as she raced to his side.

"Toth!" Seltemver called out as he saw the storm on the horizon. "Here it comes!"

Toth sprinted to the boom and grabbed the heavy rope in both hands, pulling it into place. "I've got it, Capt'n," the first mate said as he hauled it down. His corded muscles taut as the rope he held.

"Are we going to make it, Seltemver?" Amonar asked from the elven pirate's shoulder.

The *Seahaven* hit the edge of the magical storm with a wail of agony, its frame groaning in protest. Seltemver didn't answer the imp, instead, he grinned into the wind and rain, narrowing his eyes at the danger. His short white hair stuck to his face as the wind picked up even more, and his worn longcoat flapped about him like a tattered flag. "One last time into the dark, old friend," Seltemver yelled as the *Seahaven* tipped dangerously to port as the waves hammered it.

The Last Storm

This is it, the last entry of our long journey. I would like to say I will never write another one, but the truth is, I don't know what is going to happen now. The ship has been traveling for years at this point and it can only be fixed or patched up so many times,

At least I think it's been years... I lost count at five—or was it six—but it shouldn't be much more than that...I think. Anyway, here is the one that ended it all. I thank you for joining me on this trip and hopefully, if the gods above are willing, I will see some of you again, someday.

—Amonar

Unexpected Release

He spun the wheel as the *Seahaven* came out of the storm with nary a trouble, the crew looking around at the calm seas with distrust. Usually, the magical storm that threw them into different worlds was violent and menacing, but this last journey was...well, pleasant. *And completely unexpected*, he thought. The rain and wind were there, of course, but it was by far the easiest time they had ever had. In fact the storm rarely ever let them go this easily. His short white hair was barely soaked this time, and his longcoat was just hanging on his slender frame, certainly drenched by the rain but untouched by the slight breeze. The gentle storm retreated as the clouds parted and they could tell they were, once more, somewhere else.

Seltemver Ashblade frowned and looked out at the apparent dual suns of this world and squinted; his distrust written all over his elven features. over at his first mate. "Why is it that the calm storm makes me worry a lot more?" Seltemver asked the burly orc.

"To be honest, I'm right there with you, Capt'n," Toth said as he turned and started shouting orders to the crew. They didn't need to be told what to do at this point in their travels, but It was the orc's job and he enjoyed it. Toth had umber-colored skin, as most orcs did, and curved tusks protruding from his mouth. His long hair fell across broad shoulders and his heavily muscled arms bore tattoos of various weapons.

"Well if something makes us all agree then the world may very well be ending," Amonar said from his perch next to Seltemver. Amonar was an Imp bonded to Seltemver due to a curse placed on the elven sea captain many years ago. Amonar stood about three feet tall with red skin, bat-like wings, and a tail that reached two feet in length. Tiny horns sprouted from the top of his head and he had claws for hands and feet. Immortal and powerful, the imp was also afraid of violence and bloodshed; a conundrum to be sure.

Seltemver laughed at shook his head, knowing that the imp was right. "We'll face it like we have every time, old friend."

"Someone will try and kill us and then we run?"

"Precisely," Seltemver said nodding to the female elf in the Crak's nest as she signed that all was clear ahead. The Crak's nest was named that for the small orc that had been with them; the only orc that could fit up there. Crak had been killed, like so many others in Seltemver's past, and now the memory of the brave orc would live on in the hearts of the crew.

Amonar wiggled his fingers at the female elf, named Silence, and smiled with pride when she signaled back. "She says there could be an island up ahead," Amonar said grinning ear to pointed ear.

"You're getting much better at sign language Amonar," Seltemver said to his friend. Silence was found years back on a slave island and she was completely mute, her vocal chords destroyed at birth by the slave masters.

Silence leapt over the edge of the nest and grabbed the sides of the ladder sliding down and landing on the balls of her feet with a grace that told of her elven heritage. She had started growing her white hair out more and it was now past her shoulders, complementing her slight waist and shoulders. Deceptively small, she was no less deadly at the sword than most warriors on board, if not a bit more graceful.

"Toth, get the longboat ready," Seltemver called out to his first mate as Silence came over.

"You mean our last longboat?" Toth answered with a wry smile.

"Some of those weren't my fault," Seltemver countered, knowing that he had indeed lost some of the ship's longboats. They were down to one after the apocalypse world and had been for the last two worlds. Thankfully these last two were relatively calm visits and only once did things get out of hand. The last one was all fog with eerie voices drifting on the slight winds.

Silence moved her hand in a circle and thumped her chest, drawing all the orcs' attention to that region of her anatomy. Being one of the few females on the ship tended to do that, though no one had ever made any advances on her.

"Ha! You have the right of it, Len," Toth said using the nickname he had come up for her; the burly orc never felt right calling her Silence. "You'll keep him in line all right."

"She'll try," Amonar corrected.

Seltemver ignored them all with practiced ease and focused on the approaching island, praying that this one would go smoothly.

That Was Quick

Seltemver gave Sombra the wheel and strode to the rail once the island came closer. He was wary of their semi-good fortune lately and knew that something was coming sooner than later; he just didn't expect it to be sooner.

"Capt'n!" one of the orc crew called out as they sailed closer to the island. The tall orc pointed to the mass of dead trees and rotting grass and his arm visibly shook. "How can it all be dead?"

"Well that was quick," Amonar said as the imp landed upon Seltemver's shoulder. "Think the entire island is like that?"

"We'll sail around and try and figure that out," Seltemver said quietly. They could see a large ruined city now, a rubble of crumbling walls and nothing else. "Sombra, take us around within a half mile. Toth, get your looking glass ready."

"Aye, Sir. What are we looking for?" Toth asked pulling out the slender metal tube. They had found it on one of their adventures and it could see things with near demon sight.

"Life of some kind, or even an intact town. Can't resupply in ruins now can we?" Seltemver turned to Silence who had followed behind him. He swept his arm out to the ocean and pointed to himself and Amonar, then to the stairs. Silence nodded and took off at a brisk walk, heading down to the galley and packing rations for the three of them.

"You want her to get Grunhilde and send us to the bottom of the sea?" Amonar asked scratching his head. He was doing well at the sign language that Silence used, but some things evaded him still.

Seltemver ignored him and watched the waves lap against his ship as they sailed. It was a calm day, with very little in the way of storms on the horizon, yet he could feel something coming regardless. They soon found another set of large ruins nestled between three large rivers that spilled out into the sea, these ruins seemed to have better walls yet it was destroyed nonetheless. *What could've happened here that no one survived?* Seltemver asked himself as they sailed on.

Shortly after that a huge chasm came into view and most of the crew came to the rail to see it. You could see most of it without the looking glass and the sheer devastation this open wound in the earth conveyed shook them all to the core. The ground seemed black around it and spread out across the dead grass like a plague. Whatever hit to make a hole in the ground of that size had to be from the blackest heavens indeed.

"Town, Capt'n!" Toth yelled as they sailed on past the chasm. "Though I call it that loosely."

Seltemver took the device from his first mate and looked into it himself, seeing what the orc meant immediately. The town wasn't in ruins, per se, but seemed abandoned and devoid of life. Structures still stood, albeit with holes in them and some of the walls collapsed. The buildings were all dark and stained by something and nothing stirred in his view as they neared the weathered, crumbling docks. The eerie silence of the scene just added to the ominous feel of what he was seeing and he handed the glass back to Toth.

"We headed to those docks Seltemver?" Toth asked.

"Hells no. Drop anchor a ways out and we'll still plan to row in. If anything happens Amonar can come get you guys to rush in and save the day."

"Why, you plan on hitting on beautiful women again?" Grunhilde asked as she came up from below decks.

"For the love of..." Seltemver started but the female orc cut him off.

"I know, she was a shapeshifter. Gods above that's all we hear." Grunhilde laughed and slapped her captain on the shoulder. Grunhilde was a huge, grey-skinned orc with long braids and a fierce smile. The best healer Seltemver had ever seen, Grunhilde had a good eye and a bedside manner that could level a mountain. She got the job done though, and it still amazed him that she could channel the healing power of the gods, even a little.

"Yes, well, It doesn't seem to be anyone here so this could just be a quick grab and go," Seltemver said, clasping forearms with the fierce orc healer. They had a special bond and they had each saved each other's life more than once. "Besides, I trust you to come save me if I get into trouble."

"If?" Amonar questioned with a laugh.

"He's not wrong," Toth agreed as they all laughed together while the longboat was lowered.

Ur Doma

Seltemver rowed the longboat into the ruined docks with a sense of trepidation. Not that he was overly worried about getting attacked, between his skill and his enchanted blade he could fight his way out of a great many threats, no. The worry was for what could cause an entire island to seemingly wither and the folk to disappear. They passed a lone ship, abandoned as well and barely afloat, as they approached and saw that the hull was indeed cracked and flooded, the only thing keeping the ship up was a great sandbar it seemed to be resting on.

"This is not creepy at all," Amonar said from the middle seat. His beady eyes darted back and forth scanning for any signs of trouble. Not to warn his friends so much as to have plenty of warning to hide.

Silence was quiet—no pun intended—as they walked up the docks and into the quiet town. The sign hanging by one lone chain at the end of the docks proclaimed it *Ur Doma*. Orcish for something, but Seltemver had never bothered to learn the language, as the crew always spoke common. *Never thought to ask why that is though,* Seltemver thought.

[the house] Silence signed as they both looked at her. She was bred as a slave to a nation of orc masters so had learned to read at least their language.

"Well, that's odd, to say the least," Amonar said before Seltemver could answer. "But at least it doesn't mean Death Town or something like that."

They walked the streets slowly, stopping once inside at the hock of what they were seeing. Trails of what could only be dried blood were everywhere. Down sidewalks, into doorways, even up the walls of what was left of some of the buildings. Yet strangely, there were no remains of any kind. If it had been decades ago, at least the skeletal remains of the victims would have been left behind, yet there were only the blood trails.

"Uh, Seltemver? Can we go back to the ship now?" Amonar asked in typical fashion.

"No, Amonar," Seltemver said sharing a concerned look with Silence. "At this point, we need supplies at least so let's search some of the homes and see what we can salvage. Food, water, anything." You need to know what happened, don't you?" The imp asked, knowing his old friend very well.

"If this could happen to the crew, then yes I need to know what happened," Seltemver answered evenly. "If it is a curse then we don't want to bring it back."

"Don't you think we have enough curses?"

"One would think."

Silence waved from another building and the two went to see what she found. The female elf had filled two bags already and was pointing to the rear window.

"Great find, Silence. What else did you..." Seltemver stopped mid-sentence as he saw what she was pointing to. A smaller building had piles of boxes and barricades by the door, covered in blood trails and pools of dark dried liquid. Here though lay swords and axes in piles, as if whoever had done this wanted who found this to know how ineffectual they had been.

"And I bet we have to go over there don't we?" Amonar asked, his voice shaking.

"It will be fine Amonar, you know things tend to go for me first anyway," Seltemver said to reassure his friend.

"Tend? More like you always start it so they attack you."

"Now you're just splitting hairs."

Silence sighed loudly and walked between them, shaking her head.

"Times like this I bet she wishes she could talk huh?" Amonar asked as she raised one finger behind her for him to see.

"And you say I irritate people," Seltemver said as he walked after her.

The Infirmary Journal

She crept over the barricades and set down her bag of supplies carefully. In all the years she had been with this elven pirate, he had always shown a natural aptitude for getting in trouble and she had learned to be ready. Silence turned to look at him as he came over the broken barricade after her and sighed. Seltemver had saved her from the depths of a hellish existence and given her meaning again, yet he had never tried to touch her, let alone even ask; and gods above she would've relinquished easily.

"Hey look it's like a fort," Amonar said as he flew over with them.

Silence smiled at the imp and looked around. Indeed it did resemble a hastily improvised fort, complete with desks and racks for weapons. It seemed like there had been beds for the sick and maybe even test subjects. One desk had broken glass and stains that weren't blood all over it, as well as a small stack of books. Most of these were in orc, which looked like useless stories, but a couple were in common and seemed like notes on what happened. Silence handed them to Seltemver and signed for him to read them as she kept looking for more supplies.

"Ah, perfect, it's the infirmary journal," Seltemver said as he sat down Jand read. "It's stained and ripped but I can make out some of it."

The stranger first appeared in the town of Tolg, rumored to have walked down from the

Harr'ag mountains. This was two days after Starfall and most of the devastation wrought from those falling stars was still smoking.

Seltemver flipped through the pages, looking for more. "A lot of this is ruined. Wait here's more."

The fighting is everywhere and most of the orcs report total losses in all of the cities. It can't be true what they say, but we can only go by what we hear, for now. The archmage north of here is an expert in curses, so they've sent him a missive to come as fast as he can. I pray that he will help.

"Well that's not vague and scary at all," Amonar said as he fluttered around the wreckage.

"Yeah, most of this is just speculation and guessing as to what happened," Seltemver said, handing the book back to Silence.

Silence took the book and picked up another ruined book, this one by the beds with more broken glass and very large blood stains. She handed it to him and put the others away in her bag.

Seltemver skimmed the journal and sat down heavily, closing his eyes.

"That's not good," Amonar said with a whistle.

"No. It's not."

The tests all say the same thing. It's a curse that has to be broken and possibly came from the very gods themselves for our transgressions. Why it affected them specifically I can't say, but they won't stop feeding, even if threatened. We kill them and they get right back up, only to shred the flesh of those that stand in their way.

They're everywhere, in every town, and they are converging here in Ur Doma for some reason. I think they know about the Archmage's plan to lift the curse. We're sending the rest of our notes on ahead and I will follow tomorrow once the final test is complete. It all started with that man, the dark one, with onyx skin. The Ilkar are coming.

Silence shook her head and tapped the far desk with her sword. It showed a map of the town and a tower to the Northeast.

"Yeah, looks like we need to go and see this archmage's tower," Seltemver said solemnly.

"Yes because that's always ended up doing well for us," Amonar interjected. "Plus, more curses?"

"I know, but I can't leave risking that we have carried it to the ship until we find out what the Iskar were."

Silence nodded and hefted her sword and bag of supplies. *Never a dull moment with this elf,* she thought as they headed out quietly for the tower.

Tower of Chanyl

Seltemver walked with his enchanted sword out, canning the sides of the road for whatever the former residents had been overrun by, yet after an hour of walking north, there was still no sign of anything hostile.

"Here's another thing, Seltemver," Amonar said as they traveled. "There aren't nearly enough blood trails for the amount of people that must've lived in a town this size."

Silence rolled her eyes and signed with exaggeration.

"I am not droning on like a faerie!"

"Listen, both of you," Seltemver started then caught himself. "Wait, is this how Toth must feel?" He shook his head and laughed. "Anyway, the answer must be at the archmage's tower so let's just get there and then figure it out."

They passed a graveyard, with more trails of dried blood on the road leading in every direction at this point, like it had been some sort of free-for-all. Still not one body or body part could be seen. It was the eeriest thing Seltemver had ever seen, and he had seen some very eerie things.

"At least the graves aren't open," Amonar said with Silence nodding for once.

"I've told you before, Amonar, zombies are fantasy," Seltemver said laughing. "The dead just don't get back up unless the skeleton is animated by magic, and even then, those don't eat brains."

"Didn't those notes say they were feeding? What about other organs?"

"No."

"I'm just saying that it's a good thing the graves are intact," Amonar said, then stopped short when the tower came into view, the sheer sight of the battlefield stunning them all.

The grass here wasn't just dead but burned away by fire; a fire that seemed to spray away from the tower door like a cone. Trees on either side of the tower were split in two as if from a great lightning strike and all sorts of weapons stuck into the ground like some bizarre garden as they walked up the dirt path.

"Magic didn't seem to work either," Seltemver reasoned as they approached with caution. He stopped and looked at the ground now, examining the tiny footprints that seemed to be everywhere. It was the first sign of any kind and gave him hope. "Maybe the children were gathered here for defense?"

"Well let's be quick about this," Amonar said looking back at the setting sun. "Something tells me that this place gets worse at dark."

Seltemver wanted to argue that whatever did this wasn't going to wait for the sun to set, but just nodded and climbed the ruins of the front door to the crumbling tower. The inside seemed devoid of anything but piles of trash, anything they could find to bar the door that must've given way under great stress despite the magic surely keeping it up. *What could've attacked here and wiped everyone out?* Seltemver asked himself for the hundredth time.

Silence signaled from the far stairs for Amonar as Seltemver stopped to look at the wall and the scorch marks splayed across the stone. The marks were waist-high and erratic, like whatever they were targeting had to be moving fast; small and fast.

"Seltemver, more journals," Amonar said as the imp picked one up. "Written by the same hand I would guess." The imp cleared his throat and read aloud as he hovered in mid-air, his tiny wings beating loudly.

Chanyl figured out how to break the curse, alas he has died before he could try it out. I am all that's left now, a lonely apprentice that the orcs of Ur Doma look to stop this horror. Only an elf can work the spell Chanyl came up with, and yet I am only human amid an island of orcs; we are doomed with this knowledge we cannot use.

Once the sun rises and they sleep, we will make a break for the chasm, throwing ourselves into its depths. It is now the hope that if they are robbed of food, they will starve and die, ridding this world of them forever.

"I knew the sun going down was bad," Amonar said putting down the ruined journal. "There's more but it's all unreadable." Before anyone could comment a horrible scream broke the silence of the village, echoing for what seemed like miles. It was answered again and again, across all points of direction, and seemed to be converging on their location. The Iskar were coming.

THE ISKAR

Seltemver looked up at the broken stairs and the archmages' study that sat exposed to the air. "Let's get those notes and race for the ship. If we can get far enough from shore they might not be able to swim to us." Seltemver leapt for the broken stone and hauled himself up, dragging Silence after him.

"What about not bringing it to the ship?"

"If it is a curse, I don't think it can be contracted."

Amonar flew up and hid behind Seltemver. "Hurry, I did not like that cry at all, and I'm from the deep hells."

Seltemver pointed for Silence to go through the scrolls on the desk while he searched the shelves. More journals, this time in the archmage's elven script.

It seems that Krist himself had doomed these orcs, cruelly transforming their hope against them. Yet all is not lost. I can use a life curse to break what the God of Death's Incarnation has done, but it will mean my life.

Seltemver's mouth hung open at the spell described hereafter...it was the same one that the old archmage had used to curse him with Amonar; or rather a version of it. Instead of pairing a soul with an infernal presence, it was severing a presence from a soul or a collective of souls. This would've indeed killed the caster, but not immediately. It seemed like it drained the caster's very soul and eventually, they would die. "Found it, let's go."

"Can we do it?" Amonar asked as they scrambled down the broken steps.

Seltemver shrugged, unwilling to reveal the spell at the moment. The trick was that he couldn't cast magic; never had been able to. He was born that way and he couldn't ask Silence to try it since she could never recite the words. "Let's see if we can get away from here first."

They ran down the road toward the main part of town, still hearing the screams getting closer, but not nearly as fast as he would've thought. Seltemver thought they would have a clear run for the ship, yet when they skidded into town they stopped, horrified at what lay across their path.

"No, it can't be," Amonar said, his clawed hands going to his mouth in abject terror.

Seltemver stopped, looking at what could only be the Iskar. They were orc children, covered in dried blood stains and crawling towards them ceaselessly, endlessly screaming. They could only be from the ages of five to possibly fourteen or fifteen, but most were very young and still wore the tattered remains of play clothes and carried dolls here and there in their desperate hands; hands covered in the stained blood of their families.

"Don't make us feed! Please!" the children cried out, even as their hands reached for the trio and hunger made their teeth gnash together.

"We're so hungry!" another group called out, now on all fours. "Run! Please don't make us eat you too!"

Silence was in tears as she shook off the shock, grabbing Amonar and running for a gap between the children.

"Seltemver!" Amonar called out.

Seltemver was outraged. For anyone, god or man, to curse children like this was far too much; too horrible even for him. He sheathed his sword and ran, cursing the gods with every step, and leapt over one child that cried for her mother.

"Go Amonar, get to the ship and tell them to get ready," Seltemver called out as he kicked a small hand from his coat. There were so many now, swarming in from everywhere. Now he knew why the barricades and lack of weapons. No one wanted to kill their own children, or anyone else's for that matter.

As they got to the dock, Seltemver could see the *Seahaven* already incoming, the screams a natural beacon for the trained crew, yet Seltemver knew they wouldn't make it. The children were gaining strength, as if waking up from a long slumber and they seemed faster already. Seltemver stopped and unbuckled his sword belt. "Silence," he called and as she turned, he tossed the belt back to her, scabbard and all. "Treat her with dignity, she has always served me well.."

Seltemver turned back and waded into the children, kicking and dodging with a skill born of centuries, holding off the small horde until Silence could get far enough. Once the long boat was away, he turned and ran, intending to dive and swim for it, yet his coat was snagged by a small girl, her teeth clamping down on his leg. Seltemver cried out and hit the wooden deck as more crawled over him.

Last Stand

Amonar heard his master's cry and froze. "Seltemver!" The imp called up his power, that dreaded gift that made him sick and his eyes started to glow red. "A…"

"No! Amonar, don't!" Seltemver commanded in that voice he rarely used with his old friend. "They're just children!" The elven pirate kicked and punched the kids back and crawled backward, trying to get away.

Amonar's chest grew light, a weight lifted from somewhere he couldn't describe. His eyes narrowed and he flew back, crashing into the children with a defiant scream of his own, flinging them left and right off of his friend. Their teeth couldn't break his demonic skin, nor find purchase in holding him, so agile was the flying imp. Amonar screamed and roared with all the power of the deep hells, and after a brief fight, the Iskar of Ur Doma fled, rather than try and overtake him.

"Amonar!" Toth called out, as the Seahaven slammed into the docks behind him. "Grab the line!"

Amonar turned with silver tears falling and saw Toth swinging down to grab them both. The imp gripped Seltemver in his clawed hands and picked him up, newfound strength flooding him. Minutes later they were safely aboard the ship, yet it was no victory.

Seltemver lay there, bleeding from more than a dozen bites and tears, most of his leg gone. "Amonar, how...very brave of you," the elf said as the imp embraced him.

"Grunhilde!" Toth roared even as the crew stared off the side of the ship in horror at what had been fighting their Captain. The Iskar had rushed the docks once more, hu8nmger driving them past the brief fear of Amonar.

"Toth, it's all right," Seltemver said coughing. He pulled a small book out and set it down next to him as Silence came over with his sword. "No, it's yours now, Silence. I won't be using that thing again."

"That's the spell to break the curse, isn't it? Amonar asked, knowing that look in Seltemver's eyes.

"Yes, Amonar, it is."

Grunhilde came skidding in, her hands already glowing. As if it were some sort of beacon, the Iskar on the shore all cried out in pain and anguish the minute her power came on. "What?"

"Guys...wait," Seltemver said trying to sit up. "Listen, all of you. Those kids were cursed by the gods and I can break it. It will certainly kill me, but I just can't...won't let these kids suffer like this."

"Won't that condemn Amonar to hell as well?" Toth asked, concern on his rugged face.

"If he were bonded to me, yes."

Amonar's eyes widened. "No, you can't," the imp said, tears still falling. "You can't cast magic..."

"I think this will work, as I'm not calling the elements like normal; it's a type of curse instead. The spell I found in these journals is almost the same, so...yes, Amonar, I can give you to another. It would just have to be someone..."

"I accept," Toth said without pause, his own tears now silently falling. Most of the crew was gathered around now, kneeling and bowing their heads.

"Great, but let me fix those Iskar first," Seltemver said, trying to sit up. Toth helped him as he started reading the book in a whisper. Seltemver clapped his hands together and a wave of force cascaded out over the town. The screams of the children seemed louder as the wave washed over them, bursting into a crescendo...and finally, silence.

"It's done," Seltemver said and then hefted the book again, but it slipped from his weakening fingers.

"I've got it," Amonar said, holding the book for him. "You know, you're my best friend right?"

The imp could see the fading soul of his friend growing thin as he lay there; he was helpless to save him.

"You're not so bad yourself, Amonar," Seltemver said as he smiled up at the imp. "And I have loved every minute of your company."

Seltemver read the words and changed his tone slightly, then whispered and clapped his bloody hands together once more as the concussive force exploded out from him in an invisible wave around the crew this time. As the dust settled, Seltemver's head dropped...he was gone.

End of the Curse

Captain Toth walked the docks with his axe out just in case. Amonar sitting on his shoulder and silently mourning. There would be ample time to grieve the loss of his oldest friend later. Now he had to make sure the threat was indeed over and to see if any of the kids were salvageable. Toth saw the name of the town and stopped, dropping to his knees in shock.

"What is it, Toth?" Is it an attack?" Amonar flew up and circled the orc protectively, finally finding his courage, at least for the meantime.

"No, Am," the orc said wiping a tear from his cheek once more. "The name of the town is Ur Doma."

"Yeah, we saw that, so what?"

"It means - A Home."

"I don't get it."

"The sea witch said that Seltemver was doomed to sail distant waters until we found a home," Toth said quietly. "Well, we've found it."

"It can't be that easy," the imp said holding his head.

"We'll find out when we leave I guess." Toth saw some of the kids coming out and knew that he would have to take as many that would want to go with them. Without anyone else, these young orcs would perish easily. "It's all right, young ones," Toth said, holding out his massive hand. "How many are there of you?"

A young orc, not more than six winters looked down at her feet. "Just us. Most of the others are...well. They just can't live with what they had to do to survive."

Amonar had filled Toth in, albeit quickly, about the situation and he couldn't imagine having to feed off of the very ones that raised you. It was a horror that he would never shake. "Well, you are all welcome to leave with us, just as soon as we bury our friend," Toth said with a sad smile.

"He said that he would rather be burned on the water," one small orc said, his tusks just starting to come in.

"Come again?" Amonar asked, flying down to the small child.

"He came to all of us after it was over and said that he was going to someone named, Syll and that to tell his friends to burn him on the water."

"By Dava, he's not in the hells," Toth said with a whoop and a cry.

"He must've redeemed his soul by saving the children," Amonar said numbly. Fresh tears welled up in his eyes as he remembered his friend.

Toth walked back to the *Seahaven* with about twenty children, a smile on his tusks. The news these little ones would bring to the crew would make leaving easier, especially for their healer. Grunhilde was still inconsolable over the death of Seltemver, even going so far as removing her holy symbol when he passed. Silence had sat with her, crying in the bow of the ship and cradling that damned sword. Silence hadn't let it go since he passed it to her. *We all grieve in our own ways,* the burly orc thought. *I know I did after Crak died.* This one hurt more though, as it was Seltemver that had saved them in the very beginning, all those years ago.

"We're going to be all right aren't we Toth?" Amonar asked as they walked back to the ship, the imp tussling one of the children's heads as they went, messing up her hair.

Toth looked out at the vast ocean beyond the *Seahaven* and knew in his heart that the storm would indeed take them home. But what awaited them was still a mystery. Still, with friends like these, he could get through anything. "Yeah, Am, I think we are."

Epilogue: End of the Story

Karsis sat back and looked at the tears falling from the twins' eyes, realization hitting him now that he was seeing this whole story from a new perspective. These characters were real and these things must have truly happened. It was a blow to his senses for sure, but one he couldn't show the young ones quite yet. Let them have their fantasies for now. The Incarnation of Magic stood slowly, tucking the children into bed as they hugged each other and smiled up at their 'uncle'.

"Thank you, Unc...Karsis," Braelyn said sniffing and trying to fix her hair.

"It was my pleasure to share in something I have enjoyed since I was young," Karsis said, patting Brinn on the head as the boy tried to hide the fact that he was crying as well. "Now I have to see to something rather important so you two behave for your parents all right?"

"Yes, Karsis," both said in unison.

"And listen to Aunty Carana as well," Karsis added, unable to pass up the jib. The incarnation of Protection had taken to being called Aunty even worse than he had, and he still owed that woman for certain things, though collecting was always more fun than owing.

Braelyn's eyes clouded briefly and she looked right at him, the young child's face a mask of seriousness out of nowhere. "You're going to see Janna aren't you?" Braelyn asked in a monotone voice startling her brother.

Karsis frowned, knowing it was too soon for the young girls' powers to be coming in. If she were anything like her father, Gods help them all. "Yes, but never mind that, go to sleep both of you."

"Go and find the Isle, Karsis. It is needed." Braelyn's eyes focused again and she yawned.

Karsis didn't have time to think about what just happened—at only eight winters this young one was going to be trouble. He got up and collected the sheets of parchment neatly as the young twins got comfortable, Brinn hushing Braelyn as she asked what happened. The Incarnation of Magic stepped out and whispered to the ether, disappearing in a flash, never seeing his own son, Rhoe, watching from the far hill.

Karsis stared intently as Janna held the parchment, reading through the stories. He couldn't help but fail to breathe as she finally put them down. They were at a small Inn called the *Fair Prince* located in Alrin and had been there for almost two days now. "Well?"

"Yes. I can't believe it, but yes."

Karsis sat back and took a deep breath. "So that was you?"

"Yeah, but I can tell you this right now. I haven't told anyone that story. Ever. Myst would kill me if he found out."

"Janna, that's not the point."

"I know, but I'm trying to wrap my head around you reading about me hundreds of years ago and not falling in love with me," the Incarnation of Beauty said with a fluttering of her eyes.

"That's not..." Karsis rolled his eyes and stopped. *Bards, Gods above why was it always bards? I am one and still...*

"I know. So what's the plan now?" Janna asked, "I know you don't let things like this go easily."

"Well I thought we could start by taking a trip to Novrantir," Karsis said with a smile. "Maybe a long trip on a nice ship, get one cabin..."

"Oh, you insatiable...I'm in." Janna stood and threw down five coins to pay for their stay and winked at the legendary bard.

Karsis stood and locked arms with the gorgeous lady and walked out. He would inquire about Seltemver on the mysterious island and who knows, maybe they truly did come home and they would find the *Seahaven* for real. Karsis hadn't felt nervous in years, yet that thought made his stomach do flips. *Then there's the question of the demon on the sea witch's isle,* he thought. *And the fact that something spoke through Braelyn to get me to go there.* Karsis shook his head. *One pretty lady at a time. For now, this story stays with me, and can never get into the hands of anyone.*

About the Author

Born in the usual way, author **Michael D. Nadeau** found fantasy at the age of eight with Dungeons & Dragons. He loved being different people as well as casting magic. By High school, he discovered his love for reading thanks to a teacher. She fed his thirst for books by bringing her own collections from home and lending them to him, even buying one towards the end of her class. He has now read hundreds of fantasy books, living in each of their worlds along with the characters. After a while, he started creating his own worlds for his games with friends. Cities, gods, ancient and terrible beings, and histories...then he would burn them all down.

He is the author of the Lythinall series: *The Darkness Returns* Book 1, *The Darkness Within* Book 2, *The Darkness Falls* Book 3, *Dragon Caller; Rise of the Archmage* Book 1, *Dragon Master; Rise of the Archmage* Book 2, *Tales from Lythinall*—an anthology, and *Angels Among Us*. He also has several stories in Eerie River Publishing anthologies, as well as writing on his own.

9 781960 654021